A DARKLING POWER

Before they reached the door, two darkly cloaked and hooded figures slipped swiftly through and blocked the way, daggers drawn at the ready. Nyctasia had time for only a moment's regret: neither she nor 'Ben was armed.

As the assassins started forward, 'Ben took a step towards them, as if to meet their attack, but the intruders never reached their quarry. They crumpled suddenly to the ground, without a cry, before they came within striking distance. Nyctasia didn't bother to listen for the attackers' heartbeats.

" 'Ben," she said heavily. "What bargain have you made?"

SILVERGLASS
MISTRESS OF AMBIGUITIES

J. F. RIVKIN

ACE BOOKS, NEW YORK

This book is an Ace original edition,
and has never been previously published.

MISTRESS OF AMBIGUITIES

An Ace Book / published by arrangement with
the author

PRINTING HISTORY
Ace edition / April 1991

ISBN: 0-441-76601-3

Ace Books are published by The Berkley Publishing Group,
200 Madison Avenue, New York, New York 10016.
The name "ACE" and the "A" logo
are trademarks belonging to Charter Communications, Inc.

PRINTED IN THE UNITED STATES OF AMERICA

10 9 8 7 6 5 4 3 2 1

1

"Oh, I could complain
That my life is a curse,
But 'twould be in vain
All my woes to rehearse.
For one thing is plain—
Things could always be worse!"

sang Nyctasia. She ate one of the walnuts she'd been shelling,
and tossed all the hulls onto the coals of the cooking hearth.
"Corson, let me do that for you," she suggested.

Corson was trying to chop suet and scraps of meat, holding
a wooden bowl awkwardly in her lap while wielding a
crescent-shaped mincer. Her left arm was in a sling and kept
getting in her way, but she ignored Nyctasia's offer of help.
She was not in the best of humors. Her bandaged arm
hampered her, and it was very hot in the kitchen of the busy
tavern, where meats were kept roasting all day, even in the
warm late-summer weather. "That fool song of yours!" she
said. "You were singing that the first time I laid eyes on

you—cursed be the day. That's when all my troubles began, so I tell you."

"I remember it well," Nyctasia said mildly. "The moment you swaggered into The Lame Fox, I thought, 'There's the one I want. Strong, oversure of herself, and none too clever—perfect for my purposes.'"

The others laughed, and Corson turned and deliberately spat into the fire, knowing that Nyctasia found the habit revolting. "I must have been a fool, I can't deny it. If I'd had the wits of a newborn newt, I'd not have been cozened into taking your part. I'd have kept to my bargain with your enemies, and cut you into shreds." She demonstrated with the mincer. "That's what a *clever* person would've done."

"But you couldn't very well do that—you were in thrall to my artful charms and evil spells. You know I'm irresistible."

"Like a serpent," Corson agreed, "that fascinates its prey with its stare, then paralyzes them with its poison. That's you."

Nyctasia regarded her coolly. "Your braid is in the chopped suet," she observed, "which is not making either of them more appealing."

Corson cursed and tried to fasten up her long braid with one hand, but she soon dropped her hair-clasp and had to pick it out of the half-minced meat. Nyctasia let her struggle stubbornly with it for a while, then sighed and went over to pin up her hair for her.

"Don't get your hands dirty, m'lady," Corson grumbled.

The others, who had heard their bickering time and again, lost interest and went on about their own tasks. When Walden's back was turned, Nyctasia stole silently across the kitchen, intent on snatching a handful of sweet raisins from the barrel.

"Get out of that," the burly cook growled, without turning around, "or we'll be serving up Roast of Rhaicime with Raisins tonight." He sank a cleaver through a slab of beef-steak, with a threatening flourish. "If you've finished the walnuts, you can get on with the apples."

Nyctasia retreated hastily. "How does he *do* that?" she complained. "It's demonic. I never made a sound. I can stalk a deer within ten paces—"

Walden snorted. "I've a dozen children—I have to have eyes in my back. And you're always up to something. Skinny people aren't to be trusted. Don't they feed you at that fine court of yours?"

"Oh, the food's plentiful enough," Corson said with a grin, "but she doesn't dare eat much of it, for fear someone's poisoned her share."

"Saves up her appetite for her visits here," Steifann put in, "then eats me out of a month's earnings. As if it wasn't hard enough feeding Corson, now there's two of the ravening leeches, and the one just as useless as the other."

Nyctasia paid no heed to his disrespectful remarks. She knew as well as the rest that Steifann's tavern profited from the patronage of a noblewoman of her rank. Word that she frequented the Hare had reached the local gentry and brought Steifann much desirable trade from among them, and her connections to a clan of eastern vintners had made the finest wines of the Midlands available to him as well. All in all, Corson's acquaintance with the Rhaicime of Rhostshyl had proven most advantageous for Steifann, but since he had taken a liking to Nyctasia himself, he naturally treated her as a nuisance and a burden.

"Nyc may be useless," Corson protested, "like all the aristocracy, but I'm—"

"Don't forget you're a lady now yourself," said Annin, the head serving-woman at the Hare.

"That's different! I earned my title by my sword. Nyc's a lady born and bred." Though Corson held the rank of Desthene, no land or fortune pertained to the title, and she still made her living as a mercenary swordfighter—much to the disgust of Steifann, who felt that she should settle down with him.

"Earned that wound by your rutting sword too," he said sourly, gesturing at Corson's bandaged arm. "Worthless half-wit. You could have been killed, and now here you are living on my bounty as usual, not fit for a scrap of work."

"I'm as fit with one arm as you are with two! It's you who won't let me lift a hand to the heavy chores—"

"Now, Corson," Nyctasia interrupted, "we all know that you like nothing so much as an opportunity to indulge your indolence, but—"

"What did she say?" one of the scullions demanded, poking the serving-lad Trask.

"She means Corson's lazy," he explained with a grin. Trask was no better educated than the rest, but was considerably more ambitious. He never lost a chance to learn fine phrases and aristocratic ways from Nyctasia.

"—but as your pride is even more excessive than your sloth," Nyctasia continued, "you'd try to carry on just as usual if we let you, and give that injury no time to knit. You're to rest easy till you're properly healed, you heed me. I'm not so useless that I don't know how to treat a wound."

Nyctasia was a skilled healer, and Corson knew it well, but she scoffed, "Fuss, fuss, fuss—you're as bad as Steifann. It's just a nasty scratch from a hayfork, no more. None of them had proper weapons. A border skirmish with a few peasants fool enough to attack the escort of an imperial emissary. It was my own fault I was hurt. I thought we could scatter them without killing the lot." She shook her head in wonder at her own behavior. "Fight to kill or run away—one or the other— remember that," she admonished a pair of the cook's children, who were listening wide-eyed to this martial wisdom.

The others ignored her bravado, as usual. "You'd not have to kill or be killed if you stayed here where you belong, instead of traipsing all over creation looking for trouble," Steifann pointed out. "I daresay as soon as you're whole you'll be off on some other addlepated chase."

Corson laughed. "Addlepated enough, but only as far as Rhostshyl. Nyc wants me to guard those precious books of hers on the road—if Destiver ever delivers them. Though why anyone would want to steal the moldy old things is more than I could tell you."

Nyctasia was in Chiastelm to receive a shipment of books from her kinfolk in the Midlands. With each lot of wine they sent to Steifann, they dispatched, at her instruction, certain works from the abandoned library of rare scholarly lore that had been discovered on their land nearly two years before. It was not easy for Nyctasia to get away from her duties in Rhostshyl for even a few days, but she had felt that she must without fail take possession of these particular volumes herself.

"These books are especially valuable, Corson," she explained. "And especially dangerous. To let them fall into the wrong hands would be unforgivable."

"Spells," Corson guessed. "With all your learning, Nyc, you'll never learn that no good comes of meddling with magic."

"Not from meddling, no," Nyctasia agreed curtly. She

frowned. "Where *is* Destiver? The *Windhover's* been in port for hours." She had sent two of her people to the docks to see that the books were safely delivered, but she would not feel easy about them until she had them under lock and key.

"Don't worry, she'll be here in time for a meal, if I know that one," Corson said with a sneer. There had never been much love lost between the two of them, but since Corson had unwittingly taken part in the capture of Destiver's band of smugglers, their mutual dislike had grown to new heights of loathing. It was only through Nyctasia's intervention with the powerful Merchants' Guild of Chiastelm that Destiver had escaped hanging, and she held Corson to blame that she was now forced to make an honest living as a cargo-runner. Corson, for her part, resented any rival for Steifann's affections, and she knew that Steifann and Destiver had shared a memorable past. She spat again.

"When the rest of her cargo's unloaded, she'll be along with ours," Steifann assured Nyctasia. Most tradespeople fetched their own goods from Merchants' Wharf, but Destiver usually delivered Steifann's wares herself, so as to sample them, and to pass the time with her old friends Steifann and Annin.

"If she hasn't drunk up our cargo already," said Trask, smacking his lips. "That wine of yours is too good for a sot like her, Nyc. It's fit for the imperial court. I don't see why your kin in Rhostshyl disapprove of it." Trask knew nothing about fine wines, of course, but this did not discourage him from talking as if he did.

"It's not the wine itself they condemn," Nyctasia told him, "it's my impropriety in allowing our Midland cousins to export their wares to the Maritime markets. Now any commoner on the coast who has the price can purchase wine that bears our family name—as if the House of Edonaris were engaged in trade!"

"No one need be ashamed of those wines," Steifann declared with satisfaction. "They'll make my reputation yet among the gentry."

"And they'll destroy ours, according to some." Nyctasia smiled. "There can be no greater disgrace for a family like mine than the taint of commerce. I believe that not even the marriage-alliance with the Teiryn has scandalized them so much as this. The Teiryn may be the arch-enemies of our House, but they are of the high nobility, you see."

"And this latest outrage of yours will give your kin something to think of besides reconciliation with the Teiryn, no?" Corson asked shrewdly. "Divert your opponent's eye from your true objective—that's good strategy. How goes your grand scheme to unite the enemies? Has your vixen sister murdered her Teiryn husband yet?"

"By no means. Tiambria's proud and willful, but she's not a fool. One couldn't keep company with Jehamias ar'n Teiryn for long without finding him an agreeable companion. And he was madly smitten with her at once, which rather helped matters along, I fancy. Half the city think him a traitor to his House, and the rest think I've spellcast him. Ettasuan ar'n Teiryn's sworn to have his blood, and he's not the only one. Tiambria did scorn him for a coward, at first, but she's come to see that it took far more courage for him to marry her than to refuse. It's not she who worries me now, it's 'Kasten."

"Your brother Erikasten, her twin? What stone's in his shoe? Have you found a Teiryn lass for him to marry?"

"Would that I had! He's so driven by jealousy he's easily led by those who claim that the family's been dishonored by the union. I think," she added, more to herself than to Corson, "that I must find some pretext to send him off on an important mission soon, to somewhere at a considerable distance."

"Eh, jealousy?" said Corson. "But he couldn't very well expect to marry her himself—unless you Edonaris are even crazier than folk say."

"No, but no one expected her to marry so young, least of all Erikasten. It's hard on him—first he lost his brother to the war, then his sister to the peace. And no one's ever come between him and Tiambria before, not like this. He's always depended on her and followed her lead. Now that she has a husband and child to think of—"

"A *child*? I've not been away so long as that!"

"To be sure, you've not heard the news—I forget that others don't concern themselves day and night with the tidings of Rhostshyl. Of course she's not a mother yet, but she shall be, and that before three seasons are out." A radiant smile lit Nyctasia's features as she spoke of her sister's unborn child. She seemed suddenly illumined by an inner flame, and her words rang like chimes, joyous and confident. "All my hopes for the future rest with this child, the heir of two great Houses. I have dreamed of a new dynasty, and I believe that we shall soon see the birth of that bloodline—the lineage that will bring peace and prosperity back to the city, that will unite all the people of Rhostshyl at last!" The power of her vision was undeniable.

"It's as good as a play to hear that one talk," Annin said, amused.

"She wields words as well as I do weapons," Corson agreed. "And she wins, too, I'm bound to say. I've seen it at court time and again—she makes them all do what she wants, just by talking at them till they surrender."

"It seems you've learned some of her ways, then. When she's not talking, you are."

"Oh, Corson was always ready with her tongue," said Nyctasia. "You can't blame me for that."

"True enough," Steifann replied. "And talk's all very well to pass the time, but there's Destiver out back, and talk won't get those barrels down the stairs. At least keep out of the way, the pair of you." The wine casks would have to be brought through the kitchen to the cellarway, and there was little room to spare. "Why don't you make yourself useful and go sing for the taproom?" he suggested to Nyctasia.

Nyctasia obediently took up her harp. "Very well. If I stay here, Walden will only set me to peeling potatoes, after all." Though she occasionally made a formal visit to the Hare with the full retinue befitting a Rhaicime, she did so purely to enhance the tavern's reputation, as a favor to Steifann. Usually she came, as she had today, in the guise of a commonplace traveler, a student or minstrel, and no one who chanced to see her would take her for a personage of rank and importance. "You come too, Corson. I've a new drinking-song you might like to hear. Just let me see to those books first, so please you, sir," she said to Steifann with mock humility.

Corson was willing. She couldn't help unload the barrels this time, and she didn't much care to meet with Destiver, that was certain. Besides, she could tell from Nyctasia's manner that there was mischief brewing. She went out to the taproom while Nyctasia attended to the unloading and storing of her books.

They were to be kept in locked chests in Steifann's quarters until Corson was able to convey them to Rhostshyl herself. When they had been secured, Nyctasia dismissed her people, but before she could follow, Annin slipped into the room and shut the door firmly behind her. "I want a word with you,

Nyc," she said, sitting on one of the chests and gesturing for Nyctasia to take the other. "It's about Trask. You'll have to do something for him, you know. He's not a child anymore. This place has no more to offer him."

"I?" gasped Nyctasia. "What is it to do with me? Why am I to be responsible for every stray mudchild who follows Steifann home?"

"You're the only one among us who can make a place for him," Annin said reasonably. "It's not as if he'll inherit the Hare—Steifann and Corson will settle down and raise a brood of their own someday. No, you'll just have to find a position for him, Nyc. That one could make something of himself, with half a chance. And it's your fault that he has a taste for such things anyway."

Nyctasia argued, but she knew it was a losing battle. Even her powers of persuasion were no match for Annin's determination. Only by promising to give the matter her earnest consideration was she able to escape to the taproom.

Nyctasia's new drinking-song proved quite popular with the patrons of The Jugged Hare, although they were not able to hear the entire work on that occasion. It was, she announced, entitled "The Host of the Hare," and was a tribute to the estimable Steifann. She perched on a table like any common tavern-singer, pushing dirty platters and mugs out of her way, then winked at Corson and struck a few dramatic chords on her small lap-harp. When she had the attention of the house, she began:

> "In fair Chiastelm
> On the coast,
> Stands the far-famed tavern
> Of a worthy host.
>
> Tall as a tree
> Is the host of the Hare,
> Broad as a barrel,
> Big as a bear.
>
> With eyes green as jade
> And a beard of black thatch,

A neck like a bull's
And a temper to match!

The song of his praises
Could run on forever.
He's strong as three oxen
And *nearly* as clever.

He's feared for his fists
Throughout the west,
As a braggart and drunkard
He ranks with the best.

As a lover, it's said,
He's a man without peer,
And folk flock to his bed
From afar and from near.

From the woods to the water,
It matters not where,
You'll not meet the like
Of the host of the Hare!"

Steifann did indeed have quite a reputation, at least in certain quarters of Chiastelm, and not a few of his customers knew him well. Nyctasia's mockery was received with enthusiasm, and by no one more than Corson. By this time, Corson was leading the applause, pounding the table with her tankard, cheering after each verse, and shouting for more. Call *her* a useless layabout, would he? She intended to learn every word of Nyctasia's new ballad. Trust Nyc to fashion a sword out of words!

The song, Corson had realized, was Nyctasia's calculated revenge for Steifann's inhospitable reception of her when she'd first visited the Hare a year ago, in search of Corson. Goaded by jealousy, Steifann had all but flung her into the street, and though Nyctasia had forgiven his behavior, she had not forgotten it. She carried on with a few relatively tame verses about Steifann's prowess at brawling, boasting and drinking, but when he came into the taproom himself, to see what all the commotion was, he heard:

"From border to border,
Wherever you fare,
You'll not meet the like
Of the host of the Hare!

For he'll swagger and strut
For each strumpet and slut
Like a cock among hens,
Or a stallion in rut!

His—"

But much to the disappointment of her audience, Nyctasia's performance was suddenly cut short at that most interesting point. Amid calls of "Let the lass finish!" and "Give us the rest, girl!" she dashed out the door to the street, two steps ahead of the bellowing Steifann.

2

"Corson brenn Torisk! Upon my word, it could be no other!"

It took Corson rather longer to recognize her fellow traveler. She reined in the horses and jumped down from the cart to take a closer look at the man who'd hailed her, but though his face was familiar, he might have been any one of a dozen townsmen she'd known. He was handsome enough, she thought, and had a haughty air about him, for all that his clothes were worn and shabby. It was his lofty manner, as well as the pen-case hanging at his belt, that spurred Corson's memory at last.

"Surely you can't have forgotten me?" he was saying reproachfully. "Thankless wretch! I taught you to read, to say nothing of—"

"To be sure, I remember you, you bastard—Desmalkin brenn Cerrogh, 'Malkin the scholar, 'Malkin the cheat, 'Malkin the toady, who forsakes his friends when he's grown too fine to be seen with them! I've not forgotten that, you'll find. I should wring your neck—"

"Why, Kitten, it wounds me to hear you speak so," 'Malkin said placatingly. "And after all I did for you. I tried my best to teach you the rudiments of civilized behavior, but you couldn't stay out of trouble for two days together. I had my position to think of, after all—a retainer of a noble household has to be careful. I'd have soon lost my place if I'd kept company with you much longer."

There was truth in that, Corson had to admit. When she'd first met 'Malkin she'd been just out of the army, aimless and wild, with no friend but her sword. War was all she knew, and she'd seemed to be at war with all the world in those days. She had survived her term in the army through cunning and ferocity and ruthless desperation, and experience had taught her no other way to meet life's challenges.

But Corson had since lived a good deal among respectable folk, and spent time at court as well. If her nature was still far from tame, she had nonetheless lost some of her rough edges, and could even display a little polish when occasion demanded. Though she had harbored bitter resentment of 'Malkin for years, she now found that she could better appreciate his point of view. And, after all, it didn't become a lady to bear a grudge against an inferior. . . . That was what Nyc would say, no doubt.

"Well, you're treacherous scum, but let that pass," she said grandly. "What's become of your fine position, then? Here I find you tramping the roads like a penniless student again."

"Oh, it was insufferably dull, Corson. When all's said, you know, one is a scholar, not a clerk. I've held better places since, but none, alas, that gave proper scope to my learning."

Or to your ambition, Corson thought. "You don't look much better off than you were," she pointed out, pleasantly aware that she herself did.

'Malkin shrugged, as if this were a matter of no consequence. "It doesn't do for a traveler to appear too prosperous. There are thieves about—"

"And you never were handy with a sword, as I recall," Corson put in, grinning, "though I did try my best to teach you the rudiments of fighting."

"I've heard that there's work worthy of a scholar in Rhostshyl," 'Malkin continued, as if she hadn't spoken. "That's why you find me on the road. The Rhaicime has let it be known far and wide that the services of sages are needed at court. They say Her Ladyship's a cultured woman. If I could attain an audience with her, my fortune would be made."

Corson made a half-hearted effort not to gloat, and failed

completely. "I could arrange that for you, if you like," she said offhandedly. "I'm an intimate friend of the Rhaicime, as it happens. The ruffian you disdained has risen to the rank of Desthene while you curried favor with your betters and remained a common scribe. They call me Lady Corisonde at court in Rhostshyl."

But 'Malkin only laughed. "Why I'm delighted to hear it, Kitten. No doubt you can use your influence with the Rhaicime to have me made Palace Chancellor."

For answer, Corson wrenched open one of the crates on the cart and pulled out an ornately tooled and gilded leatherbound volume. "Have a look at this, then, if you think it's all a lie. I'm bringing these books to the Lady Nyctasia, and she wouldn't trust them to anyone but me."

He took it from her and examined it curiously, then suddenly gasped, "Hraestlind's *Elaborations*! Is it possible?" Reverently he turned over a few of the thick vellum pages. "And it looks to be genuine—Corson, this work is priceless! I don't know of a complete copy outside of YuVoes. What else do you have there, in the *vahn's* name?"

"Only some wine. And a lot of other rare and valuable books—for the Rhaicime's library, you see," Corson said smugly. "That's what she needs you scholars for, to help her take stock of the wretched things." She held out her hand for *The Elaborations of Hraestlind*.

'Malkin surrendered it reluctantly. "I don't doubt that they belong to Her Ladyship, but all the same, Corson, it won't do to go about claiming that you know the ruler of the city just because you've been hired to deliver these books to her. I know you mean no harm by it, but you could get in trouble in Rhostshyl for talk like that."

Corson could afford to bide her time. "Oh, don't worry about me," she said, with a smile which Nyctasia would have recognized as dangerous. "Climb in, why don't you? You can ride in the cart—just don't try to make off with any of those books, so I warn you."

'Malkin was not surprised that Corson was admitted to the palace without challenge. Evidently she undertook important commissions for the court and was known to the guards, who joked with her as she passed, asking, "Eh, Lady Corson, is that your squire or your latest conquest?"

"Him? He's no one at all," said Corson. "Just another scribbler for Her Ladyship's collection."

But when Corson led him to a luxuriously appointed chamber among the private apartments, and claimed it as her own, 'Malkin felt that she was carrying the game too far, in her desire to impress him. "Corson, let's go," he began worriedly. "If we're found here—"

When the door was flung open, he immediately started to invent plausible reasons for their presence there, but explanations proved unnecessary. The woman who raced into the room was alone, except for a huge hound, and both were plainly quite pleased to find Corson there.

Nyctasia had left orders that she was to be informed straightway of Corson's arrival, and she came at once to seek her out and assure herself that the books had been delivered safely. She threw her arms around Corson, and the dog leaped up to lick her face in welcome. Laughing, Corson picked up Nyctasia and kissed her.

She couldn't be anyone of authority, 'Malkin saw with relief. She was dressed in worn breeches and an old tunic, her hands and face were grimy, and straw clung to her clothes and her close-cropped hair. Still, she was remarkably pretty, for all that. . . .

"Corson, my love!" Nyctasia was exclaiming. "I see your arm's quite healed. And you met with no mishap on the road?"

"Oh, Milady's beloved books are all here, don't worry. I gave them over to Ioras. But what have you been playing at, you unkempt sloven? You're not fit to be seen."

"There's mange in the kennels again. I've been dosing the dogs, and this time I mean to—"

'Malkin felt that he'd been a bystander at this reunion for quite long enough. "Corson, present me to this dainty wench," he broke in, slapping Nyctasia affably on the thigh.

She whirled around to stare at him in astonishment, the dog growled a warning, and Corson gave a shout of laughter. " 'Malkin, you rutting dolt, this is the Rhaicime, not a common tart! It's most likely high treason to take liberties with her."

Nyctasia quickly recovered her equanimity. "Never mind, Corson, I'd not expect a friend of yours to have manners. But I must go bathe and dress now—I'll see you at dinner." She dashed out as unceremoniously as she'd appeared, the great dog at her heels.

It did not occur to 'Malkin for a moment that Corson had been telling him the truth.

Nyctasia thought no more of the matter, but Corson resolved to take full advantage of 'Malkin's grave offense against propriety. "Now you're in the stew, and no mistake, my lad," she said ominously. "The Lady Nyctasia may act like a stable-lass when she chooses, but she doesn't stand for familiarity like that from a stranger. I'll try to excuse your boorish behavior to her, but you'll be lucky to get out of this scrape with a flogging, I fear. She didn't say much, but she was angry, I can tell."

"Corson, if you've quite finished spinning your fancies, we'd best be on our way before someone else discovers that you keep your trysts here."

"Very well, if you insist," said Corson. "Come along." She made no further attempt to convince him of her own or Nyctasia's standing at court, but merely turned him over to a page, with instructions to find him lodgings and a place at table among the students and other rabble.

It was not a place of distinction. Educated folk of every description had been flocking to Rhostshyl since word of the Cymvelan library had been heralded abroad, and 'Malkin found himself one of a motley crowd of scholars and scribes, all hoping to turn their learning to profit. He had to squint across nearly the whole length of the great dining hall to get a glimpse of the personages at the higher tables. He was at too great a distance to recognize Nyctasia when she first entered, though had he been nearer he might well have failed to see in her the sprightly grime-stained waif of an hour before. She now wore a graceful pearl-grey tunic of the finest linen, and hose of silver-grey silk which had surely never been worn within a kennel. It was not her elegant clothes which transformed her, however, so much as the air of nobility and dignity with which she made her entrance, bowing to right and left as she graciously acknowledged the greetings of the court.

Everyone rose, and there were murmurs, at 'Malkin's table, of "There's the Rhaicime . . . the small one with the dark hair."

"Are you sure? I thought she was older."

"Look how she wears her chain of office, fool—round her head, not round her neck like the rest."

"Never mind *her*—what I want to know is, who's the tall one? *Vahn*, what a beauty!"

Corson had changed her travel-worn garments for a gown of fawn-colored silk, with a close-fitting bodice cut fashionably low, a full, flowing skirt, and loose sleeves slashed open and gathered at the wrist with a golden band. Her long hair had been woven into three plaits, braided together and entwined with strands of small gold beads. She looked even more stately than Nyctasia, and 'Malkin might not have known either of them had they not been followed into the hall by a very large and all too familiar-looking hound.

'Malkin suddenly felt faint.

"That's the Desthene Corisonde," someone was saying. "She used to be Lady Nyctasia's bodyguard, as I hear it, but they say she's more than that to Her Ladyship now. . . ."

Now that Nyctasia had arrived, the meal could commence. When she took her place at the head of the highest table, the rest resumed their seats, and food was soon placed before the company. But 'Malkin had completely lost his appetite.

3

"So this friend of yours is a scholar?" said Nyctasia.

"Well, so he says. I'm no judge of such things."

Dinner was long over, and Corson and Nyctasia had withdrawn to Nyctasia's private rooms to escape the court formalities and have a long talk in comfort. Palace etiquette had always been second nature to Nyctasia, but since her return to Rhostshyl she had begun to find it tedious and irksome. As she and Corson exchanged their news, she busied herself unpacking and examining some of the new shipment of books.

Corson had kicked off her tight, gold-tooled shoes and sat lounging on a couch, drinking some of the new shipment of wine. The dog, Greymantle, lay sprawled at her feet in great contentment as she idly scratched his belly with one bare foot. "Still, I think he must be a true scholar like you, Nyc," she said pensively. "He does nothing but talk and never says a sensible word, he doesn't know anything useful, and he's never done a day's work in his life."

Nyctasia did not look up from her task. "You surprise me, Corson. I thought your old friends were all brigands and cutthroats. How do you come to know someone reputable?"

"Reputable! I met him in prison! He was only a mangy, vagabond student then." Corson chuckled. "But I took him for the fount of all learning, I confess. I traveled about with him for a few months when I was just out of the army. I didn't know my left hand from my right in those days."

"I can't imagine how you lasted a week in the army," Nyctasia said absently, blowing dust from a fragile, faded old volume, "with your insolent tongue and your savage temper. I know little enough about it, but I'd always supposed that a soldier had to observe a certain degree of discipline and obedience. I don't believe that you could be civil to the Empress herself for long."

"Oh, they beat the nonsense out of me soon enough," Corson said grimly. "I learn quickly, you know, and I learned first of all that there were worse things than following orders." She poured herself more wine and downed it at once. "I learned other lessons too—not just weaponry and strategy—I learned that real power is something you can't fight with your fists. Where I came from I could get by because I was bigger and stronger than most—I could bully anyone who was in my way. But we were all of us poor and powerless. It was in the army I found out that the wide world was different from a little swamp village. If you don't humble yourself before the powerful, you'll be crushed, no matter how big and strong you are. *That's* a lesson you couldn't learn from those books of yours, or from all the books ever penned by scholars."

"Yes, you're right," said Nyctasia, who was now listening attentively. Corson had rarely spoken of her years in the Imperial Army. "Only experience can teach such wisdom as that. There are many things that one doesn't learn from books, and humility is among them."

"Well, I never learned to like it," Corson brooded. "I hated the army and all its lessons. I swore I'd go my own way as soon as my term was over—if I lived that long—and that I'd never re-enlist, no matter how desperate I might be. And I kept to that, too, but I'd not have survived a season on my own if I hadn't first learned how to *serve*. I was lucky to have been a soldier, in truth. Asye knows what would have become of me if I hadn't been sold into the army."

"Sold! Were your people slaves, then?"

"No, we were free folk—free to starve or scratch a living out of scrub forest and swampland. Only the strongest could hope to be taken on by the army. The others envied me the chance."

"But, Corson, how could you be sold?"

"How not? If I'd been on my own I could have had the recruitment fee for myself, but I was still under my family's roof, so they got the money for enlisting me. That was fair enough, I suppose, though I grudged it to them at the time. They'd raised and fed me as best they could, after all. They were entitled to some recompense."

"But to make a soldier of you against your will—!"

"It wasn't against my will," said Corson, surprised. "All the young folk of Torisk hoped the recruiters would take them. We knew that the army fed you well and put clothes on your back. And it was the only way for folk like us to learn a trade—don't you know that?"

"That too," Nyctasia said seriously, "one doesn't learn from books. How old were you when you were . . . sold?"

"Now how would I know? We didn't have the means to keep records. Someone once told me, 'You were born the summer that lightning burned three cottages,' but that didn't mean much to me—or to the imperial recruiters. They aren't supposed to take a child under fifteen years, but they're not choosy if one is big enough, as I was. They don't ask, 'How old is this child?' but just 'Is this child of an age to be enlisted?' And folk have learned to say just 'Yes.' No one asks more questions, and no one can prove that a recruit is underage."

"Then you don't know how old you are now?" Nyctasia asked, incredulous.

Corson shrugged. "Not to put a number to it. What difference does it make?"

Nyctasia was dumbfounded. Such numbers were of immense significance for those of her station, for only upon coming of age did one assume the full responsibilities and privileges of one's rank. Precise records of kinship were necessary to determine the inheritance of titles and property. What with the many twins in the Edonaris line, mere minutes of life might mean a great deal. Nyctasia could hardly imagine being unaware of, much less indifferent to, her own exact age, or even the ages of her kin.

"So I can't blame them for selling me, you see," Corson was saying. "There wasn't food enough to go around, and I ate more than my share. I don't know what you're so vexed at—when children are apprenticed to a trade, no one consults their wishes."

"Most professions are not so likely to be fatal, however."

"Nyc, dying in battle's better than dying of hunger, or being worked to death slowly, year after year! You don't understand at all—the poor don't have *choices*. Asye, most don't even have chances. My people gave me a chance to better myself, and that's more than they ever had themselves. Oh, they didn't do it for my sake, I know. They did it for the money, and to have one less mouth to feed. But I'll tell you this—I had sisters and brothers, and I'd wager what you like that some of them are dead now, and that none of them live so well as I do."

Nyctasia was silent for a time, pondering Corson's words. So Corson did not even know whether her closest blood kin were living or dead! This was strangest of all to Nyctasia, daughter of an ancient dynasty that could trace the fate of its every child for centuries past. At last she asked hesitantly, "Don't you ever wonder what's become of them, Corson?"

Corson shook her head. "Why? I hardly remember them now. It almost seems as if my life started when I joined the Imperial Army . . ."

But if Corson had forgotten much of her life before her enlistment, she remembered the life that followed it all too well. Though years had passed since her training as a footsoldier, yet the lessons in degradation and helplessness she'd been forced to learn then were still too raw and rankling for her to speak of them to Nyctasia. Even Steifann had heard little of those memories.

The new recruits had been marched for weeks through the wasteland of the southern barrens, into the lowest reaches of Liruvath, where the westerners would be less likely to try to desert. Here they had no friends or kinfolk to hide them, and they knew neither the land nor the language. Most had never been outside of their villages before.

But the long march did not discourage many of Corson's companions. The food was plentiful, and they were used to toil and hardship. It was not until they reached their training camp and were turned over to their commanders and instructors that they discovered the brutality and abuse that have always been a new recruit's lot. The pick of their villages for strength and prowess with their fists, these proud youths now for the first time found themselves at the mercy of others, driven and chivvied about with kicks and curses, taunted and threatened like the lowest of slaves, yet not daring—if they were wise—to answer a word, much less raise a hand, in their own defense.

When Corson had been whipped for insolence and disobedience, she learned to hold her tongue and do as she was told. When she had spent time locked in a small wooden cage, she gave up all thought of deserting. And when she, along with the rest of the assembled camp, had been forced to witness a man being flogged to death for attacking an officer, she learned to control her quick temper, whatever the provocation. Their comrade's torn body, hung at the gate to feed the crows, served to remind the cowed recruits of this latest lesson. No matter how Corson was goaded and insulted, no matter if she was spat upon, no matter what she was ordered to do, no matter how hard she was hit, she made herself stand silent, clenching and unclenching her fists instead of using them. But most of all, at such times, she thought of the cage. More than any beating, perhaps more than death, Corson feared the cage. She would do anything, endure anything, to keep out of its nightmare grip, which had left her with a horror of confinement that haunted her still, years afterward.

Like most of her company, Corson was glad when they were finally sent north to Yuvahn to join forces with the imperial legions ever defending—and expanding—the borders of Liruvath. It seemed that she'd spent a lifetime in the training camp, and any change was welcome, even at the risk of her life.

The footsoldiers feared for their lives with good reason, for they were ill-equipped and ill-defended, mere fodder for the beasts of battle. They cared nothing for victory or empire, but ran forward to meet the enemy, when ordered, only because there were archers waiting in the rearguard to fell those who retreated. Corson's only thought was to somehow survive the fray, but once she found herself in the thick of combat all thought was lost, swept away by the overpowering realization that she was finally, after her many months of training, *free to act*. She felt as if she had suddenly been released from bonds or some long imprisonment. She need no longer hold herself in check—at last she could give rein to her stifled wrath. Fury overcame fear, and she laid about her with her broadsword like one possessed by a murderous demon. No matter that those she slaughtered were not to blame for her torment—the relief of unleashing her pent-up anger was too great to be resisted by reason. Corson's training had been a complete success.

It was not long before her commanders recognized Corson's value to the regiment. She was often commended for her bravery in battle, though her superiors knew as well as she that courage had nothing to do with her prowess. Hers was the true battle-frenzy born of rage and blind hatred, not for the enemy, but for anyone or anything that stood in her way. She was worth a score of common soldiers in the field, and she was soon removed from her company of raw recruits and assigned to a place among a troop of seasoned warriors. She was taught to fight on horseback, and given further training with shield and spear and sword. In time, her skill with weapons grew so marked that she was made an instructor herself, treating those beneath her no better than she had been treated. By the time her term of service was over, Corson had risen in the ranks to become a commander, and led her own troops into battle. But she never forgot how much she was still in the power of her superiors, and though she was offered favorable terms to re-enlist, she was not tempted to accept. The army was a cage.

When she was released, Corson took her honed hatred and her deadly rage into the service of anyone who'd pay well for a skilled soldier-of-fortune. She knew enough to be respectful to her employers, but she flouted the civil authorities as much as she dared, and was soon known to the magistrates of more than one city as a troublemaker and a scofflaw. Each time she was pilloried or thrown into prison, she vowed to herself that she would behave more wisely in the future. The terror of confinement and the humiliation of helplessness would curb her reckless audacity for a time, until too much ale overcame her resolve, and the savage fury within her gathered strength to break free again.

Corson remembered those days very well indeed, but to Nyctasia she said only, "It almost seems as if my life started when I joined the Imperial Army . . . and a dog's life it was, too, but I've no cause to complain—it taught me how to survive. When I got out, I only had to learn how to live." She suddenly began to laugh. "And 'Malkin had a hand in that, to do him justice. No doubt you think it's uphill work to make a lady of the likes of me, Nyc, but 'Malkin had to make a human being of me first!"

"That must have required some courage. However did he go about it?"

"Talk," said Corson. "Neverending talk, worse even than you, I believe—or perhaps it's just that I'm better used to it nowadays. But 'Malkin was the first book-learned blatherskite I'd ever met, and I was none too pleased to meet him, I can tell you. He was scared out of his wits, so he jabbered like a jay the whole time. He'd never been in prison before, you see—"

"Neither had I, before I met you," Nyctasia pointed out. "It's an experience that seems to befall your companions as a matter of course."

"I had nothing to do with his arrest–not that time, anyway. I'd never laid eyes on him till they threw him into my cell. He'd tried to sneak out of an inn without paying—a student's trick if there ever was one."

"And why were *you* in prison on that occasion?"

"Hlann Asye, Nyc, how should I remember that? For drunken brawling, I suppose." She shrugged. "I *was* sotted, I remember that. My head was aching, and his maddening chatter didn't help. The cell was nothing but a hole in the wall, but at least it was a quiet hole before that one turned up."

"I'm surprised that you didn't just wring his neck."

"I probably would have, but to tell you the truth, I thought at first that he was crazy, and it's bad luck to kill mad people. Finally I seduced him, just to stop his talk—not that it did stop."

"I see! Then it's not bad luck to . . . ?"

"Well, he's not ill-favored," Corson admitted. "And I was curious, too. They say students are the best lovers, you know, and I'd never had one before."

"Students have their uses. I trust you weren't disappointed?"

"Oh, you could do worse, Nyc. He knows what he's about." She sipped her wine in silence for a moment. "And he was a change from what I was used to, that's certain. The only love-talk I knew was the crudest sort, and I thought he was mocking me when he called me 'Kitten.' I threatened to tear out his tongue for him, and then—I'll never forget it—he said, so quietly, so earnestly, 'Girl, have you had so little affection in your life that you don't know it when you meet it?' Gods! I'd *never* heard anyone talk like that—I was *spellbound*! After that, I started to listen to him."

"Ah, when you listen, you're liable to learn something. You

do listen occasionally, I've noticed. Not often, but when you do, you learn."

"I listen to you when you say anything worth the hearing. Sometimes you do. Not often, but when you do, I listen."

"Go on with your story, if you please. I find it most instructive. It was his lovemaking, then, that persuaded you of his wisdom?"

"Perhaps it was. But what really beguiled me was a curious story he told me . . . I don't know now why I was so staggered by the thing. It was just some moonshine about a lady who lived in a tower, with a lot of magic creatures, and a treasure . . . but then it wasn't about those things at all. I wish I remembered how it ran."

"But I believe I know the very tale—wait, I'll just run to the library." Greymantle scrambled to his feet and followed, unwilling, as ever, to let Nyctasia out of his sight. Corson, too, was reluctant to let her go by herself. She disapproved of Nyctasia's habit of going about unarmed and unguarded. Though her power in Rhostshyl was now fairly secure, she still had enemies at court who could prove dangerous if given a chance. Nyctasia claimed that her seeming vulnerability was in fact a protection, because it made her appear so confident in her power that no one dared attack her. Corson thought this a clever notion, but she was not convinced that it would stand the test. Nyc had the dog with her, of course, but still . . .

But Nyctasia was back in a trice, carrying a small, well-worn book inscribed with the title *The Parables of Albrechas the Scrivener*. "Listen," she said, dropping into a chair, "is this the one?"

"There was once a proud and powerful lady who ruled a fair and flourishing domain, where none held sway but she. Her dwelling was a tall tower, a fortress that had never yet been overthrown, for it was built of the strongest stone, and well provisioned against a siege. To guard her, moreover, the lady had two magic hounds that could defend their mistress against the threat of thief or enemy. When she ventured abroad, two magic horses drew her carriage, and these steeds could carry her to safety too swiftly for any foe to follow. Two magic eagles had she as well, that nested in the heights of the tower and flew every day through her domain to spy out all that passed, lest any danger should take her unawares.

"Now this favored and fortunate lady guarded, in the very peak and pinnacle of her tower, a certain rare crystal, carven like a woman's head, and this was the greatest treasure of all that she possessed. For this crystal was an infallible oracle that could answer any question and resolve any dilemma. Thus did the mistress of the tower pass her days in safety and security, for none in all the land might overcome her defenses nor challenge her dominion.

"But at last came a foeman more cunning than the rest, for he came in the guise of a friend, with smiles and charm and flattery, and he so won the trust of the lady that she herself unbarred the way and welcomed him within. Many visits did he make her, and ever did the mistress of the tower take greater delight in his company. Though her true friends warned her that he was a dangerous thief and deceiver, yet she heeded them not, but invited this false friend to visit her all the more. Finally she grew to love the dissembler so well that she could hardly bear to be parted from him for a day. And then one evening, when they sat together at dinner and made merry, the treacherous one slyly gave to the unwary lady a potent sleeping-draught that straightway left her senseless as one struck down by a grievous malady. And as she lay thus, all unknowing, he made his way secretly to the crown of the tower and took the treasure, hiding it away beneath his cloak.

"Now when, in his flight, the thief passed the chamber where the lady lay, the crystal head cried out to her, 'Ware thief! Hark, hark, my mistress!' But the lady awoke in such great pain and distress that she had not the strength to stop him. She called upon her hounds to seize the thief, but he had chained them in their kennels, and she found herself too faint and weak to set them free. Thus he made his escape from the tower with the treasure. She then bade her horses give chase to the thief, but he had hobbled them in their stalls, and the lady was too ill and giddy to loose them. And so he fled far from the tower with the treasure. At last she sent her birds to fly aloft and discover whither the thief was bound, but he had clipped their wings, and therefore the treasure was lost forever.

"Without the magic oracle to advise her, the lady knew not what course to take, and her domain was left undefended. Her enemies, lying in wait, showed no mercy but stormed the tower forthwith and took her prisoner. And thus did the mistress of the tower end her days in sorrow and shame, while the thief went free to deceive and despoil others, as we may witness any day we will. Now tell me the name, if you can, of this falsehearted flatterer, for you know him as well as another, and better than some."

"I remember it all now," Corson exclaimed. "And I was taken in by it, too, right to the hilt! 'Malkin said, 'What would you have done, in that lady's place?' And I said, 'She was nothing but a fool. That would never have happened to me!' "

"So he led you right into the trap—how very unkind."

"Unkind, perhaps, but very like a student."

"And then I suppose he said, 'But it has happened to you. If she was a fool, then you are one as well.' No?"

Corson nodded. "I said, 'Who are you calling a fool, you little worm?' but he only answered so rutting reasonably, 'You have called yourself so, for you are mistress of the tower, and the name of the thief is Drink.' "

" 'For do you not partake thereof by your own will and desire?' " Nyctasia read. " 'Does not drink flatter you by causing you to feel clever and strong, and powerfully pleased with yourself withal?' "

"He had me in the net, and no mistake, the smug wretch. I wriggled and writhed but there was no getting out of it—he had explanations for everything. The tower was meant to be my own body, according to him, and the land was my life, I think. 'The hounds are your two hands,' he said, 'that don't do your will when you've had too much ale. And the horses are your legs that can't carry you when you're drunk.' " Corson began to mimic 'Malkin's learned tone. " 'And what are the eagles but your own eyes that won't guide you when your senses are addled with drink?' "

"And the oracle," Nyctasia concluded, closing the book, "is Reason, the greatest treasure humankind possesses."

"I was even fool enough to ask why the crystal hadn't warned her of the thief, since it knew everything, and 'Malkin explained that she hadn't asked its advice. 'Had you consulted your reason,' he said, 'you'd not have gotten drunk and been thrown in prison.' Well, I didn't know much in those days, but I knew when I was beaten. If he'd just told me it was my own fault I was in prison, I'd probably have broken his neck, but once he'd tricked me into saying it myself I couldn't deny it. And I thought he'd made up that tale himself, just for my sake.

I'd never heard such a thing before, a story that said one thing and meant another—like one of those lying Cymvelan riddles."

"Such a tale is called an allegory."

"That's what 'Malkin said. No doubt you were raised on allegories with your mother's milk, Nyc, but to me it seemed confoundingly clever and deep."

"Yet here you sit swilling down wine," Nyctasia teased. "You can't have taken the moral of the story much to heart."

Corson flushed. "It takes more than a few glasses of wine to get the better of me! I'm not a little twig of a thing like you. And I never get myself arrested for public drunkenness any more—well, hardly ever, that is. But it wasn't 'Malkin and his allegories that cured me of that. It was Steifann."

"And not by talking, I daresay."

Corson chuckled. "He didn't use a lot of big words—just a few well-chosen, loud ones. Very easy they were to understand, too. That prating popinjay 'Malkin used to say, 'Corson, if you can't be less *conspicuous*, I shall be forced to forego your acquaintance.' And then he did," she added, "the bastard."

"For shame," said Nyctasia. "That proves he was no gentleman."

"He was a worthless, bootlicking mongrel, and I'd have realized that if I'd had any sense. He was in prison the same as me, and no better off than I was, but to hear him tell it, you'd have thought that was just some trifling inconvenience to him. He always talked as if he was going to be someone powerful and important one day, and I believed him. Eh—I was younger then, and if you only understand one word in three that someone says, of course you think it must all be great wisdom." Corson brooded over her memories for a few moments, then said slowly, "And I thought . . . that maybe if I could learn to read, and to talk like that, perhaps I'd not be poor and powerless all my days, you see. He was so sure of himself. That's why I took up with him and let him teach me things. But all I learned from him was fancy words and notions—though he did teach me to read, for all the good that's ever done me."

Nyctasia, who spent her every spare moment engrossed in her books, said only, "You're a woman of deeds, to be sure. But learning never goes to waste, they say."

"Maybe not. After all, Steifann was impressed that I could read."

"As was I."

Corson suddenly laughed. "Some learning is wasted, though. You'd agree if you'd ever seen 'Malkin with sword in hand. He wanted me to make a swordsman of him, but he could sooner have made a scholar of me. I learned my letters readily enough, but he didn't last long at his lessons."

Nyctasia had suffered through several such lessons herself. "If you dealt with him as you do with me, it's small wonder he chose to forego your society."

"Oh, 'Malkin was much worse at it than you are, so he had a harder time of it. You're not such a bad pupil. You're learning."

"That's high praise from you. Still, anyone who so much as survives an hour's instruction at your hands is to be congratulated."

"Huh—I'm *gentle* with you, I'll have you know. If I handled you the way we trained recruits in the army—"

"If you did, I'd have your head. So your friend never became powerful and important, I take it?"

"Not he. He's still nothing but grand talk. He came here on foot to look for work, like all the others of his ilk you've got swarming over the palace. I told him I could introduce him to you, but he didn't believe a word of it. He thought I was still the common ruffian who wasn't good enough for him before, but he knows better now!" Corson grinned triumphantly. "I've had a full measure of vengeance on that one at last!"

"Vengeance? What do you mean?"

"You'll see. Why don't you send for him, since you take such an interest in the fellow? I said I'd arrange an audience with you, after all."

'Malkin had eaten very little of his dinner. He had slipped out of the dining hall as soon as he could possibly do so without calling attention to himself, in hopes of reaching his lodgings and gathering his few possessions before his absence was noticed. There was nothing to be gained by staying in the city now, curse the luck! He had not relished the prospect of spending the night in the open, but a night in the pillory was even less inviting. Better to risk the dangers of the road than the wrath of the Rhaicime. If only he'd known who she was, he could have turned that chance meeting to advantage, and instead he'd ruined his prospects for preferment at court and offended the ruler of the city! But it was no use thinking of that now—the only thing to do was to get away from the palace before it was too late, and try to sneak out of Rhostshyl under cover of darkness.

But it was already too late.

As he hurriedly left his quarters, carrying his cloak and satchel, he was stopped just outside the door by one of the palace guard, who demanded, "Desmalkin brenn Cerrogh?" 'Malkin retreated a few paces, but there was another guard at his back, blocking the corridor behind him.

"Er . . . no," said 'Malkin. "He was here, but he's gone to dinner. Excuse me, if you will." He tried to edge past, but suddenly a sword was in his way, the point only inches from his stomach.

"And where are you off to in such a rush, eh?"

"Let me pass! I want to get a meal too, and I'm late already," 'Malkin protested. "You've no call to interfere with me."

"No need for games," said the other sentry, sounding amused. "This is the one. Her Ladyship pointed him out to me herself."

"I assure you this is quite unnecessary," 'Malkin said, sweating. "It's all a mistake. I'm a friend of the Lady Corisonde—"

At this, both guards broke into laughter. "A friend of hers, are you?" one of them said. "Who isn't a friend of hers? Come along, we've orders for your arrest, and that's all we need to know. We don't care who your friends are, or who your family are either." She held 'Malkin at swordpoint while the other pulled his arms behind his back and fastened his wrists with manacles. He was then led to a small cell in the dungeons beneath the palace, where he had been waiting ever since, expecting the worst. All the while that Corson had been relating her reminiscences to Nyctasia, 'Malkin had been pacing his cell in a grim silence broken only by the conversation of the warders outside the barred door.

"What did that one do to land himself in so much trouble?"

"Insulted the Rhaicime, nothing less, the rutting fool. I've never seen her in such a rage." He recounted 'Malkin's crime, and his cohort gave a whistle of amazement.

"He must be crazed, poor wretch. He'll lose a hand for that, I shouldn't wonder."

By the time Nyctasia sent for him, 'Malkin was in such a state that it was almost a relief to be summoned to his doom.

If Nyctasia thought it strange that Corson's friend arrived escorted by armed guards, instead of by a page, she found it stranger still when he threw himself at her feet, abjectly imploring her pardon and declaring his innocence of any intention of offending her. No wonder Corson had taken him for a madman at their first meeting—there seemed to be no telling what the man would do next.

Fortunately for her composure, if not for 'Malkin's, his entreaties were cut short by Greymantle, who naturally assumed that anyone who was on the floor was there to make friends with him. He came over to 'Malkin, wagging his tail, and began to lick his face good-naturedly, interrupting the flow of his eloquence, and leaving him even more disconcerted than before.

Corson was delighted beyond measure at the success of her prank, and she dismissed her comrades from the palace garrison with hearty thanks for their help in carrying out the deception. "Just don't forget the ale you owe us," one reminded her in parting.

"A lady always pays her debts," said Corson, and fell back onto the couch, overcome with laughter. She prodded 'Malkin with one foot, and ordered, "Get up, you sniveling weasel. That'll teach you not to doubt the word of a Desthene." She was laughing too hard to go on, and it was left to Nyctasia to assure 'Malkin that he had been arrested without her knowledge, and entirely at Corson's instigation. But even Nyctasia, despite her good breeding, found it difficult to conceal her amusement at her guest's discomfiture. 'Malkin rose to his feet unsteadily and looked around in dismay, unable to think of a thing to say. Never had he felt so thoroughly humiliated.

Contrite, Nyctasia tried to put him at his ease. "Do sit down, sir—don't mind the hound, he means no harm. Pray take some wine, if Corson has left any."

"I haven't," Corson said cheerfully.

"Then send for more, woman. I'm sure our guest could do with some, after the spiteful trick you've played him! Really, Corson, such buffoonery is beneath the dignity of a lady."

Corson was completely unrepentant. "I don't care," she said, between gasps of hilarity. "He deserved it. Maybe next time he'll think twice before he drops someone's acquaintance."

Nyctasia shook her head. "It's quite useless to remonstrate with her, as you no doubt know. She's perfectly incorrigible."

"I am not. What does that mean?"

"It means," 'Malkin said furiously, "that you can't be taught to behave decently by any means whatsoever!" He would dearly have liked to tell Corson exactly what he thought of her, but he hesitated to use such uncouth language before the Rhaicime.

"Now you mustn't think yourself too ill-used," said Nyctasia. "That one is capable of much worse. She tried to *sell* me once, at the Harvest Fair in Osela."

"Yet you made her a Desthene?" demanded 'Malkin, looking from one woman to the other in bewilderment. Both were laughing now.

"It was rash of me, true. Perhaps I should have her executed now and have done with it, if only for her intolerable impertinence. Do you favor hanging or beheading?"

"Flaying and disemboweling," 'Malkin said promptly, following Nyctasia's lead like a true courtier. "Boiling in oil. Drawing and quartering. I'd be honored to carry out the sentence myself."

"Alas, such penalties are forbidden by law in Rhostshyl, however deserving the culprit."

"But as sole ruler of the Rhaicimate, Your Ladyship could declare an exception in this case," 'Malkin urged. "Perhaps a pit of vipers . . . ?" he suggested.

"*You're* a viper," said Corson. "You should be thanking me, 'Malkin, for bringing you to the attention of the Rhaicime! If not for me, you'd have bided your turn with the rest of that rout of bookworms. You might never have come to Nyc's notice. But *I've* told her what a fine scholar you are."

"Indeed yes, Corson's spoken very highly of your abilities," Nyctasia said smoothly. "I understand that you taught her to read—a heroic task, I should imagine. Surely one who could accomplish that could teach anything to anyone." Then her manner suddenly grew serious. "I think of establishing a school here, for the youth of the city, and perhaps for those of neighboring municipalities as well. I shall need able teachers for such an undertaking, but in truth that is only a small part of my plans. I require scholars learned in every discipline to carry out the task at hand." She gestured toward the books she'd been unpacking. "No doubt you've heard something of the lore-hoard of the Cymvelans, else you'd not be here."

"I've heard a great deal of students' talk, Rhaicime," 'Malkin said eagerly. "But I didn't credit the half of it till I saw some of the books Corson was bringing here—and even then I was hard put to believe my own senses. The *Lost Commentaries* of Lhesandru, Hraestlind's *Elaborations*!"

"Ah, the fabled *Elaborations*—do you know, I found them something of a disappointment. The expositions are of exceptional clarity, to be sure, but the material itself, in essence, can almost all be found in other sources."

'Malkin looked shocked. "Why . . . I suppose that *was* to be expected. We are told that the text was a 'prentice effort, after all. But surely the book itself is of enormous historical significance, if it's genuine. Its very existence lends conviction to much that the learned have dismissed as legendary—not only concerning Hraestlind herself, but the history of YuVoes and the Damiellid Dynasty, don't you agree?"

Nyctasia smiled. 'Malkin had certainly passed the first test. "Oh, assuredly. Scholars of the pre-Imperial era will find it most illuminating. And a few of the paradigms are interesting in themselves. But as extraordinary as this discovery may be, I myself was even more gratified to find that all the known treatises of Rosander the Sangreot are in this collection, in full."

"In full . . . ?" said 'Malkin doubtfully. "You can't mean *The Manifestations of the Fourth Veil*?"

Nyctasia reached for one of the books and passed it to him, without a word. A ribbon had been laid between the leaves to mark the place. "But this . . . this is in Tsathonic!" he exclaimed, gazing at the pages in disbelief. "Sweet *vahn*, generations of debate over the glosses—!" He fell silent, intent on studying the dense script.

Corson, exceedingly bored by the conversation, glanced at the book over his shoulder and gave a snort of contempt. "Dead languages!" she said. "We should have left these books in the crypt where we found them." She finished 'Malkin's wine and poured herself some more.

"Mind you, the accuracy of the transcription is far from

reliable," Nyctasia warned 'Malkin. "I question whether the scribe understood the nature of the work." She joined 'Malkin and pointed out a particular phrase.

"*Mar icoji*," he mused. "Yes, I see. *Marico ji* must have been intended. It's likely that this copy was made in the north, to judge from the slant of the serifs. I daresay the scribe knew no Tsathonic at all. But however corrupt the text, it's bound to resolve the major difficulties over the interpretation of the *Fragments*."

Nyctasia agreed. She was quite satisfied with 'Malkin. Evidently he had not spent all his time swindling innkeepers and lying in prison with ignorant mercenaries. "I've sent copies of the first few pages to the Imperial University," she said, " and some of the most renowned scholars of Liruvath are on their way here now, to consult the manuscript."

"Asye's eyes! *I'd* go from here to Liruvath just to hear no more of the thing!" Corson declared.

"Indeed?" said 'Malkin. "If you start now, you could be there before winter."

"I should have known better than to introduce the two of you. Everyone knows when two scholars get to talking you can't put in a word to tell them the house is afire. When those others get here from Liruvath, all of Rhostshyl will be talked to a stupor."

"Pay her no heed," advised Nyctasia, who knew that Corson disliked being ignored much more than being reproached or reviled. "Have you noticed that the word given as 'blind' in the *Fragments* is *vuhrtev*, and not *tsegre*, as has always been assumed?"

"No! Is it?" said 'Malkin, deeply interested. "That will altogether alter the acceptation of several passages. Why, the First Fragment alone. . . ."

Corson left them to it and went off to find more congenial company, slamming the door behind her.

'Malkin looked after her with dark disapproval. "That one will go too far one day," he predicted grimly.

"She already has, any number of times, but there seems to be a charmed impunity about her. Was she any the less brazen when you first made her acquaintance?"

"Brazen! She was barely human, my lady. I thought myself fortunate to escape with my life on that occasion."

"That would be when you met her in prison, would it not?"

"Er—yes—purely the result of a misunderstanding . . . and a magistrate with an unreasonable dislike of students." At Nyctasia's look of polite disbelief, he added, "Well, be that as it may, they'd no right to lock me up with a murderous madwoman. It was like being caged with a wild beast, I tell you. She raged around that cell cursing and howling and pounding the walls with her fists—I tried to stay out of her way, but there wasn't room enough."

"She did remark that it was rather crowded," said Nyctasia, without mentioning that in Corson's account it was 'Malkin who was the mad one. "I've never seen her quite like that. She must have been very drunk indeed."

"She'd certainly been drinking, but that wasn't all that ailed her. She was in a panic terror at being confined, out of her mind with fear—and fury. And she'd no one to take it out on until I came along. So there I was, half her size, defenseless, just a peaceable young scholar, you understand. I thought my last hour had come." If the tale amused the Rhaicime, 'Malkin thought, he might as well make the most of it. "I cowered in a corner and hoped she'd let me be, but she came storming over and kicked me and shouted, 'Talk to me, curse you, or I'll beat you into butter!' "

"And that's when you told her the Parable of the Drunkard?" said Nyctasia, laughing. So Corson had *forced* him to talk, had she?

"So I did—I'd forgotten. It did keep her calm for a bit, working out the meaning. But I was hard put to think up talk enough to satisfy her." He wondered what else Corson had told Lady Nyctasia. Knowing Corson, it was unlikely that she'd been at all discreet. And Her Ladyship didn't seem easily shocked, after all. . . . "I was so desperate that I even made love to her at last, just to distract her from murdering me," he continued. "And that was no pleasure, I assure you!"

"No?" said Nyctasia, who was thoroughly enjoying the conversation. "Of course, I shouldn't dream of doubting your word, sir, but . . ."

"Well, she smelled, for one thing," 'Malkin explained. "And she was utterly inexperienced, and exceedingly suspicious and hostile. The poor girl had never—"

"What, *Corson*? After her years in the army?"

"Oh, she'd been used by others, of course, but she'd never

had a proper lover who took the trouble to please her, if Your Ladyship takes my meaning. I had to teach her *everything*."

"I see . . . ! Still, you must have found some charm in her, if you took up with her after prison and taught her to read."

"She did follow me about for a time, but I had to put a stop to that after I found respectable scribe's work with Lord Dainor of Eilas. Corson was always in trouble with the authorities, and I was liable to lose my livelihood if I was taken for her confederate. I was sorry to part with her, in truth. She was an apt pupil—and not only at learning her letters." His glance met Nyctasia's, and both laughed.

"They do say that students make the best lovers," Nyctasia murmured, as if to herself.

"I don't wish to boast," 'Malkin said demurely, "but Corson was quite devoted to me in those days. But my lord would have dismissed me at once if I'd brought a shadow of disgrace upon his household. Not all the nobility are as tolerant and liberal as Your Ladyship. . . ."

His meaning was not lost on Nyctasia. "Oh, I daresay I can find work of *some* sort for such an exceptionally able teacher," she said.

4

"Those two will take to each other like flame to flax," Corson thought, chuckling to herself. "They might have been meant for one another. He'll have me to thank if he finds favor at court, that's all!"

She was greatly looking forward to telling her friends at the Hare the story of her triumph over 'Malkin. As she rode along the coast road on her way back to Chiastelm, she was already polishing and improving the tale for their benefit. Half the fun of the thing would be in the telling.

Corson had stayed in Rhostshyl for barely a fortnight, yet it seemed to her that she'd been away from Chiastelm for months. She wondered if it seemed that way to Steifann too. At the thought of him, she grinned broadly and broke into a verse of "The Host of the Hare." Nyctasia had taught her a few new stanzas to plague Steifann with.

> "Serving spirits to others
> Does give one a thirst,
> So he makes it his practice
> To have a few first.

But whatever's left over
He's willing to share,
So I give you the health
Of the host of the Hare:

His brew's never watered,
He draws a full measure,
For ale's his profession
But also his pleasure!

The boast of the coast
Is our excellent host.
In his honor I offer
The following toast,
And fortune will favor
The one who drinks most:

Tell me, what can a taverner
Buy with his gold
That's worth half so much
As the goods he has sold?"

Corson laughed aloud. It was an old joke, that riddle, but
none the worse for wear, in her opinion. "There's true
wisdom," she thought, "and worth three of 'Malkin's lessons
or Nyc's lectures." Corson knew what Steifann would say to
the allegory of the drunkard—she'd heard him say it often
enough. "The fault's with the drinker, not with the drink," was
his philosophy. "Folk who've no stomach for drink should let
it alone—and let *me* alone, into the bargain."

One of Steifann's merits as a tavern-keeper was that he could
out-drink any of his customers and not be much the worse for
it. But his influence on Corson, as she'd told Nyctasia, had
been rather sobering than otherwise. From the first, he'd no
more approved of her drunken rampages than 'Malkin had,
though he was well accustomed to dealing with her sort, and
had no fears for his reputation. An ale-house was bound to
attract its share of drunks and troublemakers, but to house one
on the premises was bad for business, and Steifann had not
gotten where he was by neglecting the good of his business.
Corson was too easily bored, too ready to pick a fight with a
customer or fly into a murderous rage over some harmless

gibe. Steifann had found her well-nigh irresistible, but her company was a luxury he could ill afford.

He had made allowances for her many times, had even posted bond for her when she was brought before the magistrates, and had accepted her often-repeated assurances that it wouldn't happen again. But when all else failed, finally even Steifann would lose patience with her. He'd turn her out of the Hare and they'd part with a furious argument and curses that could be heard throughout the harbor district. Steifann would assure anyone who'd listen that he was well rid of the she-demon at last, and would then spend days brooding about her, drinking too much, and finding fault with everything and everyone. Corson, for her part, would go her way alone, vowing that she'd stay free and untrammeled in future, that she needed no one—not a misbegotten student nor a bull-headed dramseller, neither of them ever satisfied with her ways, plague take the pair of them!

But during the time she'd spent with 'Malkin, Corson had grown used to having someone to talk to, someone to listen to, and she'd found Steifann an even better companion than 'Malkin had been. From the moment she'd first laid eyes on the brawny, bearded owner of The Jugged Hare, Corson had liked everything about him, from the unruly black hair falling into his face to the long, powerfully-built legs that made him fully as tall as she. He'd seemed the most desirable man Corson had met with in her young life, and she'd no sooner seen him than she started a violent fight with him.

She'd already been disgracefully drunk when she'd come into the Hare that night to get out of the rain. Wet and hungry and penniless, she'd been ripe for trouble, but the appearance of Steifann had done much to raise her spirits. He'd stood scowling down at her, hands on hips, and ordered her to get out, while Corson admired his green eyes and ignored his wrath. His fists were clenched, his sleeves pushed back to the elbow, and Corson thought she'd never seen anything so beautiful as those hard, muscled forearms, dark with wiry black hair. When threats failed, Steifann had tried to put her out by force, but though he was completely in the right, Corson had soon changed his mind, and he'd ended by urging her to stay.

And Corson had meant to stay. The better she'd come to know Steifann, the more she'd found to like about him—his good-natured grin and ready laugh, his passionate, possessive nature, and especially his way of treating her as an accepted, almost necessary member of his household. Whenever she took to the road, swearing that no pompous bastard of a tapster would tell her what to do, she'd find herself missing him sorely before the day was out. After her parting from 'Malkin she had thought of him often, but with bitterness and resentment. She had never longed for him as she did for Steifann each time he sent her packing.

When next her travels took her to the coast, Corson would chance to pass through Chiastelm, and Steifann, against his better judgment, always took her back with hardly a show of reluctance—hardly able, indeed, to disguise his delight. "It's the bane of my life to be cursed with this savage spitfire," he'd declare with unmistakable satisfaction. "It's fate and no use fighting it." And Corson, once she'd grown accustomed to the constant exchange of insults, threats and boasts that made up friendly conversation at the Hare, had learned to laugh and answer, "You love it, man! Without me to kick a spur into you, you'd perish of boredom in this dull town. You wouldn't know if you were dead or alive!" Then all would go well until the next time Corson's ungoverned temper and recklessness got the better of her.

Though she would have denied it in those days, Corson had known even then that she'd have only herself to blame if Steifann one day broke with her in earnest. She had not been ready to face that frightening truth, or to accept the responsibility of deserving his affection. But what had at last turned the tide in their uneasy union was a misadventure that wasn't Corson's fault at all.

She had wisely taken work with the night watch of Chiastelm at that time, to relieve the galling restlessness that too often led to drink and a dangerously quarrelsome mood. The city guard was more like the army than Corson cared for, but at least she was free to give it up if she chose, and the work was not so tedious and dreary as the household chores at the Hare. Steifann grumbled at having her away for the greater part of the night, but still, the job kept her in Chiastelm, and kept her out of trouble.

She usually returned to the Hare just before dawn, when Steifann did the day's marketing, and Walden filled the great

oven with newly-risen loaves. When she approached the yard
before sunrise one morning and was not met with the smell of
freshly-baking bread, she knew at once that something was
amiss, and she cloaked her lantern and drew near without a
sound. The kitchen was dark and deserted. She crossed it
silently to peer through a knothole in the door that led to the
taproom, and what she saw set the bloodlust raging through her
like a call to battle.

Walden lay on the floor, motionless, while Annin knelt
beside him trying to bind his wounds with her blood-soaked
apron. Only a few of the young scullions were in sight,
cowering against the far wall and staring at the three strangers
who stood guard, shortswords drawn. The others, Corson
realized, must have gone off to market with Steifann.

The thieves had chosen their time carefully, watching for
Steifann to depart before they struck. There should have been
time enough for them to overcome Steifann's people, break
open his strongbox with an axe, and make their escape in the
darkness before he returned from the marketplace. They had
laid their plans cleverly and well in advance. Too far in
advance, as it happened.

They hadn't known about Corson.

With surprise on her side, she fell upon the unsuspecting
thieves like a sudden storm that strikes without warning, leaving
uprooted trees and overturned marketstalls in its wake. She felled
two of the three at one blow, with a heavy bench, before even
drawing her blade, but by the time the third realized what was
happening, she was ready for him, sword in hand, immediately
on the attack.

Corson had the advantage of strength and skill, and the man
could not have held out against her for long, had not the fourth of
the intruders come rushing at her out of Steifann's quarters,
wielding a heavy axe. Caught between the two, Corson backed
away toward the kitchen, hoping that they would draw together
and come at her as one, making a single target of themselves. If
one of them had the sense to circle around behind her, they might
yet give her some trouble, she thought. But before they could
make their move, Annin settled the matter for them by attacking
the man nearest her, from behind. Experienced at tavern brawls,
she handily slammed a stool into the backs of his knees, cutting
his legs from under him and throwing him down with some force.

A well-trained swordsman would have thrust his weapon

well away from him as he pitched forward, instead of allowing the force of his fall to drive the edge against his own throat. But a common thief is rarely a well-trained swordsman. Annin, who'd been about to bring the stool down across his back, stopped and let it fall, seeing that there'd be no further danger from him. Instead, she gathered the weapons from the fallen thieves and herded her underlings out of harm's way, while Corson kept the man with the axe at bay.

Shooing the scullions out through the kitchen, Annin ordered, "You, straight to Leech Street and fetch someone—you, roust folk out and tell them we've thieves here. Run!"

Corson could hear their yells as they sped off, and so could her opponent. He had no time to lose if he was to get away, but Corson prolonged the fight, refusing to close with him. She pressed in to harry him, drawing his blows, then danced back, easily dodging the unwieldy axe and letting him wear himself out with clumsy swings of his heavy weapon. "You should throw it, fool," she taunted. "It's too big for a weakling like you to wield. It's only pulling you off balance. Soon I'll get past your guard and gut you!" It was sound advice, and Corson offered it in hopes that he wouldn't take her up on it.

"Are you still toying with that one?" Annin demanded, coming in from the kitchen with rags and a bucket. "Finish him, can't you! Do I have to do everything myself?"

"Leave him to me," Corson ordered. "He can't aim that thing, but he might hit you by chance. Keep out of the way."

"Oh, very well, but get on with it, then. It's almost daylight. There's work to be done." She spilled some of the water over Walden, who snorted and muttered angrily to himself without opening his eyes.

"Ah, you won't let me have my fun, Annin," Corson complained. "I had a dull night. This town's too quiet by half."

("What was so fearful," Annin said later, "was the way she *smiled*.")

The desperate thief felt himself weakening with each swing of the axe, but still he dared not throw it and leave himself armed only with his shortsword and dagger against Corson's longer reach and warrior's broadsword. He knew that he couldn't hold her off any longer on his own, but he took heart for a moment when one of his confederates crawled free from beneath the bench that had struck him down. The other had taken the blow to the back of her head and would be yet some time recovering, but he had only been dazed. Now he staggered to his feet and looked around him frantically for a weapon. As soon as he'd taken stock of the situation, however, he made a dash for the street-door, threw back the bolts and disappeared, ignoring the plight of his fellow robber.

The remaining combatant wisely decided to follow his example, now that the door behind him stood open. He edged toward it, flailing about with the axe, then finally flung it wildly at Corson and turned to flee.

It was a mistake to turn. Had he backed out the door, he could have seen the knife Corson threw, and perhaps avoided it. He ran on for a few paces across the threshold, after it struck him, then collapsed face downward in the street.

"Well done," said Annin, "we've blood enough in here." She wrung out another cloth and applied a fresh one to the side of Walden's head. He groaned and cursed at her weakly.

Corson retrieved her knife and joined them. "How is he?"

"The bleeding's stopped. He'll come 'round—he's just stunned. It wasn't the wounds, it was when they hit him with a log of firewood. Here, help me get him off the floor."

And that was how Steifann found them, just then, as he ran into the taproom, alarmed at finding the house silent and the kitchen empty. "What's happened—where are all of you—" he called, then stopped and stared, faced with the aftermath of bloodshed and mayhem. He saw furniture overturned, blood spilled, the lifeless bodies of strangers on the floor at his feet.

He saw Walden lying wounded, supported by Annin, while Corson stood over them, knife in hand, her blade still crimson.

This time, Steifann didn't shout or curse at her. His voice was quite level, deliberate and quiet, almost soft, as he said to Corson, "The blood's on my hands. I should have known you'd never change. Just get out of my place, you mercenary trash, and don't come back here again, I warn you." His face was a mask of fury and contempt.

Corson went white. She understood now that she'd never seen Steifann truly angry before, despite their many quarrels. Not trusting herself to answer him, she turned away and went into his room, without a word.

It was Annin who explained how matters stood, as between them she and Steifann got Walden to his feet. "Corson didn't do this, Steifann, you fool! A pack of armed robbers broke in here after you left—those two are what's left of 'em—oh, and another one out there. Walden went at them with a cleaver, but they were too many for him."

"Rutting cowards," Walden said thickly, and winced.

"If Corson hadn't come along when she did, the bastards would have gotten away. You've her to thank that they didn't make off with every crescent you've saved, and cut all our throats, as like as not!" This was not likely, in fact, since the thieves would surely have murdered them at the outset if they'd planned to do so at all. But Annin, indignant on Corson's behalf, was not above a little exaggeration in the interests of justice.

It took Steifann some moments to get his bearings. "Thieves . . . ?" he said vaguely, as if he'd never heard the word before. He looked around in confusion, pushing the hair back from his forehead. "Oh . . . but I . . . Well, call for the Watch, then."

Corson stood leaning in the doorway, her pack over her shoulder. "I *am* the Watch," she said grimly. "Remember?"

"But you don't have to go," Steifann had protested. "Why should you? You weren't to blame—"

"This time," Corson interrupted, as if supplying words he'd left unsaid. "But what of next time, eh? If I try to stay pent up here forever, I'll go mad from boredom sooner or later—and I'm dangerous when I'm bored. It'll be better this way. I'll come back in a month or two, and I'll be certain of my welcome."

Corson had made up her mind, and knew that she was right. She had seen what would happen if one day she became a threat to Steifann's home and people, and she meant to take no chances on letting it happen. She never wanted to see that look on his face again.

It was the first time they'd parted without anger, and this became the new pattern of Corson's life. She followed her calling wherever it led, giving free rein to her restlessness and daring, and earning a greater reputation, and larger fees, for her prowess with a sword. But now her aimless adventuring was broken by sojourns at the Hare, visits which had taken on the nature of homecomings, over time, and given her rather random existence a stability and security she had not known before. Her stays had grown longer, now sometimes lasting a season or more, but she still took care always to be on her way before there could be trouble.

> "Seek to the ends
> Of the earth, if you dare—
> You'll not meet the like
> Of the host of the Hare!"

Corson sang lustily. When she arrived in Chiastelm, not long afterwards, she greeted Steifann with a fervent embrace hardly warranted by such a brief separation. He received her crushing hug with the deep, warm laugh Corson loved. "Here, what's that for?" he said, surprised and pleased by her unbridled enthusiasm.

"I missed you, you stupid lout!" said Corson.

5

"Word has reached me that you are conspiring to raise opposition to certain of my plans," Nyctasia said quietly. "And I must protest that it would be more seemly for you to come directly to me with your views, instead of leaving me to learn of them from my court spies. You must be aware that I shall find them out in time, but apart from that, I quite frankly want your advice on these matters."

She paused, but no one replied to her. Lady Elissa merely regarded her silently, while Lord Anseldon seemed to look through her without interest. Both were older than Nyctasia by a generation and resented her manner, which, though unfailingly courteous, did not altogether disguise her impatience. The young widow Lhejadis studied her ringed hands uneasily. She had never made a secret of the fact that she blamed Nyctasia for the death of her husband, Mescrisdan. Lord Erikasten, Nyctasia's younger brother, sat scowling at the floor, refusing to meet her eyes.

"As you know, I intend to issue the remaining pardons as part of the festivities of celebration following the birth of Tiambria's child," Nyctasia continued. "As I understand that

45

you object to this proceeding, I have taken the liberty of calling you together, that I may have the benefit of your counsel. It seems to me that we have been feeding and housing the prisoners long enough. We could put our resources to better use."

Lord Anseldon was the first to speak. "There is a simpler way to resolve that difficulty, and husband the resources of the city."

"That," Nyctasia said curtly, "is not a subject for debate. You know my views. I'll have no further butchery in Rhostshyl. We've enough to answer for!"

"Commendable sentiments," said Lady Elissa. "You've your reputation to consider, after all. 'Lady Merciful' they call you in the streets, is it not? And what need for further bloodshed, now that Mhairestri is murdered, and Emeryc's heir removed from the succession?"

With the death of the matriarch Mhairestri, the opposition to Nyctasia's rule had lost much of its force, but the matriarch's followers at court were still a power to be reckoned with.

"Mercy for the enemies of our House, but another law for those of your own blood who stand in your way," said Lhejadis suddenly. "Enough to answer for indeed!"

"You do the matriarch an injustice if you suppose that she was that careless," Nyctasia said evenly. "As for Emeryc's family, they are all three safe and unharmed, as I have repeatedly explained." She half smiled. "Though were I guilty of all you say, I could only be accused of upholding family tradition. Because in my place you would have done away with them, do not make the mistake of assuming I have done so. For your own sake, I pray you, consider how foolish you will feel when they return."

"If they live, where are they?" Lord Anseldon challenged. "And when may we expect this return which is to make fools of us all?"

Nyctasia shook her head gently. "Forgive me, but surely the fewer who know their whereabouts, the safer they will be. There is nothing to be gained at present by taking unnecessary risks."

"That is to say that you do not trust us. Why, then, do you seek our advice? Consult with Therisain and your other lackeys."

"I know their advice without asking. I can do no wrong in

Therisain's eyes, which makes him a good ally, but a bad advisor. Now, *you* think I'm mad—thus you'll see the flaws in my plans, and if you care more for Rhostshyl's welfare than for my downfall, you'll warn me of them. Oh, it's your advice I need to hear, I know that.

"Of course, I may not *follow* it," she added. "But for all our sakes, and for the sake of the city, let me hear what you have to say."

"Very well," said Lord Anseldon coldly. "It's said that you mean to dismiss half the city guard—only madness itself could suggest such folly."

"Nonsense! Nonsense and idle rumor," Nyctasia cried indignantly. "There's no question of half, or even a quarter, of the garrison—only of those who were conscripted from among the laborers on the municipal estates. We've peace in the city now, and there's the harvest to be thought of."

"And how long shall we have peace if the city's defenses are to be weakened?" demanded Lady Elissa. "Rhostshyl has barely recovered from civil war. We should be strengthening her forces now, with mercenary troops if necessary—the more so if you reject the proposal of alliance with Ochram!"

"I have not rejected it!" Nyctasia protested. "I have barely had time to consider the matter."

The Edonaris had recently received overtures from the ruling family of Ochram, concerning the possibility of a marriage-alliance between them, and only Nyctasia was of sufficiently exalted rank to enter into such a union with the High Lord Aithrenn. Her allies and opponents alike had urged her to consider the advantages for Rhostshyl of closer connections with the Maritime city-states. Ochram was a major port and center of shipping; the alliance could go far toward restoring Rhostshyl's prosperity.

The marriage itself would be no more than a diplomatic formality that would hardly interfere with the lives of those concerned, and, having arranged a marriage-alliance for her sister, Nyctasia was in no position to refuse without good reason.

"They have not made a formal proposal, merely a sugges-tion that we discuss the matter," she continued. "And I have invited His Lordship to come to Rhostshyl at his pleasure, to do so. More than that I cannot do at present. He must see for himself what the city has suffered, and how much remains to be done before she will be again the proud and powerful city she was."

"Exactly so," Lord Anseldon agreed. "Hardly the time, one would think, to invite outright rebellion by conferring these senseless pardons of yours and decreasing the city guard!"

Nyctasia appeared to be troubled by these arguments. "I don't believe there will be rebellion," she said slowly. "Folk in this city have had their fill of warfare. The partisans of the Teiryn were crushed once, and those who remain are thankful to have been spared. They'll not be eager to chance a second defeat, against greater odds. After all, we hold the city, we have more dominion over Rhostshyl than ever before. Surely even the most foolhardy of the Teiryn would not be so rash as to attempt to overthrow us now. And you must admit that most have accepted the terms of the peace."

"Of course they accepted," Lady Elissa said bitterly. "We demanded no concessions, and surrendered every advantage! Not even the Teiryn are fools enough to refuse such terms."

Nyctasia sighed. " 'Who can put a price on peace, or weigh clemency in the balance?' " she quoted, then remarked wryly, "By the *vahn*, the older I grow, the more serviceable I find the Principles of the Philosophers."

It could not be denied that the marriage-alliance of the Edonaris and the Teiryn had brought about an uneasy, but thus far stable, peace between the warring families. The majority of the surviving Teiryn had come to see that they'd been given a chance to temper defeat with dignity. They had been at the mercy of the Edonaris, and a marriage treaty, as between equals, was a more than generous offer from a victorious enemy. Those who still could not be brought to take this view of the matter were among the prisoners in question.

"I imagine we'll see outbreaks of trouble," Nyctasia concluded. "And possibly brawls between hotheaded bands of youths. But I do not anticipate a concerted uprising—do you?"

"Perhaps not, but we must be prepared for one, nevertheless. This is no time to take risks with the city's security—no time to think of reducing the municipal guard, just when they'll most be needed to keep the peace."

Nyctasia was in complete agreement, and had been so from the start. She had long since decided that the numbers of Rhostshyl's warders must be augmented when the final pardons were declared, but she had spoken of this decision to no one.

Instead, she had instructed certain of her courtiers to spread rumors to the contrary, so as to allow her opponents to challenge her on grounds where she was prepared to give way. The pardons would be carried out, but it wouldn't do to have her powerful kin believe that their views held no weight with her at all. Should they conclude that it was useless to try to reason with her, they'd be all the more inclined to try other means to gain their ends.

"There is much in what you say," she said, as if reluctantly. "Carelessness could accomplish what the Teiryn failed to do."

"Yes," said Lady Elissa, with the air of one who has finally succeeded in explaining something to a simpleminded child. "And the Teiryn may have lost much of their following, but they might well seek allies elsewhere. With Rhostshyl weakened by civil strife, it would be no difficult matter to persuade the governors of Heithskor that the time is ripe for conquest. If the Teiryn have learned that they cannot take the city, they'll stoop to serve another power that will destroy the Edonaris for them—and reward them with a place among Rhostshyl's new rulers. Can you doubt that Ettasuan ar'n Teiryn would sell Rhostshyl to her enemies, to have revenge on the House of Edonaris?"

Erikasten was startled into speech. "Lord Ettasuan! 'Tasia, you don't mean to pardon him with the rest?"

This too was a point Nyctasia was willing to concede, but she said only, "I think to do so, yes. A general pardon ought not to admit of exceptions."

"But he's tried to kill you—you know he'll try again if he's set at liberty!"

"Brother, if I were to condemn everyone in the city who's tried to murder me, the dungeons would not be adequate to hold them. Of course, if Ettasuan's fool enough to try it again—and I daresay he is—he'll be arrested and brought before the magistrates—"

"Have you forgotten that Ianesse ar'n Teiryn is dead?" Lord Anseldon interrupted. "Ettasuan will be head of the House of Teiryn if you release him."

Nyctasia never forgot details of that sort. "Only until Jehamias comes of age," she pointed out. "A matter of mere months. And I needn't restore Ettasuan to his rank, if you think it ill-advised. Yet what harm could he do, even so? He has little enough support now, even among his kin, and his health is not what it was since his imprisonment. I should not be surprised if he succumbed to the hereditary scourge of the Teiryn within the year."

At this, the others immediately assumed that Nyctasia had employed a slow-working poison to ensure the accuracy of this prediction. No one voiced this suspicion, but Nyctasia replied as if it had been spoken. "No. How often must I explain that it is unnecessary to murder the Teiryn? They will perish of their own accord, if given the least chance to do so. For that reason alone I would pardon Lord Ettasuan, lest he should die while still in our hands. Such a thing would not be to our honor, though we had no part in his death."

Nyctasia was aware that the others did not believe her, but she only shrugged, abandoning without regret all attempts to convince them. After all, they would not disapprove of her resorting to poison in such a case; on the contrary, they'd no doubt think the better of her for it. The one point where everyone in the room could agree was the desirability of Lord Ettasuan's demise. "But, for all that, his fate must finally rest with the heir of his House," she observed. "I may pardon our enemies, but his threats against Jehamias are another matter."

"Jehamias!" Lord Anseldon said with scorn. "That one will do whatever you bid him, you know it well."

To his surprise, Nyctasia smiled. "Yes," she said unexpectedly, "and very convenient I find it. Come, confess that our interests are better served by Jehamias as a willing ally than as a sacrifice to our victory. Already many of the Teiryns' supporters acknowledge him, and more will follow when he becomes titular head of the House of Teiryn."

"As he never will, if Ettasuan has his way. But perhaps the spells that safeguard you now shield young Jehamias as well?"

Nyctasia allowed this to pass unanswered. If people chose to believe that she had such powers, so much the better. Rumors of that sort could be better protection than spells themselves. "A watch will be kept on His Lordship, should Jehamias consent to his release," she said firmly, and turned to Lady Elissa. "Yet I fear you wrong him, Madame, if you believe that his hatred of our House would outweigh his loyalty to his city. A fool the man unquestionably is, but not, I think, a traitor. Still, whether Ettasuan prove treasonous or no . . ."

She had meant to conclude, "Heithskor would be no threat to Rhostshyl, even with his complicity," but even as she began to speak, an entirely different idea occurred to her. It was true that she feared no invasion from the inland city-state of Heithskor. Though Rhostshyl's defenses had been weakened, the city was still well-protected by its sister cities of the Maritime Alliance, whose members were all pledged to mutual defense. Nyctasia had often praised the foresight of her ancestors for bringing Rhostshyl into the Alliance. Since she'd come to power, she had taken pains to confirm and reinforce those ties, and she was confident that the coastal cities would honor their treaties with Rhostshyl. No doubt the rulers of Heithskor would be pleased to annex Rhostshyl and its widespread estates, but they would not take arms against the entire Alliance to do so.

Yet it might be wise, Nyctasia realized, not to insist that the city's borders were secure. What better way to unite the disparate factions at court, the remaining rivalries in the city, than to offer them a common enemy?

"Whether Ettasuan prove treasonous or no . . ." she said, and hesitated, ". . . Heithskor remains a threat, with or without his complicity. Rhostshyl is vulnerable, as you say, and I have perhaps been inclined to rely too much on the good faith of our allies."

"You have," said Lady Elissa. " 'Friends may prove fickle, but foes are faithful.' The security of the city must depend on no other power."

Nyctasia seemed to be listening to her and weighing her words with care, but she was already so engrossed in her own plans that she barely heard. She would have her people begin to spread rumors at once, she decided, that spies in Heithskor reported preparations for invasion. She nodded thoughtfully and said aloud, "We are agreed, I believe, that the safety of the city is paramount. But that is why we must strive above all to reconcile the differences that divide our people, to lay old enmities to rest. Unless the city is unified it cannot stand firm against a threat from without!" *Divert your opponent's eye from your true objective*, she thought.

"And the city guard?" asked Lord Anseldon.

"I shall see to it," Nyctasia promised. If she were to raise a force of mercenaries, it would lend substance to the rumors as well. Perhaps Corson would be willing to undertake the matter. "I was certain," she said, with every appearance of satisfaction, "that you would know where I had neglected my duty. Mhairestri always told me that I was too liable to let my visions cloud my sight. I need you—*Rhostshyl* needs you—to warn me when the welfare of the city may suffer from my misjudgment."

As ever, when Nyctasia most desired to be persuasive, she mingled as much of the truth as she dared with her deceptions. She did indeed need the help of her kin. When she had first returned to her homeland, she had been forced to assert her authority to the fullest, and compel the others to acknowledge her ascendancy, in order to carry out her plans. But she could not continue to govern Rhostshyl alone; there were other matters for her to attend to, other ways in which to serve the city. Now that the marriage-alliance had been established, and a measure of stability restored to the city, it was time to propitiate those who had opposed her, and to win their support, if this were possible. To do so, she must relinquish some of her power over them, relegate some of her duties to others. It had worried her to discover how reluctant she was to do this. She had not yet escaped Mhairestri's influence.

Now she stood, to indicate that the audience was at an end, and thanked the others warmly for their candor. It was the most courteous of dismissals, but a dismissal nonetheless.

6

Erikasten was not surprised when Nyctasia bade him to remain behind when the others took their leave. "I've been wondering why I was summoned to this counsel," he said. "You would hardly consult *my* judgment on matters of state." Though he agreed with Anseldon and his party about certain of Nyctasia's measures, his views would have little weight until he came of age.

Nyctasia resumed her seat, and motioned for him to do the same. "I'm worried about you, 'Kasten. You haven't enough to do."

"I take it you've something in mind for me to do?"

"Very good, quite right. There is a commission you could undertake for me, if you would. It will require you to travel into the Midlands, to our kinfolks' vintnery at Vale."

"In fine, you want to be rid of me," Erikasten said with a sneer.

Nyctasia matched his tone. "Indeed I do. You're like the tom whose littermate has young. I'm afraid you'll eat the kits."

Erikasten drew a sharp breath. "It's the talk of the court, how coarse and common you've grown," he spat.

"Isn't it a pity? I once had such exquisite manners, alas. Let it be a lesson to you not to keep low company. But if I shock you, I shall at least be certain of your attention. I'm sorry I've neglected you of late. I seem to have the least time for those I love the most. But I have been giving a great deal of thought to you, and how you might best serve the city. 'Kasten, you could really be of great help to me in the Valleylands."

"I suppose I'll never be seen again, like Emeryc's heir? Was he one of those you love the most?"

"If you believe that I've done away with Leirven, you should thank me," Nyctasia said sharply. "But you know better."

When Rhostshyl's civil war had claimed the life of their older brother, his title had come to his son Leirven, still a young child. But should Leirven die without an heir, Erikasten would succeed him.

"The others believe it," Erikasten said carefully. "Lhejadis says it openly." He knew he was betraying nothing that had not already been reported to Nyctasia.

Nyctasia shook her head. "Poor Jade, she'd like to believe it, but I don't think she does. She'd be glad to believe me guilty of any atrocity. She was genuinely fond of Mescrisdan, you know. But it's more than that. She's resented me since we were children, before you and Tiambria were born." She paused. "Do you remember my telling you, long ago—when I was nursing you through some ailment or other—what a very sickly child I was myself?"

Erikasten did not want to be reminded that Nyctasia had once been all but a mother to him and his twin sister. He nodded, frowning. "You said it was the *vahn* that healed you."

"So it was. Certainly it wasn't our court physicians. Their judgment was that I'd not live to come of age."

A true Edonaris, Erikasten was quick to follow this. "Then Lhejadis might well have become Rhaicime—"

"If I had died, yes. She would have stood a very good chance of inheriting either our mother's title or Lehannie's. It really was rather hard on her that I recovered."

"But now Tiambria and Deirdras are the heirs apparent," Erikasten pointed out, "*if* Deirdras still lives, as you claim. Lhejadis wouldn't benefit by your death."

"It might not be difficult to have Deirdras's claim set aside, especially now that Emeryc is gone. But even that wouldn't be necessary if I were not only dead but disgraced utterly—if my name were stricken from the family records."

Erikasten understood. If that should come about, it would be as if Nyctasia had never inherited the Rhaicimate from their mother, Teselescq. That title would pass to Tiambria, leaving Lhejadis as the successor to Lehannie.

"It would suit Jade very well if I were condemned for any number of monstrous crimes," Nyctasia was saying. "As for the others, if they believe that I had Rehal and her children murdered, so much the better. They probably respect me for it."

"Why do you think Lhejadis doesn't believe it, then?" Erikasten asked, curious in spite of himself.

"Because if she were convinced that I was that bloodthirsty, she'd not dare to say such things about me! Why, the most powerful contradiction of these accusations is that my enemies are alive to make them. It must be a sore puzzle to them that I haven't tried to have them silenced."

"Why haven't you?" Erikasten found himself enjoying the sense of being in Nyctasia's confidence. But he remained wary.

"The truth is that it would be against my principles. Not very convincing, is it?"

"Not at all."

"The truth so seldom is. That's why I prefer to lie, as a rule. And folk prefer to hear lies, for the most part. But my invention has so far failed me, in this matter. I simply cannot contrive a credible reason to spare Anseldon and those of his faction. Can you?"

Erikasten was silent, suspecting a trap.

"And yet they live, and are at liberty to scheme against me, though I've the power to prevent it," Nyctasia continued. "Quite unaccountable, unless one accepts the unbelievable— that I refuse to resort to bloodshed. Think on that, brother. And if you can devise a more plausible explanation for my behavior, I'd be grateful to hear it. I've seldom been at such a loss for lies. Well, let them wonder for the nonce. Let them believe that I've some plan in mind so demonically clever that no one can guess at it. Perhaps I'll think of one." She laughed at Erikasten's look of angry uncertainty. "Oh, 'Kasten, nothing is so mysterious and misleading as the truth."

"Then why are you afraid to tell me what you've done with Emeryc's children? I'm surely not wise enough to believe you!

If I'm to accept your word that the others wrong you, prove it—where are Leirven and Deirdras?"

"Why, in Vale of course, 'Kasten. Why else would I wish to send you there? Here, if you must have proof, read this. It's from Rehal." Nyctasia took a letter from between the pages of a book and handed it to him with a smile. "Raven and Derry are quite alive, growing fast, and turning brown in the sun."

With each shipment of wine and books from the Midlands, letters arrived for Nyctasia from the family of vintners. This last had announced, among other news, the betrothal of her brother's widow, Rehal, to Raphistain ar'n Edonaris, one of the heads of the vintnery.

Erikasten read it quickly and looked up, frowning. "Rehal's to marry one of these winemakers?"

"I couldn't be more pleased. It will be an excellent match for both. Rehal was never at her ease at court, but our cousins in Vale aren't too proud to welcome a farmwoman among them. Raphe needs just such a wife, as well, who can be of help to him at the grape-growing and the harvest. And if I know that one, he'll not mind having a *Hlaven* to wife. Rehal will seem quite the lady to her new family."

But Erikasten wasn't listening. "So you've sent Emeryc's children to be raised by peasants! Is that your game? You'd not have them killed—not you!—you'll only see to it that they're made unfit for their position!"

"Silence! You know nothing of my plans, or of these people." Mastering her anger, Nyctasia forced herself to speak calmly. "The Edonaris of Vale are not peasants. They are country gentry, and nearer kin to us than you suppose. You will know that as soon as you see them—they're our mirror image . . . or we theirs. You'll see much of Emeryc in Raphistain, and not only in the resemblance. He must have seemed to Rehal like her husband's ghost at first. And his twin sister Frondescine—oh yes, they're as prone to twins as we—is so very like me that Raphe himself took me for her when we met. We are one family, 'Kasten, or ought to be."

She paused, choosing her words, and said earnestly, "I have sometimes thought that they, not we, are the true Edonaris. They've preserved something that we've lost, something of what the Edonaris once were, a quality that made us capable of building this city. I don't know whether to call it the vital essence of the spirit, or whether to give it simply the name of honesty. I only know that we've become capable, instead, of destroying the city—you have seen that for yourself. And if Rhostshyl is to live, we must learn again to serve the furtherance of life, not the furtherance of our own power."

"A most moving speech," said Erikasten, in unwitting imitation of Lord Anseldon. "But I fail to see how the heirs to the Rhaicimate can serve the city if they're to be hidden away in the Midlands."

"Of course they must return when they're old enough, but not yet, 'Kasten. That's one reason I want to have you there, as my emissary, to see that they receive an education fitting for future rulers of Rhostshyl. Naturally you suspect me of other intentions. You suspect everyone, and rightly so. Look at the life you've led! You're still a youth, in years, but already you've been through war, lost a brother to your enemies, taken part in schemes and conspiracies—of course you trust no one. How could you? *But that's not the youth I want for Leirven and Deirdras!*"

There was a silence between them, then Erikasten, speaking each word deliberately and with unmistakable resolve, said, "'Tasia, if you're lying to me now, I warn you, you really had better have me killed before I discover the truth. Because if you don't, I'll kill you myself. I swear it, on the honor of an Edonaris."

"I'd expect no less of you, brother. You learned much from the war, I know. You made me proud. But I want the next generation of the Edonaris to learn from peace." For the first time, she spoke simply, easily, seeming to be neither on the defense nor the attack. "I agree with you, however, that they must not be allowed to forget who they are and what duty they owe the city. It is necessary that Rehal and Raphe understand this. I would send you to them because you understand it."

"You said that was one reason you wanted me there," Erikasten reminded her. "Tell me the rest."

"It is my hope that when you return, some of our Midland cousins may be allowed to come with you, and perhaps settle among us here. This House needs new blood, and theirs is Edonaris blood. We are not a prolific family, you know. But they are. We need them far more than they need us, but some of our young cousins at Vale long for Rhostshyl above all else, I know. When I was there, they were all afire to join battle with the Teiryn and defend their ancestral home. Their elders

forbade it, as well they might, but now . . . now that we
have peace in the city, now that they carry on trade with the
coast, and we're soon to have marriage-ties with them as well,
they may be willing to permit their young folk to visit
Rhostshyl, perhaps to receive an education here. You're of an
age to befriend them, 'Kasten, and whet their curiosity about
the coast and the court. You'll seem a hero to them because
you've fought for your House, and because you're a lord of
Rhostshyl who lives in the palace of the Edonaris." And it
would do 'Kasten good to be admired and made much of,
Nyctasia thought. Tiambria's celebrated marriage had put him
too much in the shade. "They'll need your help to learn court
etiquette and deportment," she continued. "But take care not to
condescend to them, or let them feel that you think them
ill-bred and unmannered. They're proud people, and they'll not
stand for that. If you show them proper respect, they'll be more
than glad to learn what you have to teach them. Indeed, they'll
demand to be taught, as I can assure you from my own
experience. But you'll learn from them as well, if you're
wise."

She spoke as if his journey to Vale were a settled matter, and
Erikasten knew that it was. He would have to go there, if only
to see for himself whether Emeryc's children really were
safe. If it was all a trick of Nyctasia's, so be it. He was
accomplishing nothing worthwhile at court, and he admitted to
himself, though not to Nyctasia, that any change would have
been welcome. "Do you know," he said suddenly, "I've never
been farther than a day's ride away from Rhostshyl?"

Nyctasia smiled, half sadly. "I know very well. And it's
time you saw something of the world. But, 'Kasten . . .
you're not being sent into exile. I'll not deny that I want you
away from Anseldon's influence, but it's equally true that
you're the one person best suited for this mission. As the uncle
of Emeryc's children, you've a right to concern yourself with
their welfare, and you're old enough now to do so. But you're
young enough still to be a companion to those of our kin who
I hope will join us—and young enough, I trust, to learn from
their way of life." Nyctasia studied her brother's countenance
for a long moment. "And then, there is one other reason for
you to go," she said, faltering somewhat. "I hadn't meant to
tell you, but I believe I'll chance it after all."

Erikasten looked up sharply. "The true reason?"

"What I've told you *is* true, but it isn't the whole of the truth. You see, there's one of our Midland cousins, Tepicacia by name, whom I'd particularly like you to bring back to Rhostshyl—as a bride."

Erikasten was on his feet in an instant, shouting, "Isn't it enough that you've married my sister to a Teiryn? If you think you can make me take a common rustic to wife—and be the laughingstock of the court—"

"You call Emeryc a laughingstock?" Nyctasia asked coldly. "A common rustic was good enough for him to marry, but not for you?"

Erikasten was taken aback. "That—that was altogether different! Rehal had borne him an heir, and . . . and he *chose* to make her his wife—everyone knew that—"

"Of course this affair is different. Tepicacia ar'n Edonaris is neither a hired laborer nor a nobleman's mistress. Her blood is as good as your own, and I'll not hear her insulted by an insolent puppy like you!"

Furious as he was, Erikasten was too well-bred to turn and go, without Nyctasia's permission. She was his elder, and a Rhaicime. He bowed and said, "If there was nothing else you wished to tell me, Madame, have I your leave to withdraw?"

"Oh, sit down, 'Kasten, and hold your tongue if you can't talk sense. I begin to regret that I've placed my faith in you. There's no question of my making you marry. You may be my ward, by law, but Tepicacia isn't, and she's far too proud to accept a bridegroom who disdains her family. She may not take to you, for that matter—I daresay you'll have to woo her if you want her."

Nyctasia knew very well that 'Cacia was besotted with dreams of Rhostshyl and her noble kin. Erikasten would seem to her the embodiment of that romantic, distant city, but it would be as well to let him think that the girl wouldn't be so easily won. Perhaps it had been a mistake to reveal her hopes for the betrothal, but Nyctasia thought not, on the whole. *He'll be half in love with her by the time he reaches Vale*, she thought, *just from wondering about her all the way*. And when he found that she bore a certain family likeness to Tiambria, not in her features merely, but even more in her bold spirit and will . . . well, let him discover that for himself.

"Her kin would approve the match, I think," she said aloud, smiling, "but they're not tyrants like me—they'd no more marry 'Cacia against her will than sell her into slavery. And I've not suggested a word to them or to her about a betrothal, I assure you. It will rest entirely with you whether or not the matter goes any further. I ask you only to meet the girl and then decide for yourself. That, I'm sure you will agree, is not an unreasonable request, so will you please *sit down*, 'Kasten?"

This time Erikasten obeyed, but muttered defiantly, "I still think you bewitched Tiambria to obtain her consent to the match. You gave her a love-philtre, or a charm—"

Nyctasia broke into a peal of laughter. "And the Teiryn think I did the same to Jehamias—as if either of the pair weren't desirable enough to inspire love, without the aid of witchery! I grant you that I would have spellcast them both, if I'd had the means, but fortunately it wasn't necessary. You see, in my experience, the directions for such potions invariably call for ingredients I couldn't possibly obtain. In fact, they don't exist.

"There are charms that arouse lust, yes," she added, grinning, "but love can no more be mastered by magic than by reason. As ever, all of you credit me with powers far beyond my poor abilities. But after all, you've nothing to fear, 'Kasten, even if you believe such nonsense. I can hardly give you a love-philtre while you're in the Midlands and I'm on the coast."

"You needn't mock at me," Erikasten said, between his teeth.

"True. It's an odious habit, but hard to break. Please forgive me." She sounded disgusted with herself, and genuinely contrite.

Erikasten wondered, not for the first time, whether his older sister really was mad. But, as always, he gave up trying to make sense of her. Tiambria had told him, "She's crazy, to be sure, but that doesn't mean that she's wrong."

"All the Edonaris are crazy," he said resignedly. "When am I to leave for the Midlands, then?"

"At once. If you delay, you might be stranded in Osela till the spring thaw, if the snows come as early as they did last winter." Nyctasia did not need to ask what had prompted his remark about the Edonaris. "So look to your preparations. But mind you don't run to Anseldon and the rest with word of Rehal's whereabouts, 'Kasten. If you do, any harm that befalls the children will be on your hands."

"Why should they harm Emeryc's children? They were his allies! They want Leirven to take his place—"

"And Deirdras to take mine? Yes, but do they want my undoing even more? Is it beyond belief that they'd make an attempt on the children's lives in order to fix the blame on me?"

Erikasten hesitated. "Surely you—" he began, and stopped abruptly. "I don't believe they'd resort to that," he said finally.

"No? Well, neither do I, in truth. But I'm not so sure of it that I would give them the opportunity. Are you?"

"I won't tell them," sighed Erikasten. "But I mean to tell Briar where I'm bound." He meant to tell a few others as well. If no one knew his destination, it would be a simple matter for Nyctasia to see that he disappeared without a trace. Why should he make it easy for her?

But Nyctasia responded at once, "By all means, tell everyone where you're bound. I'll *not* have it said that I've done away with you as well as Emeryc's heir. A certain reputation for ruthlessness may be advantageous in my position, but only in moderation. Tell them . . . tell them that I think to arrange a marriage-alliance with the Edonaris of Vale, but that nothing has been settled, and that you're being sent to see how the land lies. *That* will give them something to think about! It's not *your* whereabouts I would keep from them, you understand, but that of Emeryc's family—at least for the time being."

"What I don't understand," Erikasten said, after a silence, "is why you would trust me to know their hiding-place." He did not so much doubt Nyctasia as feel that he ought to doubt her.

"Ah, I wondered when you'd ask me that. It does seem unlikely that I'd trust you with the truth, I admit, but I can explain. I don't trust your judgment, brother, but I do trust your honor. I know you'd die to defend Emeryc's heir, even though he stands between you and the Rhaicimate."

"He stands between me and you as well, sister. I'd as soon throw away my shield in battle as wish Leirven out of the succession. While he lives, I'm no threat to your ambition."

Nyctasia covered her face with her hands. "Spoken like an Edonaris," she said.

7

Steifann had much enjoyed Corson's account of her vengeance on 'Malkin. He'd heard more than he liked about 'Malkin over the years, and he'd been none too pleased, at first, to learn that Corson had encountered him again. But now he felt quite satisfied that this scholar would want nothing more to do with Corson, after the nasty game she'd played him. Steifann could almost feel sorry for the fellow. "Well, I'd not turn my back on that one, if I were you," he advised Corson. "If you used me that way, I wouldn't rest till I'd made you regret it."

"He brought it on himself! I told him that Nyc was the Rhaicime. He should have believed me."

"You know very well no one would take Nyc for a Rhaicime—not unless she took the trouble to play the part. I thought she was some feckless vagabond student when I first laid eyes on her. I all but swatted her myself."

Corson shook her head. "The *first* time you saw her, you thought she was Destiver's cabin boy," she reminded him.

Destiver laughed. "*I* thought she was an imperial spy, or an assassin. I threatened to keelhaul her if she didn't keep herself out of my way! If I'd known she was a runaway Rhaicime, I could have held her for ransom."

62

"And you'd have been hung for a smuggler," Annin said tartly, rapping her on the head with a large ladle. "You're lucky that our Lady Nyc doesn't hold a grudge."

When the *Windhover* was in port, Destiver spent far too much time at the Hare, in Corson's opinion. True, she'd spent the night with Annin, not with Steifann, but what happened when Corson wasn't in town, and Destiver was? "Nyc has a forgiving nature," said Corson. "But I don't."

"Neither do I," Destiver put in. She kissed Annin's hand and went off to the docks.

"She says that mercy is the mark of true nobility," Corson continued, ignoring Destiver. "But I'm not of noble blood. Now that I'm quits with 'Malkin, I'll forgive the bastard. Besides, Nyc made me promise not to do that sort of thing at court again. That's all right, though—I don't know anyone else like 'Malkin."

"Good," said Steifann, and added wryly, "Very forgiving our noble Nyc is—until she starts singing her little songs about you."

Trask snickered. "Ho, you *like* that song. You've been singing it yourself, I heard you."

"You hear too much that doesn't concern you. Go open the taproom, we'll have folk here soon enough. And fetch in that wheel of cheese from the cart! If I have to tell you again—"

"It's too heavy for me," Trask complained. "Now Corson's back, let her do it. Or has milady grown too grand for that?"

Corson stood and stretched, grinning down at him. "Nyc says no honest work's beneath the dignity of a lady, but I have yet to see her carrying cheeses about—eh, not that she could."

"*You* could," Steifann pointed out. "I've been to market and back this morning, *and* chopped the wood, while Your Ladyship was still abed."

"I could sleep *all* morning, at court, and have my breakfast in bed if I liked, waited on by maids and minions. I don't have to toil like a scullion."

"You do if you want to stay under my roof! Asye! Not here a week, and already longing to run back to Rhostshyl again. I wonder you give yourself the bother to visit us lowly commoners at all."

"I don't blame you," Trask said wistfully. "*I'd* stay at court if I could."

Steifann glared at him. "Well you can't, so *go open the taproom*!"

Trask, who knew exactly how far he could safely provoke Steifann, obeyed at once this time, and Steifann turned on Corson again. "As for you, *Desthene*, if idleness and luxury are what you want, you know where to find them! No one's keeping you here."

Corson shrugged and made for the door, without a word.

"Corson!" Alarmed, Steifann started after her. "Where do you think you're going?"

"To fetch in the cheese, where else?" Corson said, laughing.

The house was full of customers by midday, and everyone was kept busy drawing the ale, turning the spits, carving the meat, cleaning the platters, serving and carrying, and keeping order. Corson, for all her chaff about her exalted station, did her share of the work, only occasionally reminding the others what an honor she did them by her presence alone.

No one paid her any heed except Trask, who honestly couldn't understand why anyone who could live the life of a courtier would choose to spend her time—much less earn her keep—in a common ale-house. The Jugged Hare had been Trask's home for years, and it was as good a home as he could ever have expected to have. A castoff beggar's brat, scrambling to survive on the streets and wharves of Chiastelm, he'd been lucky to find a place with Steifann, as he well knew, yet he dreamed of somehow becoming something more than potboy of a tavern—something finer, grander. . . . Ever since he'd been to the palace of the Edonaris in Rhostshyl to see Corson receive her title, he'd been under the spell of the splendor and glamor of the court. He longed to cut a figure among the noble lords and ladies he'd encountered there, eagerly observing their every gesture and expression. He had persuaded Corson to take him along with her to Rhostshyl now and then, but such tastes of court life, far from satisfying his hunger, had only made him more discontented with his lot. He was more sure than ever that he could master their elegant manners and turns of speech, if given a chance. He could already mimic Nyctasia's aristocratic accent with considerable accuracy—and often did so, much to the amusement of the others and the annoyance of Nyctasia. She assured him that there was more to the life of a courtier than looking and acting the part, but Trask was not put off by that. He was even willing to learn to read, if need be, but Steifann was too busy, and Corson too impatient, to teach him. If he only had the right clothes, Trask thought, with a little practice he could surely pass for a youth of good family. Even Corson could assume an acceptable demeanor at court when she chose, and Corson was common as dirt, as ill-bred and vulgar as any soldier. He could hear her cursing like a peasant as she hauled a heavy cask of ale up the stairs from the cellar.

"To think I could be dining in state now, off silver plates, instead of serving a lot of rutting drunken louts and tosspots," she remarked, setting down her burden and wiping her face with her sleeve.

"Our little starveling Rhaicime says the food's better here than in her own palace," said Walden, who repeated this often and with considerable pleasure.

Corson knew better than to argue the point with him. "So it is," she said, "but at least I can find time to sit down and eat a proper meal there, and let others make it ready and serve it to me."

Steifann was not likely to let that pass, however busy he was. "You find time to eat enough for three whenever you're here! And what's more—"

"Do they really eat off silver plates there?" Trask interrupted, ever interested in details of the life of the nobility.

"Well, not anymore," Corson admitted. "They did, but Nyc had most of them melted down to feed the City Treasury. She told her steward she'd concern herself with cutlery when the poor of Rhostshyl had enough to eat. Her kin were furious, but of course they couldn't disagree. All the same, silver or no, it's still a far cry from trenchers of wood and bowls of earthenware."

"Why don't you stay there, then?" Trask demanded. "You must be crazy to give that up for this." He gestured scornfully at the pile of onions he was supposed to be peeling.

"Ah, but she doesn't have *me* there, you see," Steifann explained, pinching Corson in passing. "What's the use of a bed as big as a barn if I'm not at hand to share it? Better straw with your sweetheart, they say, than silk sheets without."

"I have admirers aplenty at court, I'll have you know—"

"But none that measures up to me, I'll wager. Admit it, woman."

He would have won that wager, but Corson had no intention

of admitting it. Ignoring him, she told Trask, "The truth of it
is, I get bored at court after a while. There's not much for me
to do there, now that Nyc has matters in hand. No one's tried
to assassinate her for months."

"Well, here's something for you to do, take this," said
Annin, handing her a platter piled with roast beef. She took up
a pitcher of ale in each hand and pushed open the door to the
taproom with her hip, waiting for Corson to follow.

Corson caught the door with her foot and started after her,
but suddenly backed into the kitchen again, letting the door
swing shut after the surprised Annin. "Corson!" she heard,
"bring that meat here! What ails you?"

Corson cursed softly. Now he'd heard her name called out,
even if he hadn't seen her! But he had seen her, she was
certain, though he'd given no sign of it. Their eyes had met for
only a moment, but that had been long enough for Corson to
recognize Erystalben ar'n Shiastred, and so for him to know
her as well. . . .

She thrust the platter of meat at one of the serving-girls and
grabbed Trask, dragging him to the door to look through the
knothole at the taproom. "The dark one," she said, "sitting
apart from the rest, near the window."

"Mmm, the beauty with the blue eyes?"

Corson nodded. "Find out who he is and what he wants
here."

"It'll be a pleasure. You're nowhere to be found, I suppose?" He was gone without waiting for an answer. For some
things, Trask could be relied upon. Corson watched him
moving from table to table, mopping up spills with a wet cloth,
and joking with the other customers before he approached Lord
Erystalben's place.

"Trouble?" Steifann asked, joining her. He'd seen her reach
instinctively for her sword—the sword he had insisted she not
wear in his house. It was hanging high on the wall among
copper pans and iron skillets.

"I don't know," said Corson, "maybe." Trask had reached
his quarry now. He was pretending to scrub at the table near
Shiastred, and addressing him in his most flirtatious manner.
Corson couldn't hear him, but knew he was saying, "You're
not from these parts? A traveler?" Shiastred shook his head,
smiling, and said something that seemed to surprise Trask,
then laughed at his reply.

Corson straightened up, frowning. Could she have been mistaken? He looked like Erystalben ar'n Shiastred, and yet . . . this man was haggard and unkempt, his clothing drab and worn, commoner's garb that the man Corson remembered would never have worn. And that was not the only difference—it was his expression that was unfamiliar, Corson decided, not his features. Lord Erystalben wouldn't bandy words with the likes of Trask in that open, friendly way. He was the sort who gave orders to his inferiors and, apart from that, didn't notice them at all. As soon as Trask came through the door she pulled him aside and demanded, "Well? What did he say to you all that time?"

"Ow! Corson, would you stop hauling me about!" he complained, straightening his sleeve. He was clearly enjoying himself not a little.

"I'll tear you into shreds if you don't stop preening yourself and answer me!"

"All right, all right, I'm trying to—no need to get into a lather. Well . . . ." he paused, drawing out the drama, "that one's a strange lot, and no mistake. He calls himself Veron, for want of anything better, but he claims he doesn't know who he is, that he's lost his memory and his name! Did you ever hear a tale the like of that?"

Corson shook her head. "If that's true, then why is he here?"

"He says he's been told that he has the accent of a Maritimer—and he does, too—so he's been working his way along the coast looking for someone who knows him. He didn't ask for you."

"He must be after me, to come right into the Hare!"

"He's been to a few other places in town already," Trask explained, "but he says folk told him to try his luck here."

That was not unlikely, Corson realized. Anyone who was searching the coast would try Chiastelm, and anyone who was searching Chiastelm would sooner or later try the Hare. People of all stations frequented Steifann's tavern, even the gentry, of late. It was the advice anyone in the city might give a stranger. "What did you tell him, then?" she asked Trask.

"What else?" Trask grinned. "I said if I'd ever seen him before I'd surely have remembered him."

"Corson, who is he?" Steifann asked impatiently.

"Asye, I'm not sure—I think he's a lord of Rhostshyl, of

Jhaice rank. A magician. And an arrogant, vicious cur," she
added with feeling.

"He could be a Jhaice, I suppose," Trask said doubtfully.
"He's well-spoken, like a nobleman, but any cozener can
manage that. And he doesn't look to have much money about
him; his shirt's worn to a thread."

"He's not the Jhaice who gave you that whorish silk dress?"
Steifann said, suspicious.

"*He* wasn't a Jhaice, I told you, his sister was. This one is
Nyc's paramour, none of mine. If he's the same one."

"Oh, well, if he's a friend of Nyc's, where's the worry? Let
her see to him."

Corson didn't want to explain the deadly struggle for
power—and for Nyctasia—that had taken place between Lord
Erystalben and a rival mage. In that battle she'd sided against
him, perhaps unwisely, and she doubted that he would forget
it. But suppose he had really forgotten everything, what then?
In answer to Steifann's question, she said only, "I don't trust
him."

"Do you think he's really lost his memory?"

Corson didn't know what to think. "It could be so," she
admitted. "I know he did some dangerous spell or other, and
Nyc said it would take its toll of him—that he'd lose something
by it—but there was no telling what it would be. . . ."

The more Corson thought about it, the more likely it seemed
that Shiastred—if indeed it were he—had truly come there by
chance. If he knew who he was, why wouldn't he have gone
directly to Rhostshyl? Finding Nyctasia would surely be more
important to him than hunting down a mere hireling like Corson.
The proud Lord Erystalben would probably consider it beneath
him to seek vengeance on an inferior; even as an enemy he'd think
her of no importance.

"If he keeps on along the coast, he won't come to Rhost-
·shyl," she said uneasily. Rhostshyl was at least a day's ride
inland, a Maritime city only by alliance. "He'll not find his
people that way."

Steifann shrugged. "What do you care, if you think so little
of him?"

"I *don't* care! He could stay lost forever, for all of me—but
Nyc cares, the little fool. She still grieves over that bastard."
*And she'd never forgive me, if she lost him again because I let
him go off none the wiser.* Corson sighed. "I'd better try to see

if it's really him. I'll warrant it is, too. That would be just like my luck."

She might as well know the worst. If she didn't find out what his game was, she'd have no peace, wondering if he'd come to cast some foul spell on her. Corson took down her sword-belt and buckled it on. Weapons would be of no use against Shiastred's sorcery, she knew, but she felt the better for it all the same. And she took heart as she remembered Nyctasia explaining that the source of Shiastred's power was the mage-land where he'd established his stronghold. If Corson had understood her aright, he ought not to be so dangerous now that he was far from that spell-haunted place. Unfortunately, Corson also remembered that she hadn't paid very close attention to Nyctasia's explanation. She usually didn't.

From near at hand, the stranger looked more than ever like Erystalben ar'n Shiastred. Corson was not likely to forget those vivid blue eyes, all the more striking because of his dark skin, but blazing with murderous wrath and inhuman power when she'd seen them last.

He was still beautiful, Corson thought, for all that he looked wayworn and weary now, and older than she would have expected after only two years' time. His long black hair was shaggy and disheveled, carelessly tied back with a leather thong, and Corson was surprised to see streaks of grey at his temples.

He had only glanced in her direction when she entered the taproom, with no more than the casual interest commonly inspired by Corson's unusual height and pulchritude. He paid no further attention to her at all until she sat down across from him, leaned over the table and said, "If you're looking for me, here I am. What do you want?"

He stared at her in seeming bewilderment for a time before he gasped, "You know me?"

"We've met," Corson said drily. She studied him rather than listened as he hastily explained what she'd already learned from Trask, but she could read nothing in his features or manner except intense eagerness and excitement. It was a relief to her that he maintained the story—if he were still a powerful magician, he'd have no need to invent such a tale. He was either really as he claimed to be, or he was desperate enough to resort to deception, and either way he could not be much of a threat, Corson assured herself. Still, she had no intention of revealing anything to him before she'd warned Nyctasia of his return. Whatever she might tell him would lead him to Nyctasia, and Corson didn't mean to let her be taken unawares.

When he asked her for his name, she said, "If you're the one I think you are, I've a friend who used to call you 'Ben. But that was short of some fancy long name with a string of titles to it. I only heard the whole of it once, and I didn't trouble myself to remember it."

Her tone was mocking, meant to provoke, but he said hoarsely, "Don't toy with me, for pity's sake. If you know who I am, tell me!"

"Why should I?" Corson spat. "When I saw you last, you tried your best to kill me."

He looked startled, then, recovering his self-possession, he said coolly, "I'm not in a position to deny it. But how am I supposed to have done that, pray? One thing I've learned about myself is that I'm no fighter."

If he didn't remember his sorcerous powers, Corson was certainly not about to remind him. Let Nyctasia decide what to tell him and what to keep from him—she understood the ways of witchery. "You were a lord and I a lackey, in those days. But now I'm a Desthene, and you'll remember *that* if you expect any help from me."

He spread his hands helplessly. "Very well. But am I to expect any help from you? You've told me nothing."

Corson scowled. "I know little enough about you myself— and what I do know I don't like. But I can arrange for you to meet with someone who knows you all too well, if she wishes it."

"And if she doesn't, what am I to do?"

"For my part, you can go drown yourself! I'm doing this for her sake, not for yours. But you needn't worry," Corson said reluctantly, "I expect she'll meet you. If I know that one, she'll not rest till she's seen you. All the same, maybe she's come to her senses, who knows? You'll wait till I know for certain whether she wants any part of you. You'll abide by my terms or you'll never see so much as her shadow, I promise you."

"Why then, I accept your terms, Desthene," he said with an ironic smile, "since you leave me no choice."

Corson stood. "Then we understand each other," she said. "Wait here." Turning her back on him, Corson strode across the taproom to the kitchen, shoving aside anyone who got in her way. "Something like this always happens to me," she muttered. "It's not fair." There was some satisfaction in making Lord Erystalben bear with her arrant effrontery, but she was not looking forward to telling Steifann that she had to go back to Rhostshyl again so soon.

And with Destiver still in port, too.

8

The moon was full, and Nyctasia stepped in and out of pale
pools of moonlight as she paced her bedchamber, weary yet
restless, unable to dismiss the cares that kept her from sleep.
What more could she do to placate her kin, without jeopardiz-
ing the stability of the city? How much of her responsibility did
she dare to turn over to others? Which was the greater risk, to
act or to wait? And what of Lord Aithrenn's proposal of
alliance with Ochram . . . ?

At least Erikasten was out of harm's way, though—that was
something gained. She need no longer fear that he would be
drawn into a plot against her, that she would be forced to deal
with him as with an enemy. The thought chilled her. The
greatest danger was not from the conspirators, but from the
woman she herself might become if she were to sacrifice her
principles to safeguard her position. It would be easy—all too
easy—to persuade herself that she had no choice. She must be
strong, for Rhostshyl's sake, yes, but sometimes it showed
strength to yield, rather than to conquer at the cost of one's own
spirit. If she was not to be mistress of her own actions, how
could she be fit to rule over others?

Nyctasia sighed. Corson would tell her that she thought too much, no doubt. Corson would tease her out of this mood somehow. But there was no one at court now whom she felt free to confide in. For a moment she toyed with the idea of sending for 'Malkin, who would be glad enough of the summons, as she well knew. But though she found him amusing, it was not his companionship she wished for tonight.

If only she could have gone to the Midlands with 'Kasten! It seemed the height of luxury to her now, to be free to travel aimlessly from place to place, with nothing to worry her except where she would spend the night. If 'Kasten met with no delays, he might reach Osela in time for the Harvest Fair, she thought wistfully. And no doubt, instead of enjoying his luck, he felt himself ill-used to be sent away from Rhostshyl. But soon enough it would be his turn to share in the burden of governing the city, and only then, when it was too late, would he learn to appreciate the freedom he'd lost. But 'Kasten, surely, would not be alone with his duty. . . .

"Is it too late, in truth?" Nyctasia asked herself, ashamed of her self-pity. She had much to be thankful for—the city was at peace, her plans were bearing fruit. "Regret deceives the spirit," she reminded herself sternly, "and mourning denies the Discipline." Perhaps she *should* leave the city for a time. Might she not serve Rhostshyl best by preserving her own peace of mind? Suppose she were to visit Maegor the herbalist, who always spoke sense to her, or Corson's mad friends at The Jugged Hare, who treated her as one of themselves . . . ? Her hold on the city was not so weak that a few days' absence would break it. And it might serve her purposes, as well, to let the others see that she was not afraid to let them out of her sight. She could all but hear Corson commanding her, "Come along! It'll do you good to get away from here."

She paused before the tall mirror, examining herself critically. Her nightdress of silver-grey watered silk caught the moonlight and shimmered with a rich luster, but her shoulders sagged, her head drooped like a wilting lily, and her face was wan and careworn.

Nyctasia straightened her back. Really, this would not do. She could not go about looking weak and worried. However she might feel, she must appear strong and confident before others. She must not go without sleep.

She glanced at the table by her bedside, where a goblet

waited, half-full of a powerful sleeping-draught of her own preparation. It would give her the rest she needed, but she had resorted to its aid all too often of late. She must try to do without it.

She threw herself across the bed and lay gazing about the moonlit room, looking everywhere but at the silver goblet so close at hand. Moonlight streamed through the tall windows to strike the mirror and splash against the walls and ceiling in soft, rippling waves. "Neither sea nor sky," Nyctasia murmured, trying to recapture a fleeting memory hidden among those dancing lights and shadows. She was as wakeful as ever. Even when she closed her eyes she was aware of the bright glow flooding the chamber, but she did not think to draw the curtains about the bed. Instead, she turned toward the mirror again, watching it from where she lay as if it could answer her questions—just as she had done as a child, when she had so often been confined to this very bed by wasting illness and frailty.

The mirror had been hers for as long as she could remember, a legacy from the remote ancestress whose name she bore. The warped old glass gave an unclear, shadowy reflection which had fascinated her from the first. She had mirrors of better quality, but none that knew her, she thought, so well as this one. It was as tall as she, and had always seemed to her like a door, with the twin pillars that supported it serving as uprights flanking the lintel and threshold formed by the frame. As a child, she had imagined that this door would one day open to receive her, that it was the portal to another place where she would not be always sickly and aching and bedridden. She had kept the mirror drawn near to her bedside, that she might talk to the reflection she had pretended was her twin, the sister who shared her longings and her loneliness.

She had first attempted to cast spells with the aid of the mirror, long ago, when she'd had only the faintest notion of what such spells meant, and had achieved little enough to show for her efforts. Yet . . . hadn't she once, while still a young girl, succeeded in weaving a spell of Reflection—or believed that she had done so? How could she have commanded such power before she had mastered even a fraction of the necessary Discipline? Was it this teasing memory that eluded her? Had it ever really happened?

She had been ill at the time, she seemed to remember, but

when had she not been ill, as a child? No—she had been more gravely ill than usual, and had, moreover, overheard her elders discussing the court physicians' view that she was not likely to live out the year. She had determined to attempt a Reflection of the Future, to learn for herself the truth of their prediction.

Perhaps the fever itself had given her the detachment that allowed her to enter into a trance of spellcasting, but more probably the experience had been only one of the febrile dreams, half-remembered, half-invented, that had haunted her nights and days. That dream had left her with only the dim memory of a ghostly figure robed in shining silver, a woman—or perhaps a boy—who bore the familiar Edonaris features, resembling many of her kinsfolk without seeming to be any one of them. Had the reflection of that long-ago Nyctasia, the mirror's first mistress, returned to the glass at her summons?

Standing in the mirror as if framed by an open doorway, the vision had answered her unspoken questions before she herself had known quite what they were, or how to give them voice. She had awakened with the conviction that faith in the *vahn* would save her, that she would not only live but grow well and strong. Her fever had broken at last.

It was after that night that she had begun to apply herself to the Discipline in earnest, immersing herself in study of the Influences, Balances and Consolations, the Manifestations and Reflections. Had she not been given up for dead, her family would have sought to turn her from such impractical pursuits— respectable enough, but hardly appropriate for an Edonaris who must one day devote herself to the duties of the Rhaici-mate. But it could be of no consequence how a dying child passed her remaining days, and she was allowed to indulge her fancies in peace, until it became apparent that she might very well live to come of age after all. And by then it was too late to shake her deeply-rooted faith. She remained firm in her belief that she owed her newfound health—indeed her life—to the *vahn's* magic and its messenger, though she had never been able to remember just what the presence in the mirror had said to her, and as time passed she had all but forgotten the appearance of that half-seen visitant as well.

But now as she tossed restlessly in the great bed, it seemed to her that the memory, whole and unfaded, was almost within her grasp, like a familiar tune that one could recall in full if one heard just the first few notes. If only she could remember it at last, she thought, perhaps she could sleep. . . .

A moment later, she stood before the mirror again, gazing steadily into its brightly-veiled depths as she bade it to show her the past, just as she had bidden it, so long ago, to show her the future.

> "Seek in this enchanted mirror
> Images reversed but clearer.
> Patterns of shattered shadow yield
> Their mysteries, in silverglass revealed,"

Nyctasia whispered, her eyes closed, her fingertips lightly pressed to the cold glass.

> "Read if you will the gleaming's meaning.
> Pierce if you please the dreaming's seeming.
> Let far be near, and first be last,
> Let time return that hath gone past,
> Let old be new, and last be first,
> Their mysteries in silverglass reversed."

The words meant little. The words of spells served only to focus the mind of the magician on the task at hand, to point the way the spirit must follow. Nyctasia knew that true masters of magic needed no chanted rhymes to work their will, but it had been a long while since she had aspired to such mastery herself. She requested, rather than commanded, the vision she sought, expecting little, yet she was not surprised, when she opened her eyes again, to find that she no longer cast a reflection in the glass.

Instead, a wan, frail girl-child looked up at her in wonder, her eyes bright with fever, her small hands held out unsteadily to meet Nyctasia's. And then, after so many years, standing in the same place, in the same way, and faced with the ghost of the child she had been when she heard them, Nyctasia at last remembered the words she was seeking, and spoke them softly.

> "Though thou seekest far and wide,
> Yet within thee lies the guide."

It was but an old nursery-verse, a first lesson in the way of the Indwelling Spirit. Nyctasia had known it long before the stranger in the mirror had spoken to her. But hearing the familiar words thus, in a mysterious glow of enchantment, she

had known that they held a new meaning for her, not a precept
but a promise. She had replied, she remembered, with just such
another couplet, the one which evoked the landscape of death
in traditional Vahnite imagery—the black waves, the dark
shore—the rhyme the child sadly recited to her now.

> "Where the headland meets the tide
> There the heart and spirit bide."

She seemed almost to make a question of it, and Nyctasia
knew well enough what she was asking. She was seized with
pity for the pale, fragile little girl, shadowed by a mortality she
barely understood, and ready to seek among ghosts for the
comfort she had not received from the living.

"But you shan't die, little one," Nyctasia said. "You will
learn to heal yourself through the grace of the *vahn,* and so
learn to heal others as well, I promise you." She longed to
warn her young self of so many mistakes yet to come, but there
was no time—already she could sense the spell beginning to
fade, and the reflected moonlight seemed to shine through the
still, solemn figure in the glass.

And even if there were time to tell her, she would forget!
"Only remember that you are a healer," Nyctasia cried. "Let
nothing persuade you to forget that!" She thought the child
smiled at her for the first time then, a curiously reassuring
smile.

Sunshine filled the windows and spilled over Nyctasia's
pillows, waking her suddenly. She lay still for a time, eyes
closed against the light, remembering everything but uncertain
whether or not she had really left her bed during the night. It
would have been utter folly to summon a Reflection for such a
trifling reason—indeed for no reason at all—yet even if she had
only dreamed the spell, it need not have been the less real for
that. . . .

Nyctasia yawned and stretched luxuriously. It was useless to
ponder the matter further; she was not likely ever to discover
the truth of it. But she had the satisfaction of knowing that she
had passed the night without the aid of the sleeping-draught.
And she knew, now, where to find the peace she sought.

9

The man who called himself Veron wondered if he were perhaps a criminal. He had considered many possible answers to the riddle of his past, but that particular one had never occurred to him. He'd gone so far as to consult fortunetellers, but the false ones had told him transparent lies, and the honest ones had admitted that their arts could reveal nothing of his history. It was one of the latter who'd searched his palms for a clue, without success, then told him, "You're no laborer, that much is certain—look at your fingers, smooth and uncalloused, like a gentleman's. You look like a gypsy, but you belong to the gentry—it doesn't take the second sight to see that."

His hands were harder now. He'd been working on trading ships to earn his way from city to city along the coast, and that was as humbling an experience as life has to offer, but he suspected that the seer had been right about his origins. He remembered nothing about himself, but he knew enough about many other subjects to be sure that he was well educated. He could read and write, he was familiar with a good deal of history, philosophy, poetry—no, it had not seemed at all likely that he was a criminal.

But the tall swordswoman, the lout who called herself a Desthene, certainly seemed to think that he'd done something reprehensible, and he'd not be the first of the gentry to commit crimes. Unless she was lying, unless she'd taken him for someone else, it would appear that he'd led a far from blameless life. But was she to be believed? He'd been duped before, by others who'd claimed to know him, who'd offered to lead him to his people, and led him instead into the clutches of outlaw slavers. A nameless, kinless man was their perfect prey. The supposed Desthene was far more likely to be a criminal than he.

But her reluctance to have anything to do with him had made him feel inclined to trust her. The others had always been all too willing to accost him, to engage him in amiable conversation. He'd learned to be wary of anyone who was eager to be of help. And her claim to be a noblewoman—it was hardly the sort of lie she'd expect a stranger to believe. Why invent something so unlikely, then? He doubted that she was subtle enough to feign hostility, to deliberately offer an unbelievable lie, in order to convince him.

Indeed, the very insolence of his guide was reassuring. When she'd found that he had no horse, she'd sent the potboy to hire one for him, and asked sneeringly, "You've not forgotten how to ride too, have you?" It was not only that she knew—or guessed—that he could ride, but that her whole manner suggested that she suspected *him* of some deception. Perhaps these were poor reasons to put faith in her, but he wanted desperately to believe that this time he'd found someone who knew him—even if she hated him.

But when they'd started out, and she'd taken an isolated route along the shore, he'd been sure it must be a trap. Even though slavery was forbidden by law in the city-states of the Maritime region, it was not unheard of for solitary travelers to be waylaid and smuggled south in the holds of bandit ships. There, riverways led inland from the coast to the Midlands, where the slave-trade flourished. No doubt the woman's confederates waited somewhere on this dark stretch of beach to seize him and row him out to the ship lying at anchor offshore, unlighted and invisible.

More disheartened than afraid, he'd reined in his horse and said, "Far enough. Your friends will have to wait. What a

disappointment you are, after all. I'd almost come to believe
that you were something more than a rogue slaver."

He watched closely to see how she would respond to the
accusation, expecting either a denial or an outright attack, but
he was not prepared for the sudden storm of rage she turned
upon him. "You miserable hound!" she shouted. "You dare to
call me—?" Wheeling her horse around, she pressed close
enough for him to see her shaking with fury. "I've killed better
than you for lesser insults!" she hissed, and spat full in his
face. She looked half mad and very dangerous, but he only
wiped his sleeve across his face and continued to watch her
narrowly. When he made no answer, she said more calmly,
with bitter scorn, "I've wanted to do that for a long time. Now
go your way if you like! I could stop you—and I wouldn't need
any help to do it—but that's the last thing I want to do. You can
even keep the horse—I'll pay for it. I'm going on this way, and
I don't care where you go. You can follow me or not, as you
choose—but if you do, you'll take care what you say to me."

And he'd followed. It was impossible to doubt the sincerity
with which she'd said, "I've wanted to do that for a long
time." She knew him.

It was too late for doubts now, at all events, no matter what
befell. He was as good as a prisoner here, though the noble
residence where his guide had brought him, with its well-kept
grounds and liveried guards, was clearly not the den of
outlaws. The sentries had obeyed her orders readily enough,
treating her as a person of some authority. He was under guard,
not precisely in a cell, but in cramped, windowless servants'
quarters that looked to be a converted storeroom—chosen, no
doubt, because there was only the one way out to watch. He
supposed he should be grateful that she hadn't locked him in
the cellars instead.

She'd taken undisguised satisfaction in leaving him there,
apologizing with mock servility that she was unable to offer
him accommodations more befitting to his rank.

"And what rank is that?" he'd asked evenly. "If you won't
tell me who I am, will you tell me what I am?"

"You're trouble, that's what you are!" she snapped. She
turned her back and strode from the room in two steps.

Her continued rancor had come as a great relief. If it had
been merely pretense, she'd surely have dropped her mask now

that she had him safely secured. "If I've wronged you, I've paid for it, believe me," he said quietly, to her back.

At the door, she hesitated and turned back reluctantly. "If you're not the one I take you for, then I—I'm sorry," she said uncomfortably. "But if you are, then I'll be the judge of when you're quits with me. And I don't have a forgiving nature."

He merely bowed in reply. Clearly it was useless to reason with the creature. But, straightening up again, he saw her looking at him with a puzzled frown. At last she said, "I think you're a Jhaice. With 'ancillary distinctions,' whatever those are. But maybe you're not—we'll know soon enough." She gave him another long, uncertain look, then shrugged and left him there to wait, to study his unfamiliar hands and wonder what kind of man he was.

◆   ◆   ◆

"Curse her! Why does she always have to do something unaccountable?" Corson complained, though in truth that was one of the things that drew her to Nyctasia. She had arrived in Rhostshyl only to learn that the Rhaicime was nowhere to be found. "Didn't that scatterwit tell anyone where she was going?"

"She didn't so much as tell anyone *that* she was going," Lady Tiambria explained, sounding rather amused. A year ago, she'd have been offended by Corson's offhand manner, but she'd grown accustomed to the ways of her sister's favorite. Nyctasia oughtn't to have ennobled such a person, of course, but there was nothing to be done about that now. Corson was one of the few people Nyctasia trusted, and though many at court looked down at her lowly origins, there were not many who dared refuse her an audience. The Lady Tiambria dared, but did not choose, to turn her away. "She only left a note to say that she expected to return within a few days' time. I thought *you'd* be able to tell *me* where she was."

Lady Tiambria reminded Corson of Nyctasia, when she'd first known her. This one still had a lot to learn, of course, but she showed promise. "Nyc's probably sneaked off to practice more of her mooncalf magic," Corson said disgustedly. "Whenever she disappears, you can be sure she's up to some crazy spell or other, and usually it's a harebrained business anyone with a grain of sense would let alone!"

Tiambria looked anxious. "Do you think she's in danger, then?"

"I've never known her when she wasn't, have you?" But then, remembering that Nyctasia's sister was with child, she added, "But don't fret yourself over that one—she's proof against a horde of demons or a nest of vipers. If a viper bit her, it would die. And as long as she's got that hound with her, nothing that's human will attack her and live."

But despite her assurances to Lady Tiambria, Corson was worried. How dare Nyc run off like this, without asking her to come along, without even letting her know where she was bound? If something happened to her, Corson wouldn't even know! How could she protect her? For the first time, Corson understood Steifann's complaints about her own wanderings. No wonder he always insisted that she write and tell him where she was, she realized, remembering guiltily that she very rarely did so. But at least she could take care of herself—she wasn't a delicate, sheltered little hand-reared songbird like Nyc!

Corson was at a loss. It was no use scouring the countryside for Nyctasia. She could be anywhere. Well, if she didn't see fit to tell Corson what she was about, she could just go ahead and get herself killed, and serve her right, the silly, sly, secretive minx. But what was to be done about Lord Erystalben?

Ought she to wait here for Nyctasia's return, or could she safely entrust the secret to someone at court? Nyc's kin had come between her and Shiastred before, but they wouldn't dare interfere in her affairs now—would they? Tempting as it was to leave the responsibility to someone else, Corson couldn't be sure that they'd not find a way to use Nyctasia's lover as a weapon against her. She knew who Nyctasia's allies were, but they too favored the marriage-alliance with Ochram. They might well think it best to keep Nyctasia and Lord Erystalben apart. Corson thought as much herself, though for different reasons, but she would not take it upon herself to make such a decision for Nyctasia. She believed in letting people make their own choices, and their own mistakes.

Could she turn Lord Erystalben over to his own family, then? They'd be able to affirm his identity, after all, and if he really was their kinsman, they had a right to know of his return. But Corson knew nothing of the Shiastred. Could they be trusted? And how could she make inquiries about them without arousing suspicion? It would be assumed that there was a reason behind anything she asked. She'd never been given to idle court gossip.

How fortunate, then, that she'd let Trask wheedle her into bringing him along, this time. . . .

"They've been supporters of the Edonaris for years, since before the war," Trask reported.

He had carried on a number of fruitful conversations and flirtations with pages and maids of the palace, leaving them with the impression that he was merely curious about Nyctasia's past. Since he was, in fact, curious about Nyctasia's past, this had not been a great challenge.

"But there have been different factions among them, it seems, since the heir to the Jhaicery left Rhostshyl." He grinned knowingly. "So that's the mysterious Jhaice you carried off from the Hare, eh?"

"Never you mind about him. If you've told anyone—"

"What do you take me for, a milktooth babe?" Trask said indignantly. "I know a secret when I meet one. If you don't trust me, get someone else to do your spying!"

"Just remember, if you so much as hint that you know anything about this, I'll tear out your tongue and make you eat it! Now what's this about divisions among the Shiastred?"

"Well, listen then—there are all sorts of stories about, but most agree that the Jhaice Erystalben made trouble for his family with the Edonaris, because his affair with Nyc was interfering with their plans to marry her to her cousin, Lord Thierran. They wanted it broken off—"

"I know all that," said Corson, who had killed Thierran ar'n Edonaris. "What about the Shiastred?"

"They ordered him to stay away from Nyc, but he refused, so finally they sent him away—disowned him, some say."

"His own blood-kin turned him out? I thought it was Nyc's family that drove him from Rhostshyl."

Trask shrugged. "I heard that too, but the Shiastred couldn't afford to anger the Edonaris. Some say that they made him go for fear that the Edonaris would have him killed, but it's also said that most of them weren't so very sorry to see the last of him."

"I can believe that," Corson said glumly. "And they probably wouldn't be glad to have him back, either."

"There's those that might. A few of them said openly that Nyc was to blame for the whole business, that she'd 'witched Lord Erystalben, and they turned against the Edonaris in the war. Much good *that* did them. Nyc pardoned them, of course, but they don't pretend to be grateful. The rest of them remained loyal to the House of Edonaris, though, and they claim that when Nyc's swain left the city he forswore his title and inheritance. Fancy doing that for love of Nyc! His cousin Lord Jhasteine has taken his place, and *he's* about to be married to a lady of the House of Lesevern, and it's said that *her* family—"

"That'll do," said Corson, discouraged. She had heard more than enough to convince her that she'd be ill-advised to leave her prisoner with the Shiastred. Half of them hostile to Nyc, the rest unlikely to welcome a rival Jhaice. "There's no help for it, we'll just have to stay here till Nyc gets back."

Trask didn't mind in the least.

10

"Where the headland meets the tide . . ." mused Nyctasia, watching in quiet amusement as Greymantle frisked in the spray, chasing waves and barking excitedly.

As always the sight of the limitless expanse of the sea calmed and comforted her. The moon was waning now, but full enough still to send its bright path from the far horizon to her feet, and show her the dark glow of the waters between. The hushed murmur of the waves welcomed her, reassuring her that all would yet be well.

Perhaps it had been foolish to read a message in the child's words, a meaning she herself had never intended when she'd spoken them, years before. But as she gazed out over the breaking waves, she was sure she'd been right to come to the oceanside to find respite from the demands and dangers of Rhostshyl. Even on her way here, she had received a sign that had seemed to affirm her decision.

She had almost crossed Rhostshyl Wood when she'd met with a group of students and scholars on their way to the city, and passed the night in their camp. She had let them believe she was a court scribe, and had answered their many questions

with assurances that Rhostshyl was all they'd heard, that
nothing but dire necessity could ever make her leave its walls.
When they asked about the Rhaicime, she boasted that she
knew her well, that Her Ladyship was wont to dictate secrets
to her that she'd entrust to no other scribe, but naturally, as
Nyctasia intended, they hadn't believed much of that.

"But have you seen her?" one of the students persisted.
"The truth now—is she as beautiful as folk say?"

"Oh, not half so pretty as you," said Nyctasia gallantly.
"The truth, if you must have it, is that she's as plain as I am
myself. And she looks like an unkempt kennels-hand more
often than not. Her own courtiers scold her for her unseemly
appearance."

"I've heard something of the sort about her," one of the
older men said seriously. "They say there's a good deal less
finery to be seen at court, since the Rhaicime set the fashion for
simplicity. It seems she thinks it ill becomes the nobility to
wear a fortune on their backs while folk suffer want in the city.
She's set them an example, and the others are shamed into
following her lead."

"And how do *you* know so much about it, Wren?" the youth
next to him jeered. "Since when are you a follower of
fashion?"

The first man swatted him. "Show some respect for your
elders, brat! I've not seen it for myself, but I believe what
I've heard. You know folk always want to emulate their
betters. And if it's true, I think it's much to the credit of the
Rhaicime."

The firelight concealed Nyctasia's blushes. "There's some
truth to it," she said, "but My Lady can be as vain as anyone
betimes, and that much I can swear to. Perhaps I may not know
her quite as well as I claimed, but I do know her ways and
those of the court. You'll see me there when I return, I promise
you."

"And will you ask the Rhaicime to receive us?" someone
teased.

Nyctasia laughed. "Remind me to do that when we meet
next," she said. "I have always so many affairs of state on my
mind that I might forget."

That night she had dreamt that she continued her journey
alone, with only Greymantle trotting at her side, easily keeping
pace with her horse. But as she rode on toward the coast, she

chanced to look back over her shoulder, and she had seen all of Rhostshyl following behind her in a long, lively procession that stretched for miles through the woods, all the way back to the gates of the city. Yet, instead of dismay, she'd felt great satisfaction to find that she hadn't after all left the city behind her. She had called out to her people to make haste, to join her on the way to the sea. She had awakened with a feeling of deep peace and contentment.

As she shared a morning meal with the travelers, one of the students told her that she had cried out in her sleep, and she answered, smiling, "I was dreaming that all of Rhostshyl was on the way to the sea, not just my dog and I."

As students will, they at once sought to interpret her dream, but Nyctasia was sure that she already understood its meaning. Without doubt, the *vahn* had revealed to her that she was not deserting her duty by making this journey, but rather acting for the good of the city, as she had hoped. To the students she said only, "I suppose it means that I'm such a true Rhostshylid that Rhostshyl is with me wherever I go, in my heart. It's as I told you before—there's no other city to compare with her."

But the man called Wren cast a different light upon the vision. "It may be as you say, scrivener," he said politely, "but I take it to mean that Rhostshyl herself will widen her borders, and one day reach toward the sea."

For a moment, Nyctasia could only contemplate his words in spellbound silence. It was exactly what she wished for her city—that the forest that stood between Rhostshyl and the coast should be cleared, and new roads built; that the walls bounding the city should be broken down and Rhostshyl grow to double her size, till she reached all the way to the coast, a true Maritime city. Could it be that this stranger had read the significance of her dream more truly than she?

"No riddle has only one answer," she said pensively. "I believe you possess the gift of prophecy, sir."

He bowed. "Not I, but you, Madame, are the dreamer."

But it was not to dwell upon such dreams that she had come here, she reminded herself. Time enough for such matters when she returned to Rhostshyl. She must make the most of her stolen moments alone at the edge of the land, where the boundless sea began. There were lessons to be learned here that would help her to realize her dreams one day.

She had always meant to practice the sequence of Consolations known as The Legacy of the Heirs of Ocean, but she had never found the time and the chance together to devote herself fully to the Discipline, the contemplation of the manifold qualities of the sea, its timelessness, its illimitable power, its unimaginable vastness, its unchanging rhythms that revealed the order and harmony of nature. And above all, its ceaseless work of transformation upon everything it touched.

From her first sight of the sea, Nyctasia had felt that she could look upon its waters forever, and never tire of a view in which no walls stood as barriers to the eye or the spirit. In the presence of the ocean, one understood how transitory and insignificant one's own affairs were—a lesson particularly valuable, Nyctasia thought, for those in positions of power over others. The sea humbled one, yes, but it thereby set one free. . . .

She had been pacing the shore as she meditated, gathering bits of stone and bone, driftwood and shell, but now she chose one smooth, white fragment from among them, and let the rest fall through her fingers, back into the sand. Settling herself among the boulders at the foot of the cliffs, she studied the small featureless object she held, as if it were a priceless treasure. Here was the entire secret, the essential unity of all things, revealed.

It was over a year ago, she realized, that she'd last walked on the strand here, with Corson, and shown her just such a piece of polished rubble, picked up from the beach. She had wanted to come alone, to pursue the Discipline in solitude, but Corson had insisted—and quite rightly—that it was too dangerous. Her enemies could well have set a watch for her here. But now no one, not even Corson, knew where she was. She smiled, remembering Corson's impertinent questions and indignant dismissals of the answers. Nyctasia had not achieved much of her purpose that day; instead, she had found herself trying to explain to her increasingly impatient bodyguard something of the Principles of Unity and Transformation, endlessly manifested by the working of the waves.

"The sea takes a shell, a stone, a branch, or a bone, and wears away its form, washes away its color, breaks and blanches and burnishes it, cuts and carves it, smooths and shapes it, till the stone is hollowed to a shell, the wood is tempered to a stone, the bone whittled to a twig, the shell fluted to a splinter of bone. The sea incessantly transforms all things."

"Well, what if it does?" Corson said. "Why fret yourself about it?"

"Because in doing so it reveals to us the indwelling nature of those things, and shows us that form is mere mask, disguising the truth that all things are one and the same. That is what we must always remember—"

"Why?"

"So as not to be deceived by mere appearance. So as to understand that we ourselves are made up of the same substance as all other things. We are no different in essence from the stones, the trees, the shells. That which divides us is superficial and will not endure."

"Now I see what you're at," said Corson, exasperated. "It's just more of your fancy lies. Magic's all lies, and this philosophy of yours is nothing but more lies. You say that night is day, and shells are stones, and hens are hats, and you're so daft you believe it yourself. Asye, you say it so prettily *I* could almost believe it! But a stone's a stone and a shell's a shell—*that's* the truth of it, whatever you say."

"What's this, then?" Nyctasia had asked, laughing, and handed her the smooth shape, so worn by the sands that it was impossible to say whether it had originally been driftwood, shell, stone, or bone.

Corson turned it in her hands, examining it. "I don't know," she said in annoyance. "What difference does it make?"

"That's it exactly. It makes no difference. It's true that a stone's not a shell, as you say, but it's also true that they are one, and these truths do not contradict one another. Their opposition is apparent, not actual."

Corson had only snorted in contempt. "If you like to think that you're really a lot of rocks and rotting bones and sea-slugs, you can," she said. "And much good may it do you!"

Alone on the dark shore, Nyctasia smiled and clutched the unknown fragment tightly in her hand. *Much good*, she thought, *may it do me indeed*. She remained looking out over the water, and recited quietly:

> "There is power,
> There is peace,
> There is refuge,
> There, release."

Then for a long while, she sat listening to the steady, regular splashing and sighing of the waves, letting the sound and smell and sight of the sea wash over her, wear away her cares and concerns, soothe and caress her and slowly shape her anew, until she became the smooth, hard stone, the hollow shell, the polished branch or bone. All of these and none of them in one. And over time this too, in its turn, was further purified, refined to identical grains of sand, mingling with all that had gone before. Each still ceaselessly burnished the others and was burnished by them, to be worn away at last to invisible motes of dust that dissolved in the waves, and so became again one with the water, from which, it was said in the earliest legends, all life had arisen at the beginning of the world. . . .

Nyctasia did not know how long she had been resting there among the great rocks before Greymantle bounded up to her, barking and shaking a shower of spray from his coat into her face. He dashed away, along the path up the cliffside, then turned around to see if she was following, and pranced back to her, barking insistently. Nyctasia rose to her feet unsteadily and patted him. "Good lad," she said. "Very well, let's go then." Further meditations would have to wait for the morrow. The tide was coming in.

11

"I much regret that you've been detained here, sir," the woman said briskly as she entered, followed by the guard and an immense dog. "I assure you—"

And then she looked at him and suddenly fell silent, staring in astonishment. A lady from the look of her, Veron thought, despite her plain attire and the scribe's pen-case at her belt. He saw the color ebb from her face completely, leaving her as starkly white as sun-blanched bone, and she made a gesture he recognized as a sign of Unveiling, to ward off sorcerous illusions—though he had no idea how he knew such things. "I'm real," he said hoarsely, taking a few steps toward her. "That is, I think I am." His heart raced, pounding in his throat, and he felt that he could barely breathe. In her eyes he saw what he had been vainly seeking in every face for two years' time. Recognition. And something more.

So softly he barely heard her, she whispered, "There the heart and spirit bide," and swayed giddily as if about to fall.

Without thought he reached out quickly to catch her, realizing only too late that the dog would take this action for an attack upon its mistress. The guard too started forward, but the

dog had sprung at him even before his hand could close upon
her shoulder to steady her. The beast's great weight threw him
to the floor as it seized his wrist in its jaws, growling savagely,
but it released him at once, on the lady's command, and sat
back on its haunches, panting and looking pleased with itself.
Blood soaked his shirt and seeped between his fingers as he
clutched the wound, but he scarcely thought about his torn arm
as he struggled to sit up. This woman knew him—he was
certain of it—and nothing in the world mattered except that.

She was kneeling beside him now, laughing and crying at
once, while she gripped his upper arm, squeezing at it
desperately with both hands. "Lie still, love, don't try to rise.
Hold your arm up now, to slow the bleeding. Oh, 'Ben, you
should know better than to move like that before a strange
guard dog!"

"You know me!" he gasped. "Tell me!"

But she only kissed him quickly and said, "Hush! We'll talk
later—let me see to this wound now. I don't mean to lose you
again the very moment I've found you!" Turning to the guard,
she ordered, "Press hard—right here—and don't leave off till I
bid you."

There were so many questions he must ask her! But when he
tried again he found that he was too weak and dizzy to make
the effort. And why was he suddenly so cold? He let his head
fall back again and closed his eyes, the better to occupy himself
with the task of breathing, which seemed to require all of his
attention.

In a moment the woman had slit the length of his sleeve with
her quill-knife and bound the cloth firmly about his biceps.
"Good," he heard her say. "Give me that blanket, then *run* to
Teissa and tell her to fetch me hot water and clean cloth as
quick as she can."

He felt her lay the blanket over him and put something
beneath his feet, then she sat beside him and gently raised his
arm again, holding his hand against her face. With her free
hand she unlaced his shirt at the collar and lightly felt for the
throb of blood in his throat. It must have satisfied her, for she
sat back with a sigh and said only, "You've still the most
beautiful collarbone in all creation. My poor 'Ben, what a
welcome for you, after all this time. First you're locked up like
a common thief by Corson, then all but murdered by my
watchful hound, and the both of them only trying to protect

me. You know I've always been fortunate in finding loyal servants."

She doesn't know, he thought, and opened his eyes to look anxiously up at her. But before he could speak he had already forgotten what it was he had to tell her. She stroked his cheek and brushed her fingers across his lips. "Don't try to talk yet, my dear. Rest. Words will wait, cares can keep. I shan't leave you. Rest, love. Sleep."

He slept fitfully for a time, drifting in and out of dreams, dimly aware that the pale, delicate lady—she who had called him by name—was still tending to him, watching over him. The others came and went, following her orders. She seemed to be mistress of the household, and a healer. She had washed and bandaged his wound with her own hands, then had him lifted carefully onto the cot. He was warm now, swathed in quilts and coverlets. She'd said, "You lost a good deal of blood, but you'll soon be well, I promise you." But what was the name she had called him?

"A dogbite wound never mortifies or brings on disease," she'd said, "unless the beast itself is ailing. And yet the bite of a healthy human being may be deadly, so I've read. It's a thing I've never understood." But she was no longer speaking to him. Someone else answered her, and both had spoken in low, hushed tones, so as not to waken him. He turned to them and said quite clearly, "I'm not asleep."

"No?" she said, smiling. "Then have a little more broth, if you will." She took up a copper mug from a small brazier and tasted it, then tempered its heat with liquid from a pitcher and blew on it to mix it. She was alone.

More broth? He hadn't had anything to eat. And what had become of the other woman, the servant who'd said, "There are many things the leeches don't know, my lady, for all their grand airs"?

And what was the name she'd called him?

But when she raised his head and held the cup to his lips, he recognized the rich, salt, wine-spiced taste of the broth at once, and remembered that she had indeed given him sips of it from time to time during the night. The fragments of talk he'd heard must have been spoken some time ago. She had been sitting at his bedside for hours, he realized. Each time he'd opened his eyes to see if she was still there, she'd smiled at him and caressed his hair or his brow, sometimes just touching the pulse at his temple. Her hands were like a child's.

She'd fed him the warm, savory broth a few drops at a time, and when he'd tried weakly to question her, she'd put him off, murmuring soothing endearments and promises. "Later, my dear. Don't worry." Had she called him by name?

It occurred to him fleetingly that she might be his wife. Or his sister? But that was not likely—she was so fair-skinned, nothing at all like him. Perhaps now she would tell him who she was—who *he* was. He turned his head toward her again, but she was no longer beside him, and he saw to his confusion that he was in a different room altogether. This was a large bedchamber with fine furnishings, tapestries, carpets, and a glowing hearthfire. Broad windows in the far wall let in a faint grey light and the sound of waves breaking on the rocks below.

She was standing at a window, looking out to sea, motionless, a statue silhouetted against the half-light of early dawn. She had changed her roadworn tunic and breeches for a long white robe that looked soft and silken where the firelight touched it. She was barefoot. Her silence was like a shell about her, pearl-like, perfect, inviolable.

Somehow reassured, as if his questions had been answered, he slept again, deeply, lulled by the sound of the sea.

She had come to the sea to put the troubles of the city behind her for a time, Nyctasia thought wryly, and she had succeeded—*vahn* knows!—far beyond her expectations. Since she'd set foot in the Smugglers' House, she'd not had a thought to spare for Rhostshyl or anything else save 'Ben alone. When she'd arrived without warning, and unescorted, her people had assumed that she'd come on his account, and when she'd called for only a bath and a cold supper, her steward had naturally inquired if she had any orders concerning the Lady Corson's prisoner.

Nyctasia had been outraged. Another of Corson's childish pranks! It was inexcusable! After the affair of 'Malkin's arrest, she'd made Corson promise not to misuse her authority in such a way again, yet here she was up to the same game at Nyctasia's Chiastelm residence. This sort of irresponsible behavior could not be permitted to continue. It would reflect badly on Nyctasia if one whom she had chosen to distinguish with a title should prove herself unworthy of the honor.

Nyctasia decided that she would first see to this prisoner of Corson's, then go directly to the Hare and demand an explanation—or rather, she would send someone to fetch Corson to her, later, after she'd bathed and eaten. As a citizen of the Alliance, Corson was not obliged to obey such a summons, but as a Desthene of Rhostshyl she was very much obliged to do so, and if Nyctasia's messenger had to roust her out of bed, so much the better!

She was already planning the exact terms in which to express her displeasure to Corson as she hurried after the guard to attend to the unfortunate victim of Corson's malicious humor. The barbarian virago must be made to understand, once and for all, that she could not carry on in this way! Nyctasia had hardly looked up when she'd walked into 'Ben's room, uttering apologies, but still intent on the recriminations she meant to make to Corson.

When she'd seen him standing before her, she'd felt her lips grow cold with shock, and her first thought had been of the demonic spirit that had appeared to her in his guise, amidst the ruins of the Cymvelan temple. He might be a ghost, a revenant—it would not be the first time the dead had communed with the living at the haunted Smugglers' House. She'd stood stunned, as if thunderstruck, and for a moment the floor had seemed to shift beneath her feet. How desperately anxious 'Ben had looked, uncertain of his welcome, uncertain of her love.

But Greymantle's attack had left little enough doubt as to his mortality, and there had been no moment, from then to this, to think of anything but keeping him alive. Precious minutes had passed while she'd frantically tried to remember—and apply—what she knew of stemming the flow of blood. She'd learned from books that one should force the flesh of the upper arm against the bone, but her books had not told her how to go about it while 'Ben's—*'Ben's*—lifeblood was flooding from him before her eyes, when she had not yet recovered from the shock of seeing him! She had thought she would never find the right part of his arm to press, that he would be dead in another moment, that it was already too late.

Then had come the long vigil beside him, waiting for the Balance to tip toward life or death. She had been ready to take up arms against death at any cost, ready, if need be, to throw

herself into a healing trance from which both of them might
emerge, or neither.

But in time the vital heat had rekindled in his flesh, and the
beat of his blood had begun to quicken, little by little, and grow
stronger. Only when she was certain he was out of danger had
she dared to have him moved to her own quarters—orders
which had aroused much speculation among her guards and
attendants. They'd had no idea who it was Corson had left in
their custody. Some of Nyctasia's people in Rhostshyl would
have recognized him, but her retinue at the Smugglers' House
were mostly folk of Chiastelm, hired by her steward, and they
had not even seen Nyctasia herself very often. She had rarely
made use of the place since her return to Rhostshyl, though
she'd seen to it that it was kept in readiness for her, in hopes
that she would find time to visit the oceanside.

She'd bought the house years ago, when she'd first come of
age, and even then she had thought of it as a haven from the
burdensome duties of the Rhaicimate, as well as an ideal place
to try her hand at sea-spells and the Discipline of the Legacy of
the Heirs of Ocean. Even its reputation as a haunted house had
appealed to her, since such places were often sources of
Immaterial Influences. But there had been another reason she
had wanted the property, then, and she remembered it now as
she looked from her window out to the steep cliff with its sheer
drop to the rocks and the surging tide. It had seemed such an
easy escape, if she should need it, as swift and free as
flight. . . . She had taken comfort, at times, from the knowledge that the waters waited, and would always wait, to receive
her. But what she saw now, when she gazed out to sea, was a
Manifestation not of a Consolation Toward Death, but of an
Influence Toward Life.

She turned from the window to look at 'Ben again, to
reassure herself that he was still resting quietly—that he was
still *there*, indeed, truly returned to her, and not some passing
dream. Noiselessly, she crossed to the bed to watch him sleep,
as she had been doing without pause all through the night. Yet
she had hardly satisfied her need to look at him. She could
never have her fill of studying the dark, sharp planes of his
face, the sweep of his black, hawk's-wing eyebrows, his
curving lashes and chiseled lips. She longed to touch him, but
would not risk waking him, for she saw that he was sleeping

soundly at last. There was no need to hover over him any longer; she would do better to get some sleep herself.

Very cautiously, she laid herself beside him on the wide bed, taking care to make no jarring motion or noise. If she slept here, she reasoned, she would wake if 'Ben should stir or speak.

He gave no sign of doing either, however, even when she reached across him and drew the bedcurtains, to protect him from the morning light. Nyctasia settled beside him again, confident that he would sleep undisturbed for some hours yet. She too had always slept well in this room, within sound of the ocean.

12

He dreamed of the spell-haunted Yth Forest again, though he did not know if he had ever really been there, or if the Yth was in any way like his dreams of it. He was wandering through the Forest, listening to a distant singing, and though he knew he should turn back before he lost his way, the singing drew him on irresistibly. In a grassy glade, he stopped to rest beside a deep, clear pool, and at once he felt parched with unbearable thirst. It would be folly to drink the waters or eat the fruits of the Yth, yet he leaned over the pool, tempted, driven by the maddening thirst.

The sight of his reflection troubled him, for he had forgotten what he looked like, and he was reluctant to recognize himself, to be reminded that he belonged with his own people, not among the Yth-kind. He broke the image with his hand, then made a cup of his palm and tasted a few drops of the bright, cold water, but it only seemed to increase his thirst. Then, abandoning his misgivings, he bent down to the pool and drank freely and for a long while, yet when he rose his thirst was still unsatisfied.

But he could hear the singing more clearly now, near at

hand, and he set off again in pursuit of it, forgetting all else, and unaware that his reflection still remained in the forest pond. It rose from the water, laughing without a sound, and followed, unseen and unheard, not running but crawling through the tall grass like a serpent, as swiftly as water flowing downstream, as silently as a drifting fog.

At a branch in the path he stopped, uncertain which way to take, and he thought someone called to him, but try as he might, he could not make out the name. And as he stood listening, his reflection came from behind and fell upon him like a savage animal, bearing him to the ground in a grip of iron and tearing at him with teeth as sharp as knives. He fought to escape, but it was like struggling against a raging torrent that carries off all in its path. The inhuman strength of the creature overpowered him easily, snapping his bones like brittle twigs and slowly crushing the life from his chest. Yet, dying, defenseless, he was somehow unafraid at the last, and even content to surrender to the deadly embrace of the reflection.

It devoured him, flesh, blood and bone, leaving nothing, not a shred of sinew, splinter of bone or drop of blood on the path to show that he had ever existed. And when its feast was finished it stood upright, graceful and unhurried, and went its way on foot, choosing a path without hesitation.

He woke in a panic terror, his heart racing, his mouth dry with fright. The dream was always different, but each time it left him with the same mad fear—that he remembered no past because he had no past, that he was no one, a creature in man's form, somehow called into being two years before, for a purpose he could not even guess at. . . .

But with wakefulness came clarity as he remembered where he was and how he'd come there. The curtains had been drawn about the bed, but sunlight filtered through them and pierced between them, and he recognized his surroundings in triumph. Of course he was someone, for the lovely, grey-eyed woman knew him; she had told him, "I don't mean to lose you *again*." His memory of the past night was confused and cloudy, mingled with dreams, but surely she had said that? She *had* recognized him . . . ? Had he not woken once, for a moment, and seen her lying beside him, or had that been only another dream? No—for the other pillow showed the hollow where her head had lain. He touched it gratefully, and his heart grew calm, his breathing steady. He would go find her at once, and put an end to this torment of uncertainty.

He sat up slowly, supporting himself with his left arm, and leaned back against the headboard to rest. The dizziness brought on by this effort passed quickly, however. He was still weak, but no longer felt helpless and enfeebled. Determined to go on, he drew back the bedcurtains—but she was there, perched on a high inner window-ledge, waiting for him to wake.

Today she had dressed with some care, he noticed. Black knee-breeches with silver buckles, and a close-fitting sleeveless tunic of the same finespun wool, trimmed in silver, covered a silvery, silken shirt with trailing sleeves, and matching hose. Her close-cropped hair was damp, shining in the sun, and a silver earring caught the light with a burning gleam as she turned to face him. She had been eating a pear, and feeding the peel to a greedy gull, but now she tossed the rest out to the bird and dropped down from the windowsill, landing lightly on the balls of her feet, with her knees bent and her arms held out for balance.

"A rope-dancer taught me that," she said, laughing. "How do you feel now?"

His mouth was still so dry that he answered, half-choking, "Thirsty!"

She nodded. "I should think you would be, indeed. You're to drink a dozen cups today, of water or broth or what you please. And I hope you're hungry as well, because I want you to eat a good deal of meat." As she spoke, she took a silver pitcher and mug from a cupboard in the stone wall and poured out a measure of a pale golden liquid. "Still chilled from the cold-cellar," she said, watching as he took it, to see if his hand was steady.

It was only barley-water, with a scent of mint about it, but it seemed the most refreshing drink he had ever tasted. He eagerly drank the second mugful she gave him and sighed with relief. "I was dreaming of spell-waters that never slake the thirst," he said, dismissing the rest of the nightmare.

She frowned slightly, but said only, "It means nothing. The flesh has its dreams as well as the spirit, especially in illness. But you'll soon be whole." She arranged the pillows behind his back and took the empty mug from him. He could smell the fresh-crushed mint on her fingertips.

"Whole . . ." he breathed. "Yes, tell me now, in the *vahn's* name, tell me everything! Who are you, what do you know of me—?"

The mug slipped from her fingers and clattered to the floor. He saw horror dawn in her eyes, and he thought in dismay, *she doesn't know.*

Nyctasia fought to keep her composure, not to give way to alarm. She had thought nothing of his bewildered questions of the night before, taking them for mere delirium, but he should have recovered his senses by now! " 'Ben, what are you saying?" she whispered. "Don't you know me?"

"I don't know *myself*—didn't she *tell* you that?" he exclaimed, outraged. "Didn't she warn you that I'd no memory?"

"She—? I—I don't understand."

"The southerner! A Desthene, by her account of herself. She left me here and went to fetch a friend of hers, she said, who knew me. Didn't she send you?"

"Corson . . . no, she must have come too late to find me. I . . . received another message to come here." She sat on the edge of the bed, looking as weak and shaken as he. "She really is a Desthene now," she said dazedly, still trying to sort out where matters stood. *The spell of Perilous Threshold.* . . .

"Very well, she is a Desthene, but what am *I*? That one told me nothing. You called me Ben just now, but—"

"Not even your own name?" cried Nyctasia. "Oh, no—!" *I can't bear any more of this!* she thought. But she must be calm, for his sake. He was so racked with anticipation already, such feverish excitement could do him harm, in his weakened state. Calling upon the *vahn* to help her master herself, she said gently, "Yes, now I understand. I shall tell you all. You are Erystalben, son of Descador, of the House of Shiastred, in Rhostshyl."

She watched him anxiously. "Erystalben?" he murmured. "Rhostshyl . . . ?"

The names meant nothing to him. He'd heard of Rhostshyl, of course, but did not remember ever having been there. And who was Erystalben? "I took the name of Veron when I found myself without a name," he said dispiritedly. "But such a name is anyone's for the taking. The name you offer me is not to be had so easily, it seems." He looked defeated, hopeless. "How can I be Erystalben when I know myself only as Veron?"

Unlike Trask, Nyctasia recognized the name. Veron was the

hero of an ancient legend, a man who had lost his name through dealings with demons. For *veron* was not a name, but the Old Eswraine word for "lacking," for "bereft."

"You must not call yourself that any longer," she said firmly. "Name and place are yours. You are the Lord Erystalben Cador Jhaice brenn Rhostshyl ar'n Shiastred."

He shook his head wearily and sank back against the pillows, stricken by disappointment so keen it seemed to gnaw at his heart like the specter of his dream. "I've believed, all this time, that if I once learned who I was, all the rest would somehow come back to me. But you might be speaking of a stranger!"

"Despair destroys the spirit," Nyctasia said softly. *And despair could kill him now*, she thought. "It will take time, 'Ben, I daresay, but when you see the city again, your home and your kinfolk, then you'll begin to remember. You'll soon be strong enough to travel, and we'll go back to Rhostshyl together. That's sure to make a difference." She did not believe it herself. A spell of Perilous Threshold would not be undone so easily as that. But she was a very convincing liar.

And Erystalben longed to be convinced, above all else. "It may be so," he said thoughtfully. "Perhaps names are not enough. But even when I saw you I remembered nothing."

"Have you not looked in the glass? If you don't know yourself from your own face, how should you know me from mine? A name, a face—these are nothing, but to return to your birthplace is another matter. There every stone, every nail, will speak to you of your past. Rhostshyl holds your memories, 'Ben, as it does mine, and that is where you must seek for them." This argument almost persuaded her that she was right. But even if she were proved wrong, he would be strong enough in body, by then, to bear the blow to his spirit.

Erystalben sat up straighter and fixed his flame-blue eyes upon her. "Tell me the rest," he said.

"The Shiastred are a respected family," she began, "and you're the principal heir to the House. Your—"

He waved this aside. "No, wait. First, who are you—you've not yet told me that! And who are you to me? Not kin, I think."

Nyctasia flushed. "More than kin."

"Forgive me, it's a galling thing to have to ask, but are we—?"

"We're not bound by law, you and I," Nyctasia said

evasively, but her look was answer enough. "But how very discourteous of me, sir, not to have introduced myself." She rose and bowed. "Nyctasia Selescq Rhaicime brenn Rhostshyl ar'n Edonaris, and at your service. You generally called me 'Tasia."

He stared at her as if for the first time. "Rhaicime!" he gasped. "But I— But you— Do you mean to say that *you're* the Witch of Rhostshyl?"

"It's not a title to which I lay formal claim," said Nyctasia, smiling, "but, yes, I'm called that. I'm called 'The Mad Lass' in some quarters, so I'm told, but it seems no disrespect is meant, since folk in those trades often call themselves worse. You yourself used sometimes to call me 'Mistress of Ambiguities,' which perhaps means much the same thing. I've a taste for paradox and masquerade, you see."

He suddenly remembered that he'd first seen her in scribe's guise. A woman of good family but little means, he'd thought her, following a scribe's calling from inclination or necessity. He'd met many such on his travels through the coastal cities, all of them bound for Rhostshyl in hopes of finding service with the Rhaicime. Ignoring her attempts to distract him with her chatter, he persisted, "I've heard talk of you in Cerrogh, in Ochram—they say you saved the city by your spells, that you're the most powerful sorceress in the west of the world!"

"So my spies tell me, but surely you don't credit such wild tales? I encourage them, of course, in order to daunt my enemies, and the enemies of Rhostshyl, but most of what folk say is merely moonshine. I've some skill at healing, as you've seen, but what mastery of magic I ever had was weak, because I hadn't the time to devote to the Art. And now I've hardly any time at all. You were always a better magician than I."

He started. "I?" The idea struck him with the force of a revelation. It was the first thing he'd been told about himself that seemed somehow in keeping with his nature. It was as if she had confirmed something he'd suspected from the first. "I myself am a magician?" he asked, looking into the distance, lost in thought.

"You were, 'Ben. I don't know whether you are now." She had almost said, *I don't know what you are now.* He seemed suddenly far from her, as if an unseen barrier divided them. "'Ben . . ." she said, frightened, "you ought to be resting. I shouldn't tire you with so much talk, not yet. No, be still for a moment." She came nearer and brushed back his hair to touch the pulse at his temple. "Ah, your heartbeat's even stronger, that's well, but all the same you must have a day's rest and another night's sleep before I shall feel easy about you." She ached to take his face between her hands, to lean still closer to him, but she reminded herself that she was a stranger to him. She had no right to treat him as if he were still her own. She stepped back.

But he seized her hand, saying, "Don't go—you mustn't. Please—"

She pressed his hand. "Let me fetch you some soup. You need food, to renew your strength."

"Presently, whatever you will. Only tell me this first. That other one . . . Corson? It's plain that she thinks me a villain. Have I wronged you too?"

"Not me, but yourself. It is you who paid the price."

"For what, then? Why did I leave you?"

"Why do we do anything in this life?" Nyctasia sighed. "For power."

"And did I find it?"

"You did. And this was the result."

He looked away, then, and said slowly, "I never thought I was a fool, whatever else I might be."

"But you weren't to blame, love. You'd no choice but to leave the city. My kin were after your blood."

"Because a Jhaice from a respected family has no business to court a Rhaicime?"

"A Rhaicime of the Edonaris, and she betrothed to her cousin. And they believed that with you out of the way, I'd give up my studies of magic and settle down to more responsible pursuits—protecting the power of our House and plotting the downfall of our rivals. You encouraged me to neglect my duties, you see." She had been speaking with a bitter humor, but suddenly a sob caught at her throat as she said, "Oh, 'Ben, I should have gone with you! But—but—war was brewing in the city, and some of us thought it could still be stopped. They needed my support, I was the only one among them who belonged to the Rhaicimate. I hadn't the right to go, do you understand?"

He was not altogether sure that he did. Why did she ask this, what did she expect him to say? "And so you were caught up in the war?" he hazarded.

"No, I did follow you before then. I always meant to keep my word! I did! But I waited too long, and all to no purpose. I failed to prevent the bloodshed, and I let you fall prey to the Yth—"

"The Yth!" His grasp of her hand tightened. "Have I been to Yth Wood? Tell me!"

"I think so, 'Ben. I don't know the whole of it. But I have been there, in search of you, and it was so much more dangerous than we thought—nothing we had learned prepared me to resist its power. If I'd been with you, then none of this might have happened. You were waiting for me, but I didn't know—" She was crying openly now, shaking helplessly. "I didn't know what the Yth was like! 'Ben, I swear, if I'd known, I'd not have let you go there alone! Please believe me!"

She had seemed so in command that her abandoned weeping was all the more shocking. If she needed his forgiveness, she must have it. His questions could wait. He pulled her to him, circling her waist with his good arm, and clumsily drew her down beside him. "I believe you," he said, and kissed her, tasting the tears on her lips and eyes, the legacy of the salt sea. "Of course I believe you, my Mad Lass. Don't cry." He stroked the soft down at the nape of her neck, which her cropped hair left so bare and inviting.

Nyctasia shivered and pressed herself against him, allowing the sweet, familiar desire for him to envelop her like the rising tide, for the space of a few heartbeats, before she tore herself away, saying, "This is exceedingly unwise, of all things that sap the strength, the most dangerous."

"But what better way to die, answer me that," he teased, pulling her back for a moment to kiss her throat, before he let her go.

"You've not forgotten some things, I see." She stood and straightened her clothes, smiling, then leaned over him, took his face in her hands and gave him a lingering kiss. "Some food for you now, and then nothing but rest—you're not so strong as you think, not yet."

He had to admit that she was right. When she'd gone out, he fell back, exhausted and lightheaded, and lay with his eyes closed, listening to the sea. Perhaps, he thought drowsily, perhaps he was really lying asleep on the deck of some coastal trading vessel, dreaming that he'd found his home and his people . . . that he was a lord, the heir of a noble house, loved by a desirable and powerful lady—a Rhaicime, ruler of a city. . . . What else should a nameless man dream for himself, after all?

When Nyctasia returned, she found him fast asleep. "I'm sorry to wake you, but you should eat this soup now. Then you may sleep all the afternoon, if you like." As soon as he smelled the savory meat soup, thick with shreds of beef and venison, he realized that he was not only thirsty again but ravenously hungry as well. She gave him bread and wine with it, and he managed awkwardly to make a good meal, relying on his left hand and occasional help from Nyctasia. When he had downed a second bowlful, she was well satisfied, declaring that a good appetite was the surest sign of healing. "Now you may sleep till suppertime," she said, but the meal had wakened him.

"I've had enough of sleeping. I was dreaming just now that you were only a dream, and I want to keep you in sight for a bit, so as to be sure you're real."

"We are both real," Nyctasia said seriously. "Do you remember—vahn, was it only last night?—the first thing you said to me was, 'I'm real. Or I think I am.' I didn't know what you meant by that, and I hadn't much time to think about it—and yet I should have known, for I dreamed once that I'd found you, but I couldn't make you hear when I called your name, and you walked past me like a stranger.

"I'd done spells of seeking, but all in vain, and because your spirit remained hidden from me, I was certain that I'd never see you again. Of course, if you were lost to yourself, I could not find you, but I never thought of that. And so when I saw you here . . ." She shuddered. "But no illusion ever bled like that!"

"You, however, may yet prove a dream," he said. "The more I consider the matter, the less likely it seems that I could have such extraordinary good fortune. No, if I fall asleep again, I'll only wake in some filthy dockside inn and laugh at myself for dreaming that a beautiful Rhaicime was feeding soup to a nameless vagabond like me."

Nyctasia shook her head, as if at a willful child. "You needn't sleep, then, so long as you rest."

"But I feel quite fit now, not at all dizzy or weak. Why shouldn't we walk to the shore? It can't be far."

"Certainly not," Nyctasia said firmly. "Tomorrow, perhaps, if you rest today, and sleep tonight. You don't—"

But he was laughing at her. "I was only baiting you, 'Tasia, for the pleasure of hearing you scold me. I promise to rest as quiet as an unfledged chick, if you'll stay here and talk to me."

Pleased that he had at last called her by name, Nyctasia said with a smile, "You could always win your way with me."

"That's good to know. Sit here by me."

"But what shall I say, where shall I begin? Would you hear of your family? Your parents are living, and you have a younger sister."

He found that he didn't care to hear more unfamiliar names, names that suggested no faces, no feelings. He wanted to ask about the Yth, yet he was half afraid to hear the answers. And such a question might distress her anew. They both needed time to recover themselves, he thought. "Tell me more about the past—our past," he suggested. "How long have I known you? How did we meet?"

"That's a tale indeed!" Nyctasia laughed. "I was only fifteen or sixteen years of age, and you not much older. And from the moment I first heard your name, until the time we met, I loathed you absolutely."

"Why?" he asked, dismayed. "What had I done to offend you?"

"Nothing at all, but you existed, and your existence happened to interfere with my plans. You see, I was very taken with astromancy at that time, and I'd learned that an extremely rare alignment of variable stars was to take place one summer night—"

"Now how could I interfere with that?"

"Patience. I'll come to that in good time. There was to be a banquet and ball that same night, at the palace of the Edonaris, but I didn't concern myself with that. I rarely attended such affairs, and didn't suppose I'd be missed on this occasion. But that morning my great-aunt, the Lady Mhairestri, summoned me to say that I most certainly would be expected to make an appearance, and that I was not to absent myself for any reason whatsoever. And that was on your account. I was to make your acquaintance, engage you in conversation, and the like."

"But you said your kin disapproved of me."

"To be sure they did, later, when you proved such an undesirable influence on me, and threatened to come between me and the duties of an Edonaris. But at this time, the Edonaris were courting the support of the Shiastred, and you were to be head of the House of Shiastred one day. Our feud with the Teiryn was becoming serious, and your family had not yet declared themselves for one side or the other. Because I was close to you in age, my task was to charm you with my attentions, discover where the sympathies of your House lay, perhaps to sway you to our cause.

"Mhairestri was one of the heads of the family, very respected and influential. It would never have entered my mind to disobey her outright, and it took all the temerity I could muster even to question her orders. I explained, with all due courtesy, about the stars and the powerful Influences created by such a rare confluence of elements, but Mhairestri gave it as her opinion that this celestial event could very well come about without my assistance. She said, 'It's time you gave less thought to witchcraft, and more to statecraft!' Then she pointed out that my duty to my House, my estate, and my city all required me to set aside my own interests, that responsibility and rank entailed sacrifices, and that the family asked little enough of me as a rule. But she had no doubt, she assured me, that I, being an Edonaris, would willingly put the performance of my duty before all else, when duty so plainly presented itself as in this instance."

"Poor girl!"

"She could always get the better of me by appealing to duty. Or nearly always. I ventured to observe that my cousins, Thierran, Mescrisdan and Lhejadis, were also Edonaris, also young, and indeed better suited than I to win your regard, being more accustomed to society and more at their ease in company."

"Why was that?"

"Oh, I was a sickly child, and a scholarly youth, who'd never mixed much with others, aside from my kin. I'd been allowed to go rather my own way. But Mhairestri had made up her mind that I could be useful in this matter, and it was a waste of breath to argue. My manners, she insisted, were perfectly satisfactory when I chose to use them, and quite good enough for a young lordling like you. The others would do their part, of course, but there could be no question of their taking my place, because I was of Rhaicime rank. My notice would be more flattering to a boy of the lower nobility."

"The insolent harridan!" Erystalben exclaimed with real anger. "A curse on her for a brazen procuress! How dare she?"

He had not lost his pride along with his memory, Nyctasia realized. "She's dead now," she said. "By her own hand, rather than see the Edonaris united to their enemies, and the city under my rule. She never could reconcile herself to the idea that I would one day have a voice on the council of the Rhaicimate." She seemed to be speaking more to herself than to Erystalben, now, as if she were trying to understand her own history. "It was of no consequence while my mother lived, since I was to have the title from her, and the women of our family are long-lived. No one expected me to inherit until I was well into my middle years, and had outgrown my youthful notions. Mhairestri's position looked to be secure. She wasn't of Rhaicime rank herself, but she wielded a good deal of authority in the city nevertheless. The Edonaris dominated the Rhaicimate, and Mhairestri exercised considerable influence over them, especially my mother and elder brother, both of them on the council. But then my mother died unexpectedly, at a young age, and Mhairestri was faced with the prospect of seeing me take possession of my title and my powers as soon as I came of age. That's when she set out in earnest to make a proper Edonaris of me. I think she hardly knew me by sight before then. But perhaps it was already too late."

Nyctasia gave a little shake of her shoulders, recalling herself to her tale. "And so I was to occupy myself with young Shiastred, like a dutiful daughter of the Edonaris, and I detested you in consequence."

"I regret that my existence was an inconvenience to you, dear 'Tasia, but I think it would have been more just of you to detest your great-aunt."

"I couldn't very well do that, it would have been disrespectful. No, you were to blame that my plans were upset—and that wasn't the worst of your offenses. Not only would I be prevented from witnessing the Critical Alignment, but I was expected to dress in an elegant new gown of ivory silk, trimmed with rare black pearls."

He laughed. "Was that a hardship?"

"It had tight lacings," Nyctasia explained, "and stiff brocade drapings down the sides of the skirt, and delicate little slippers stitched with seed pearls. I never gave myself the trouble to wear anything but breeches and blouses and boots, at that age—and I still don't, if I can help it," she admitted. "If a garment wasn't suitable for hunting, it didn't interest me."

"You weren't always studying or stargazing, then. But I'd not have taken you for a huntress."

"You used to tease me about my passion for the chase. You found hunting a bore and a waste of time. But my dislike of long skirts was due as much to considerations of vanity as of comfort. I thought they drew attention to my short stature. I complained to Mhairestri, 'I'll look like a dwarf in such a gown!' but she said, 'Not if your hair is properly dressed, as it shall be.' I had hair down to my hips in those days—it had never been cut—and it took hours to arrange it about a cornet. I simply bound it with ribbons or plaited it, when it hampered me. I was willing to tolerate an elaborate weave of braids, at worst, when formality was called for, but I hated a headdress above all things."

"And that was my fault too, I suppose?"

"Naturally. There seemed no end to the amount of bother you were prepared to cause me."

"I'd not have thought myself capable of such infamy. However did I appease your wrath?"

"You didn't care a straw for my wrath! You were as sullen as I. Your people were no fools, 'Ben; they saw which way the victory would fall, if it came to open warfare, and they didn't mean to find themselves among the defeated. They'd come to offer their support to our House, and you'd been brought along—much against your will—to cultivate the goodwill of the younger generation of the Edonaris."

"Especially that of the Rhaicime-to-be?" he guessed.

Nyctasia chuckled, remembering the scene. "We *were* a pair—a brace of wild geese. When you were presented to me, you bowed and kissed my hand in an accomplished manner, then said, 'I've been ordered to make myself agreeable to you, my lady, but I must confess that I hardly expected to find my duty such a pleasure.'"

"What impertinence—I trust you slapped me soundly for it."

"I should have, but I was so smitten by your beauty that I forgave you everything, even your disruption of the destinies of the stars. If Mhairestri had but taken the trouble to describe you to me, she'd have had no difficulty with me. Still, I had pride enough to inform you that I had been charged with the same obligation, lest you should think I had any desire to make your acquaintance. Then I suggested, quite coldly, that we both might best accomplish what was expected of us by treading a dance together. 'Perhaps it will satisfy our elders to see us so engaged,' I said, but the truth was that I wanted an excuse to touch you."

"You'll make me forget my promise to rest quiet, if you say things like that," he warned.

Nyctasia grinned wickedly. "You didn't seem averse to touching me either, and we began to get on better before long. The situation amused us, we were both fine dancers, and we soon discovered that we had more in common than scheming relations. We both professed to be students of Vahnite philosophy, both our families thought we took insufficient interest in the affairs of our Houses and our city, we both aspired to be scholar-magicians, though your studies of the Art were more advanced than mine. We both wanted to attend the Imperial University, and neither of our families would hear of it. I was enthralled. I'd never met anyone remotely like you—except myself. You seemed nearly perfect to me."

"Why 'nearly'?" he demanded, enjoying himself.

"You didn't care for hunting. Still, despite that flaw in your character, I was growing more enamored of you by the moment, and when you proposed that we withdraw to some-place more private to continue our interesting conversation, I agreed with most immodest haste. You said, 'I've heard that the palace gardens here are exquisite,' and I assured you that they were—especially by moonlight. It must have pleased our families no end when we slipped out of the hall hand-in-hand.

"What a perfect summer night that was . . . the trees were in blossom, the leaves sighing in the sweet-scented evening breezes, the fountains chiming and shining in the starlight. . . . It was a night meant for young lovers to stroll through the terraces and trellised walks, to cross the arched bridges and tarry on the parapet together listening to the music of the stream murmuring and purling in the darkness below, to linger in the lilac-bowers, hidden by the sheltering branches and clustering flowers. . . . And indeed, we weren't the only couple enjoying the spiced night air in the arbors and under the willows on the banks of the pools. I'd known those gardens since my childhood, every path and corner, but they'd never seemed so lovely to me before. I was in an enchantment of bliss. It's not like me to live in the pleasure of the moment, but I felt that I could have wandered the gardens forever with you by my side. Even though you were a stranger to me, I didn't doubt that I understood your thoughts, that your feelings at that moment were the same as mine.

"I had a small, enclosed garden of my own, where I grew healing herbs and other useful plants. It was perfectly private, surrounded by a high wall to which I had the only key, and I led you there almost without thinking, as if it had all been foreordained, and we had only to carry out fate's decree. The door was always locked, for some of my plants were highly poisonous, and I kept the key in a secret niche in the wall, covered by ivy. I'd never revealed that hiding-place to anyone, yet I didn't try to keep it from you, when I offered to show you the garden. 'Here no one will observe or overhear us,' I said. 'We may be quite alone and undisturbed. If it please my lord, shall we enter?' And I held out the key to you."

Nyctasia paused coyly. "Shall I tell you what you did next, or can you guess?" she asked, giving him a mischievous look.

"If I didn't unlock that door and carry you through it, I must have been a madman or an imbecile."

"I confess I was expecting something of the sort," said Nyctasia. "I thought you might at the least hand me in with a bow, or offer me your arm. The one thing I didn't anticipate was that you'd say, 'There is nothing that would please me more, my lady, but the night is yet young. Could we, I wonder, climb the tower yonder? A most interesting conjunction of stars will shortly take place tonight, and the view from up there would be excellent.'"

"I deny it!" moaned Erystalben, hiding his face in his arms. "You've made the whole tale up, to torment me. I *can't* have been such a booby, I refuse to believe it."

Nyctasia rocked with laughter. "I swear it, on my honor, by the *vahn*. I remember your every word." (She stopped herself in time from adding, "And I never let you forget them either." For she had let him forget everything, had she not?)

"You'd enticed me out of doors," she continued, "not for the purposes of romantic, moonlit dalliance, but so as to be able to keep the skies in sight!"

"I tremble to ask, what did you do next?"

"Well, my first impulse was to call the guards at once and have you disemboweled, but then I'd have had to face Mhairestri's wrath. Besides, I was never one to give myself away.

The only possible thing to do was to act as if I weren't at all disappointed or surprised. And then, once you'd reminded me of it, I realized that I did still want to see the alignment myself. So I said, 'Of course, the Periodic Conjunction! I was so enjoying our talk that I'd quite forgotten it for the moment. Come, the stars won't wait. I've been looking forward to it all the year—' and more nonsense of that sort, which had the advantage of being true. Only the way I said it was a lie.

"So we climbed the tower—no easy matter for me in that cursed skirt—and you explained to me a great many things I already knew about the rare and significant event we were to witness."

"Mercy," Erystalben said faintly.

"Never mind, your zeal for the spectacle quite rekindled my own. We were intent on observing the exact configuration, whether it would appear as bow or lyre, which would determine any number of possible interpretations of matters both material and immaterial. You made involved calculations, which impressed me as favorably as the Shiastred could have wished, since I did such things so poorly myself."

"And which pattern was revealed?"

"At first I saw the lyre, but when you declared it the bow, I became unsure. It was no common bow—as you'd have known if you took a proper interest in hunting. Yet it was not like any lyre I knew of either. I had a fit of inspiration and told you exultantly that archery was a true Discipline, as well as a Manifestation of the Principles of Elemental Balance and Harmony, just like the art of harping. I said, 'It is clear to me that these are but two guises of one Discipline!' I wanted nothing so much at that moment as to sit down with my commonplace book and record these momentous discoveries."

"No wonder I called you Mistress of Ambiguities."

"You too were excited by the possibilities of such an interpretation. You said that it would make the Influences twice as powerful. Then you told me the Ahzid legend of Asye's bow, which was weapon and harp in one, and I was simply staggered at its aptness."

"You hadn't heard of it before?" Erystalben asked, surprised.

"Most Mainlanders of noble family aren't schooled in the lore of the Hlann. I only knew of Asye as a name to curse by when I stabbed my thumb, cutting a quill. You'd been told the tale only because there's Ahzid blood in your family, on your father's side."

"Ah, *Descador*, of course. An Ahzid name. I thought I must have native Ahzid ancestry, what with my coloring. In Celys, folk sometimes took me for Lieposi, but none of that tribe has eyes like mine."

"So you've been to Celys! We so wanted to go there in our youth."

He dismissed the Imperial City with a shrug. "I knew I was well educated, so I hoped to find someone at the University who knew me. But I had no luck in that cursed city—" He broke off abruptly, making a Vahnite gesture of repudiation awkwardly, with his left hand. "But what of our adventure in the gardens? What followed these revelations of mystical talismanic Principles? Did I come to my senses finally, and throw myself at your dainty, pearl-shod feet?"

"You might put it that way," Nyctasia said playfully. "We were neither of us much in our senses by then. We were wild to run to the library and consult some tome of ancient astronomical philosophy. I was impatiently gathering up my skirts, to descend the steps of the tower, and perhaps the sight of my delicate, silk-clad ankles affected you, for you bowed and said, 'Permit me, Rhaicime,' then picked me up and carried me down the stairs."

"Thank the *vahn*! I was beginning to despair of myself."

"There were indeed powerful Influences at work that night," Nyctasia said dreamily. "By the time we reached the foot of the stairs, I'd discovered how very well my face fit against your collarbone, and you too seemed to have forgotten our urgent scholarly researches. Instead of setting me on my feet, you whispered in my ear that you still had the key to my garden about you, and I—I said nothing, but only kissed the hollow of your throat, as I'd been longing to do since I'd first seen you." She sighed. "How you contrived to unlock the garden door and shut it after us without putting me down, I can't tell you, but you somehow managed it."

"You can't have weighed more than thistledown. But don't leave off now, pray. What happened next?"

"Oh, it was all so long ago," Nyctasia said with a grin. "How should I remember every last thing?"

◆   ◆   ◆

But of course, Nyctasia remembered that night in the garden as if it had happened mere days, not years, before. Erystalben had been so different from those she knew, from herself and her kin, all of them pale and colorless and cold, with their ice-grey eyes and dull black hair. Erystalben's burnished, dark skin and piercingly blue eyes had made him seem more intensely alive, more vivid and vital, than other people. Even his hair was a different black from hers, a gleaming raven's-wing black that the sunlight kindled to purple and blue. And when she was with him she felt that she too was more alive, powerful, imbued with possibilities.

She and Thierran had made love from time to time, without secrecy or impropriety. They were betrothed, they could visit one another's chambers unchaperoned at any hour. It was perfectly proper, almost expected of them, and Nyctasia had never known the glamor of the forbidden and unknown, the thrill of a stranger's embrace. She remembered every detail of that first tryst with Erystalben, the delight of lying with him under the stars in the fresh night air, the scent of the flowering herbs, the feel of the tender, yielding grass beneath her. She remembered picking mint leaves and crushing them against her throat, between her breasts, leaving their keen, intoxicating fragrance for him to savor on her skin. Never before had it occurred to her to do such a thing.

He had laid her down carefully and knelt over her, a shadow in the darkness, whispering, "Your beautiful gown will be spoilt, my lady."

"I don't care, I hate it," she'd said, pulling him down beside her and kissing him greedily. "Let it be spoilt."

"Oh, you'd best take it off, don't you think?" he teased, opening his own shirt. "Think of the scolding you'll get, careless girl."

"I *can't* take the wretched thing off without a lady's maid. That's why I hate it!"

Erystalben gathered her into his arms and began deftly to unlace the back of the tight dress. "Why then I'll help you," he murmured into her hair. "You shall see what a good lady's maid I'd make you. You'll never have a better."

She kissed his jaw, his neck, his throat, as her hands explored the ridges and hollows of his back and shoulders. "I think I'd like you for groom as well as maid," she said with a contented sigh. There was some point to such bothersome garments after all, she found. It was worth the trouble of wearing them to enjoy having Erystalben remove them. When he undid the ribbons of her bodice and bent to kiss her small,

soft breasts, she felt weak and helpless with pleasure. She
could only cling to him with one arm while with the other hand
she clutched at the long grass and dug her fingers into the earth.

Then he was gently loosing the clasps and bands from her
hair, freeing it from the hated cornet and letting it flow over
both of them in caressing waves. How could she have failed to
notice before how wonderful her own hair felt against her bare
skin? She showed him how to detach the dove's-wing draperies
that sheathed her hips, and watched in amusement as he laid
them ceremoniously over a juniper bush, to be followed by her
sash and silken skirts.

At last he knelt at her feet and drew off the narrow kidskin
slippers, then slid his hands beneath her last underskirt to
unfasten her gossamer hose. Nyctasia closed her eyes and
shivered, reaching out without thought in the darkness, to
pluck a sprig of mint.

◆   ◆   ◆

"You told me," Nyctasia concluded, "that students of
Vahnite philosophy were the most desirable lovers, because
mastery of the Discipline gives one such remarkable self-
control."

"No! I must protest, this isn't fair—I can't defend myself. I
didn't really say that?"

"Well, we were very young," Nyctasia said leniently. "And
after all, it was perfectly true."

13

"I must have been sotted," 'Malkin thought drowsily. "How could I have been so rutting careless . . . ?"

It was not at all like 'Malkin to allow mere fleshly attraction to interfere with his aims and purposes. As a rule he was thoroughly circumspect, as a courtier must be who hopes for advancement, but to have spent the night in Corson's bed like this had not been in the least discreet. He knew very well how malicious gossip could be at court—any court. True, the Rhaicime was away, but he did not doubt that she would hear of anything that went on in her absence. He was aware that he already had enemies in the palace, other scholars, jealous of the ease with which he'd gained the favor of the Rhaicime, while they'd been here longer and failed to come to her notice. (And he had Corson to thank for that, he grudgingly admitted to himself.) They'd be all too glad to see to it that Her Ladyship heard of this affair.

Not that the episode was very likely to damage his standing with the Rhaicime, even if it did get about. It was not as if he'd trifled with a palace scullion, or bedded a stableboy. After all, it was the Rhaicime herself who had brought Corson and her

base-born friends to court, and allowed them the freedom of
the palace. Still, one could not be too careful. The Lady
Nyctasia—not even in his thoughts did he call her "Nyc," as
his ill-bred bedmate did—the Lady Nyctasia might take a broad
view of these matters, but it was one thing for her to be on
familiar terms with such people herself, and quite another thing
for her followers to carry on with them. Different behavior was
expected, 'Malkin knew, from those of different stations. The
Rhaicime was above the rules. She could afford to flout
convention. A mere court clerk and scholar could not. It had
probably been unwise to permit himself to be seduced in this
way. Enjoyable though it had been, he must keep his wits about
him and not let it happen again.

Well, it was not yet dawn, he'd plenty of time to be on his
way before he could be discovered here. But he made no move
to bestir himself yet. If only he weren't so comfortable. . . .
He looked around Corson's lavish bedchamber with resentment.
It was exasperating to think of a coarse ruffian like Corson
enjoying this great feather bed, these spacious quarters, while he
shared a narrow room with half a dozen other students and
scribes. He could probably get himself better accommodations if
he complained to the Rhaicime, but it was not yet time to ask
favors of Her Ladyship. First, he intended to make himself
indispensable to her, and then the shows of favoritism would
come without the asking. This, however, was hardly the way to
go about it, he thought, glancing at his still slumbering companion.

Or, was it . . . ? he pondered. Galling as it was, this
common, ignorant creature knew things about the Rhaicime
that he didn't—things that no one else at court seemed to know
either, as far as he'd been able to determine. It should be
possible to turn that fact to his advantage.

And—plague take it!—there was no denying that the bag-
gage was attractive. Against his better judgment, he reached
over to stroke Trask's tousled hair.

◆   ◆   ◆

Trask was well satisfied with his night's work. He'd laid
plans to ingratiate himself with 'Malkin as soon as Corson had
told the tale of her revenge and its consequences. This was
someone who knew the things he wanted to learn—the
manners, the courtly customs—but who wasn't a nobleman
himself. If he was so well known to Corson, he wasn't too
grand for Trask to approach, surely. And Corson had said he

was a handsome fellow, too, though she might have meant that just to bait Steifann.

He'd lost no time in marking and stalking his quarry, once he had the chance, and had soon run him to ground in Nyctasia's great library, where her chosen scholars and scribes spent their time recording, studying and copying the works assembled by the learned Cymvelans—and where Trask, unfortunately, could not pursue him. Many of these volumes were rare and valuable, and no one could gain access to the guarded library without Nyctasia's sanction. But Trask was not one to let prohibitions stand in his way. Corson's authority was recognized throughout the palace garrison, and he demanded a warrant from her to enter the library, in return for the information he'd so painstakingly gathered about the Shiastred, at her behest.

"What do you want in there?" Corson asked suspiciously. "You can't even read. Nyc will, have you flayed and gutted if you get into any mischief with her precious books, don't think she won't."

"It's not the books that interest me," Trask explained, "it's one of the readers."

"Oho, that was quick work. Which one? It might be someone I know."

Trask could have lied, but he suspected that Corson might prove an ally in this matter, so he chanced the truth. "It is," he said. "It's your friend 'Malkin, if you must know."

Corson was delighted. She not only arranged an authorization for him to visit the library, but wished him luck, and even provided him with some useful hints, of an intimate nature, about 'Malkin's tastes and predilections. The only condition she set was that he tell her all about it later.

"A gentleman wouldn't agree to that," Trask pointed out.

"A gentleman wouldn't need my help to lay siege to the likes of 'Malkin. Look here, Trask, call him 'sir.' He'll take to that like a hog to muck, you'll see."

"Would you be Desmalkin brenn Cerrogh, sir? Lady Corson sent me. She wants to see you at once."

Corson hadn't been lying about his looks, Trask noted. He wished he knew how to bow properly.

"You may tell Lady Corson to go hang herself, with my compliments," 'Malkin said, without raising his voice. It was very quiet in the library, apart from the constant scratching of quills. "Now get out of my sight."

Trask was taken aback. Though he knew 'Malkin had good grounds for a grudge against Corson, he hadn't been expecting a flat refusal of the fictitious summons. Corson *was* a Desthene, after all. "She said it was important, sir," he said earnestly. "I'm not to come back without you."

'Malkin quietly cursed Corson, her messenger, and the misguided moment in which the Rhaicime had seen fit to confer a title on her. But, like Trask, he was mindful of that title. It was infuriating to be at Corson's beck and call, but the bitch was a Desthene, and he was a commoner. And then, she just might have a legitimate reason for sending for him. He knew that Lady Nyctasia had forbidden her to play any more of her tricks at court, and he thought that even Corson would know better than to defy her orders outright. It might well be that this matter somehow concerned Her Ladyship, he reflected. The rumors in the palace said that Corson was the one person likely to know where the Rhaicime had disappeared to. . . .

"Very well," he said to Trask, "but *Hlann* help Corson if this is just more of her foolery!"

"Yes, sir," said Trask meekly. He led 'Malkin directly to Corson's quarters, where he had already lit the candles and set out the wine. Corson, of course, was nowhere to be seen.

"Well, where is she?" 'Malkin demanded.

"I'm sure she'll be here straightway, sir. May I serve you some wine?"

Trask knew very well that Corson had gone off to The Lame Fox to get drunk with some of her disreputable friends, and that she was not at all likely to be back before dawn. He also knew where Corson kept her wine. As 'Malkin paced impatiently about the chamber, Trask refilled his goblet several times. He didn't mean to take any further steps until the good Edonaris wine had had time to mellow 'Malkin's temper.

But 'Malkin only grew more vexed as time passed and Corson failed to appear. "How dare she keep me waiting like this! Go find her at once, boy. Tell her, if she wants to see me—"

"She doesn't," Trask said, looking down at the floor, as if afraid to meet 'Malkin's eyes. "*I* do."

"*You* do? Who are *you*?"

"Nobody much," Trask admitted. "But, you see, I don't find that satisfactory." He spoke with the air of one appalled by his own presumption, but bravely determined to persevere. "I'm Trask brenn Chiastelm, I'm only potboy at the Hare. Corson brings me along sometimes to run her errands, that's all. But I've dared hope that you might help me make something of myself, sir."

'Malkin was at first more astonished than angry at Trask's confession, and then more relieved than astonished, as he realized that this affair did not, after all, concern Corson. He was not at all confident that he knew how to deal with Corson, but this young lackey of hers—or whoever he was—was another matter. Raw, hungry ambition was something 'Malkin understood thoroughly. Feeling in control of the situation, now, he seated himself again and gestured imperiously for Trask to serve him more wine. "You have, have you?" he said. "Come, explain yourself! Why do you come to me, why not to Corson?"

"Corson's a lout, and content to remain so," Trask said contemptuously, certain that this would please 'Malkin. "And *I'm* a lout," he added, with a convincing show of desperate humility, "but I know I could learn better ways, sir, if you'd teach me. I thought, since you taught Corson to read, you might be willing to give me some lessons too. . . ." He faltered and let his voice trail off uncertainly. Now to resort to flattery. "Corson says there's nothing you don't know, and Nyc thinks so highly of you—"

"How do you know that?" 'Malkin asked, before he could stop himself.

I've got him, thought Trask, who of course had no idea what Nyctasia thought of 'Malkin. "Oh, she tells Corson everything, and Corson tells us," he said, thinking fast. "But I usually know Nyc's mind about most things. She hasn't much time for the likes of me when she's at court, of course, but I see a good deal of her at the Hare." Straying even further from the truth, he said offhandedly, "And then, I have the run of the Smugglers' House, whenever she's in residence there."

'Malkin naturally was not taken in by such a web of half-truth, imposture and fabrication. If this mongrel's whelp was an intimate confidant of the Rhaicime, then he, Desmalkin brenn Cerrogh, was King of Tièrelon. But clearly Trask enjoyed *some* familiarity with Lady Nyctasia, and that was enough to interest 'Malkin. What was the Hare, what the Smugglers' House, and why should Her Ladyship frequent them? Trask knew these things, and he also seemed to know their value to someone in 'Malkin's position. Really, the little guttersnipe showed some sense. He might prove useful if properly handled. . . .

Dismissing Trask's pretensions with the scorn they deserved, 'Malkin said, "If you were at all in the Rhaicime's confidence, my downy chick, you'd know better than to say so. The first thing you'd better learn is to master your own tongue."

"Yes, sir," said Trask, in an abashed tone, hanging his head again. But his eyes shone in secret triumph. 'Malkin was going to be *very* useful to him. . . .

"Now what exactly is it you want from me?"

"I want to learn how—how to conduct myself at court," Trask said eagerly. "How to read, how to talk, how to dress—everything! Nyc said she'd find a place for me if I learned those things." Well, she had said something of the sort, though in jest. "I know she'd be pleased if you took me in hand, sir," he went on, half believing it himself. Why shouldn't she be pleased? "She wants me to learn, and she wants you to teach, doesn't she? Corson told us that," he added hastily, and with perfect truth. "I learn quickly, sir, and I'll do whatever you say," Trask promised, availing himself of his most appealing manner.

And Trask could be very appealing when he chose. He'd taken a great deal of trouble over his appearance before making his approach to 'Malkin. He'd ordered a hot bath for Corson, as soon as she was safely out of the way, and washed himself thoroughly, paying particular attention to his shaggy hair, and even remembering to clean his fingernails. He'd dressed in his best, the brown velvet doublet and the fine hose and shoes that he'd been given when he'd attended Corson's investiture. They were the only clothes he'd ever had cut to his measure, and he'd taken very good care of them.

Then, borrowing Corson's good silver hairbrush, he'd brushed and brushed his golden-brown hair till it glowed like dark honey in the candlelight.

"And I'd be so very grateful to you, sir . . . " he told 'Malkin warmly.

◆　　◆　　◆

'Malkin was all Corson had said, and more, Trask thought with satisfaction. He was quite looking forward to his lessons. Nyctasia had warned him that the skills he desired would take a great deal of hard work, study, and practice to acquire, and since Trask was known for avoiding work as much as possible, she had confidently expected this to discourage his foolish aspirations. But she had underestimated the strength of his ambition. He'd been resigned to the necessity of a long, wearisome apprenticeship of sorts, and was prepared to endure any amount of drudgery to achieve his goal. But now he suspected that his tutelage at 'Malkin's hands might prove to be anything but dull. One might even get to like 'Malkin, he thought, rather surprised at the idea.

He stretched contentedly, without opening his eyes, and nestled closer to 'Malkin, rubbing his cheek affectionately against 'Malkin's shoulder like a cat. When he felt 'Malkin caress his hair, he smiled sleepily and mumbled, "Will you teach me how to make a bow, sir, please, before Nyc gets back? I want to show her I can do it right."

'Malkin took hold of his ear and tweaked it hard. "First of all, *never* refer to Her Ladyship as 'Nyc'! It's simply not done. Such a thing is in the worst possible taste for anyone except her close kin."

"But there's no one here but us!" Trask protested, sitting up and rubbing his ear ruefully. "Where's the harm?"

"That's of no consequence," 'Malkin said sternly. "It's a question of breaking yourself of bad habits. If you allow yourself to speak carelessly in private, you'll make mistakes in public." He crooked his elbow around Trask's neck and pulled him down to lie with his head on 'Malkin's chest. "And don't argue with me, puppy," he added. "Why should I take the trouble to instruct you, if you don't listen?"

"Yes, sir, I'll remember," said Trask, with a chuckle. "It's just that everybody calls Her Ladyship 'Nyc' at the Hare. If I used court manners there, they'd stick my head in a bucket of slops."

"Always remember where you are, and behave accordingly."

Trask nodded against 'Malkin's chest. "That's what Nyc—I mean Lady Nyctasia—says. When she's at the Hare, you'd never guess for a moment that she's a lady, much less a Rhaicime." He yawned, then turned his head and nuzzled the inside of 'Malkin's elbow.

'Malkin pensively ran his knuckle along Trask's jaw, thinking, *I'll grow fond of this brat if I don't take care.* "Now tell me about this Hare of yours," he ordered.

14

"That's all I can tell you about it, 'Ben," Nyctasia said wearily. "Kastenid may still be in possession, or some other mage may have wrested the land and its power away from him. Perhaps he can hold it without succumbing to the Yth's Influence, but I believe that it will finally destroy all who try to make it their own. You were spellcast by the Yth, as I nearly was myself, and I thought that if I stayed I might be able to reclaim your spirit, but I see now that I was deceiving myself. If I'd stayed, we would both have been lost. Even as I determined to win you from the Yth, I was already in its power. I told myself that I didn't want to leave without you, but the truth was that I didn't want to leave. . . . And I had been there for only a few days—you were subject to its Influence for so much longer." She sighed. "That was the last I saw of you, till last night."

"You saw me vanish," Erystalben brooded, "and I found myself alone on that same hillside, with no idea how I'd come to be there." He gazed within, at what was now his earliest memory. "Perhaps no time had passed at all, and I was there all the while, hidden from your sight by the spell."

"And I from yours?" The idea was somehow more chilling

than his disappearance had been. "Surely I'd have known, if you were so near to me." Yet how could she have been aware of his presence, when the man she knew had ceased to exist at that moment?

Echoing her thought, he said, "Not I but Veron was near to you."

"It may be so, who can say? I performed a spell of Reflection while I was yet there and might draw upon the Yth's power, and it told me that you lived, but no more."

He nodded thoughtfully. "What did you do then?"

"I didn't know what to do. I was utterly at a loss. Corson took me south from Hlasven to Osela." She smiled, glad enough to turn the talk. "And before I knew quite what was happening, I was thrown in prison."

"Prison! Why, in the *vahn's* name? I've thought I might be a criminal, but hardly you."

Nyctasia laughed. "That's a tale for another day. It's growing late. I'm tired, even if you aren't."

"I am," he admitted. "Though I've done nothing but rest the whole day."

"A night's sleep will set you right." She kissed him and said, "I'll leave you to your repose, then. Good night, love."

"But aren't you going to stay here? You slept by me last night."

She was surprised that he knew she'd been there. "Last night I was afraid to leave you alone, lest you take a turn for the worse before dawn. Tonight you don't need watching."

"Stay anyway," he urged, pulling her back to him. "Why not?"

"Because I want you to *sleep* tonight."

"You know very well there's nothing else I can do, with my arm too sore to be touched. And I'm half-asleep already from all the wine you've made me drink. Am I not to be trusted, even crippled and drunken?"

"No," said Nyctasia. "And perhaps I trust myself even less. But 'Ben, it's your arm I'm thinking of. I might jar it. You'd be more comfortable with the bed to yourself, no?"

"You don't take up much room, little one. You didn't disturb me last night." He touched the tip of her nose lightly. "You don't even snore."

Nyctasia suddenly giggled. "Greymantle does, though. But I'll make him sleep on the hearth tonight, where he belongs."

"Greymantle? Do you mean—?"

But before he could object, Nyctasia had already crossed the room and admitted the huge hound, who had been pacing the corridor for most of the day, gazing mournfully at the door. He bounded into the room and greeted Nyctasia as if she'd been missing for weeks, his wildly wagging tail and reproachful whines clearly expressing his delight at seeing her and his indignation at having been banished from his rightful place, on the night before.

"Poor fellow!" laughed Nyctasia, tugging his ears fondly. "I shut him out last night when you were restive and feverish. I didn't want you to wake and see him. Yes, poor Grey, then. Poor lad!"

"I'm not best pleased to see him now either," Erystalben pointed out. "Poor Grey indeed! That man-eating creature half-killed me, and you've more sympathy for him than for me."

Sitting on the edge of the bed again, Nyctasia put her arm around Erystalben and kissed him. "There, now he'll see that you're a friend. Come here to me, Grey. Give him your hand, 'Ben, so he'll know your scent."

"I've already given the brute one of my hands! I've only the one left!"

"Idiot!" said Nyctasia, kissing him again. She effected the introduction, despite the mutual suspicions of the two, and ordered, "Now lie down and be still, Grey." Turning to Erystalben, she said, "And you're to do the same. Shall I really stay here tonight, 'Ben?"

"Stay," he said. "I want to see you there when I wake." (*I want you to keep me from dreaming of the Yth!*)

Though he smiled, Nyctasia thought she saw fear shadowing his eyes. Perhaps he still needed watching after all.

◆ ◆ ◆

This time the reflection seized him by the throat as he leaned over the water. It drew him under, drowned him, then climbed from the pool and stood at the edge, looking down at him with a smile. Staring up through the clear water, he could see it laughing, but no sound penetrated to the depths where he drifted helplessly, as cold and lifeless as an empty shell. Then it merely turned and walked off, out of his sight, leaving him there to take its place forever. Above the pool there was nothing to be seen but the colorless leaden sky.

* * *

" 'Ben? 'Ben, what is it? You cried out—"

He lay shivering and gasping for breath, unable to answer, while she drew back the bedcurtains to let in the early morning light. When he could see her, he grew calmer and managed to say, "It's—it's only dreams . . . sometimes, I . . ." He shuddered again, and Nyctasia folded the blanket more tightly about him and lay close beside him, with her arm across his chest. Her breath was warm and comforting against his throat. "I'm all right now," he told her shakily. " 'Tasia, you've been to Yth Wood—is it always twilight there, never day or night?" He used the old word *lirihran*, that means "half-darkness," rather than "half-light."

"Yes. It's always the same there. There's no change to mark the hours. Have you remembered something about it?"

He heard the anxiety in her voice and answered only, "I don't know. I was dreaming of it, but dreams aren't memories." There was no need to burden her with his dread nightmares. "Let's leave for Rhostshyl today," he said. "I'm well enough to travel now." If he could recover his past there, surely the maddening dreams would cease.

"Today?" Nyctasia said doubtfully. "That wouldn't be wise, I'm afraid. You've not even been on your feet yet. I meant to send a messenger ahead, first, to arrange for our lodgings on the way. We can skirt Rhostshyl Wood and stay one night in Fenshelm, then the next in Salten. It will take us longer, but the road's an easier ride than the woods, and you'd find it hard to sleep on the ground with that arm still so painful."

And she had hoped to spend a few peaceful days alone with him here by the healing sea, before returning to her duties in Rhostshyl, and returning Erystalben to his family. But he sounded so distraught that she offered, "We could ride along the coast road this morning, if you like, and see how you fare. If that tires you, we'll come back here, and if not, we could go on to Fenshelm."

He wanted to set out at once, without waiting to make preparations. He wanted to ride straight through Rhostshyl Wood by the shortest route, and travel all night without making camp, without stopping for rest or sleep until they reached the gates of Rhostshyl. But he knew that was nonsense, of course. She was clearly right. "Yes, very well, let's do that," he said, and tried to smile at her.

"We'll ride for Rhostshyl soon, if not today," Nyctasia promised.

But as Nyctasia had anticipated, he found it no easy matter to ride a strange horse while his right arm was bound in a sling. He soon tired and was willing enough to turn back before the morning was out. By daylight, the memory of his sinister dreams was not as racking, and the Smugglers' House was a welcome sight. Its tall stone walls seemed part of the surrounding cliffs, as if it had always stood there and would stand there forever. It was good to return to a familiar place. "A handsome house," he said.

"I've always thought so," Nyctasia agreed. "From the first time I saw it, I wanted to live there. When I heard that the property was abandoned, I determined at once to have it. As soon as I came of age, I sent agents to purchase it from the City Governors. I told my elders that our court physicians had recommended me to take the sea air—as indeed they had—but my reasons for buying the house were quite different. Not the least of them," she added, almost shyly, "was that you and I might have a place to be together, without interference from our kin."

"Then I've been here before?" he asked, dismayed. If a place he'd known in the past was to spur his memory, why had this place not done so?

"Not often," Nyctasia assured him. "We hoped to spend a good deal of time here, but there was always something to prevent us. We did explore it together when I first bought it, and we found the smugglers' tunnel beneath the cellars." She laughed. "We rather hoped for a few chests of forgotten booty, but all we got for our trouble were some nasty cuts and bruises. It was glorious fun!"

"Show it to me," he suggested, hoping that the sight would bring back some trace of remembrance, but Nyctasia shook her head.

"You'd need two hands to clamber about down there, for climbing and hanging on and feeling your way. I'll show you over the rest of the house, if you like, but there's not much to see."

Nevertheless, after a midday meal, she led him through the house, beginning with the trapdoor beneath the cellar stairs. Raising a flagstone, she leaned it against the wall and lowered her lantern into the opening, to show him the passageway below. "We left that ladder there, you and I. When we first discovered this hole—it was you, actually, who found it—there was no way down save to jump. You dropped down first, then caught me, which was all very well, but when it came time to get ourselves back up, you could lift me through the opening, but I wasn't strong enough to pull you back up. You were trapped down there for some time before I could find a rope to throw you. I tied it to that sconce."

Erystalben looked from the wall to the trapdoor, then down into the underground chamber. He could envision himself and Nyctasia climbing over the edge, laughing and scrambling and scolding each other, but the scene was the fruit of his imagination, not of his memory. Nothing he saw recalled the adventure to his mind. "That's your notion of glorious fun, is it?" he said finally, trying to sound amused. "Leaving me stranded in a pit! I hope we didn't have too much fun of that sort."

Nyctasia was not deceived by his tone. "Oh, very well," she said, "I won't do it again. Let's go on now, it's cold down here."

From the cellars they made their way up from floor to floor, stopping in this room or that as Nyctasia related something that the two of them had done or found there. None of it was in the least familiar to him. By the time they reached the topmost story, he was deeply discouraged and growing tired as well. But he had never known this place well, after all, he told himself. It might be different in Rhostshyl, where he'd spent most of his life. . . . "What secrets are in there?" he asked idly, as Nyctasia passed by a door without opening it.

To his surprise, she colored and looked uneasy. "Nothing now," she said, with a slight hesitation. "It's only another empty room, but it's locked. I don't like anyone to use it, because my cousin Thierran died there."

"But didn't you say that you never brought anyone here but me?"

Nyctasia led the way down the stairs, and he couldn't see her face as she replied, but her voice was level, betraying no emotion. "I didn't bring Thierran, he brought me—against my will. He tried to keep me from running away from Rhostshyl to follow you. I was betrothed to him, you see."

Erystalben felt an unreasoning stab of jealousy. "Small

wonder he objected to your leaving, then. But how did he die?"

"Corson killed him," she said flatly. "She cut his throat."

"I might have guessed as much. I only wonder that she hasn't yet cut mine."

" 'Ben, she was my bodyguard. She thought he meant to kill me."

"Are you sure it's not just that she takes a murderous dislike to any man who comes near you?"

"Quite sure."

"*I'm* not so sure. If this cousin of yours was so anxious to keep you, why should he want to kill you?"

"He didn't want to . . . but he might have, in the end. He was truly mad by then. You may as well know that the Edonaris are famed for their lunacy."

"Of course, if he'd been in his right mind, he'd have tried to kill me, not you."

"Oh, but he did try to kill you. That's when I repudiated the betrothal." They had reached the landing, and she turned to face him, with a sad smile. "Poor Thorn—he and I were inseparable until I met you. When we were children, and I was always so ill, he was my only companion, aside from my nurses and attendants. My mother didn't want to remember that she'd produced such a sickly weakling child—and I don't think my father *did* remember. My brother was kind, but he was older than I and hadn't much time for me. I could rarely leave my bedchamber, you see, but Thorn used to visit me often and bring me things from outside. Flowers and feathers and stones . . . an antler shed by a young buck . . . I thought that was the loveliest thing I'd ever seen. I have it still. I had plenty of jewels, and trinkets of silver and gold, but I treasured most the things Thierran brought me. Sometimes I'd sing for him, or read him stories. He liked tales of heroes and adventures best. . . . He was always my champion. When I grew well, he taught me to ride, to hunt—and later, when the others called me traitor, he defended me. Oh, 'Ben, he even fought a duel for me once, because someone said I practiced black magic. I was furious with him when I heard of that, but I was proud too."

"You did love him, then," he said gently.

Nyctasia nodded, fighting tears. "We weren't well suited, in truth, but we were too young to realize that. And I'd never met anyone better suited to me—"

"Until I took you to look at the stars." He put his left arm around her, and they sat on a windowseat on the landing, with the sea at their backs. "But you weren't to blame for that, 'Tasia."

"No one was to blame," she sighed. "He simply couldn't accept that I might prefer anyone else to him. How could he? He would never have done that to me."

Thierran had been brought to see her, when they were children, because it was fitting for them to know one another. They were to be married if Nyctasia, contrary to all expectations, should live to come of age. One could not begin too early to teach the young their duty.

He'd come reluctantly at first, rather scared of the white, frail child with her thin, peaked face and fever-bright eyes. She was said to be dying, too, though he was not supposed to know that. But Nyctasia had been so glad of his company, so eager to please him, that he had soon fallen under her spell. She listened with flattering attention to his doings and his opinions, much impressed that he should learn to ride or to fly a hawk, since she could not do such things herself. It was pleasant to be admired, even by his pitiable little cousin, and she charmed him with her secrets and fancies as well, making him her confidant and cavalier. She could do little but read, and she told him the stories and legends she found in her books—and the still-stranger tales from her fevered dreams of a far-off land beyond the mirror. There she met her twin, she grew strong and climbed mountains, she braved the sun and the snow to do heroic deeds. There, demon-haunted passages beneath the earth led her to enchanted treasures and mortal perils. Thorn, who had a twin himself, agreed that 'Tasia too should have one. He liked nothing better than fetching her volumes from the library and listening to her read spells and stories, and the chronicles of the Edonaris of old, their forebears, defenders of Rhostshyl, warriors, enchanters, lawgivers. Among them were other Thierrans and Nyctasias, and many pairs of twins.

When she felt strong enough, she would play her small lap-harp for him and sing the old ballads she'd read, to any tune that fit them. Or they might play at casting spells from the worn, worm-eaten books with strange scripts and unfamiliar

words. Thierran would willingly scour the fields and hillsides
for hours, seeking the particular plant whose picture Nyctasia
showed him in an old herbal. She meant to brew a potion, she
said, to make her well, or to make him invincible in battle, or
to make them both understand the languages of birds and
beasts. And though it was a game, both felt that it might just
work, someday. . . .

When Nyctasia's health began to improve, they were together more than ever, indoors and out, and as she grew
stronger he was eager to share with her the world she knew so
little. It was delightful to be able to show off for her, and to
help teach her to ride, to hunt, to fence, to dance—for she had
always been the teacher before. Even when her skill with a bow
surpassed his own, he did not mind overmuch. She was his
pupil, his betrothed, and her success did him credit. He was
proud of her.

Their elders viewed these developments with satisfaction. It
had seemed for a time that Nyctasia might make Thierran as
dreamy as herself, but if he took her in hand and made an
Edonaris of her, all would be well. The pair did get into
mischief, betimes, but high spirits were to be expected in
youth, and were to be preferred to too much meditation and
melancholy. Perhaps an early marriage would be best for them,
in a few years' time.

Nyctasia was responsible for their transgressions. Released
from her years of confinement, she was afire to go everywhere,
to experience everything she had only been able to imagine for
so long. She persuaded Thierran to take her to other parts of the
city, places they were strictly forbidden to visit.

"They lecture us on our responsibilities as future rulers of
Rhostshyl," she complained, "but they don't let us learn what
our people's lives are like. We must know the whole city, not
just our own corner of it."

Disguised as beggar-children, they explored the back streets
and markets, the poor cookshops and taverns of the city,
fascinated by the different districts, each a city in itself, within
the walls of Rhostshyl. Sometimes Nyctasia took along her
harp and posed as a minstrel-lass, earning pennies or perhaps
a meal of cheap sausages, which they thought delicious, and
which generally made them ill.

When they were caught, Nyctasia was quick to admit that
she had been the instigator, but Thierran was the one blamed,

the one who should have known better. Yet despite reproaches and the risk of punishment, he could never refuse Nyctasia when she next proposed some forbidden venture. Suppose she should think him less daring than herself? He could bear to lose his elders' approval, but not Nyctasia's admiration.

Their family was indulgent of their escapades for the most part, however. They were reprimanded, not so much for disobedience as for repeating the vulgar oaths they'd heard in the streets, or for pronouncing Rhostshyl "Rozchill" as the common people did. But they would outgrow such childish behavior in time. The boy understood his duty. He was a good influence on Nyctasia, drawing her away from the library and her Vahnite notions. There was no need to keep them on too short a rein.

But Nyctasia did not by any means abandon her studies. She enjoyed her new doings, and took pride in mastering the fitting accomplishments for a lady—though lessons in deportment and etiquette bored her—but the Discipline claimed her as well. She was fully convinced that it had saved her life, and her studies had remained serious and demanding since then, no longer an amusement for her or an entertainment for Thierran. He listened patiently enough to her excited explanations of Vahnite philosophy, but he soon saw that her discoveries did not interest him. But to his relief, she did not think the less of him for that. She only said solemnly, "It is written, 'What is right for one is not so for another.'" And for his part, Thierran, though he could not share her passion for such dull labors, nevertheless took pleasure in defending her to the others—even taking her part against his own twin brother—and receiving her gratitude for his loyalty. 'Tasia was different, special, clever, he insisted. If she was to be a scholar, a healer, that was to her credit.

And she was always glad to see him, still. She'd lay aside her books to listen to him, to sympathize with his concerns, to join him for hawking or riding. She sought him out whenever she was lonely. They grew more devoted to one another than ever, even as they were growing ever further apart.

"And so he persuaded himself that you had cast an enchantment over me. He knew that you were a student of magic, and he preferred to believe that I was under a love-spell than to believe that I would betray him. If I were bewitched, it would

be his duty to rescue me from your evil influence at any cost."
Nyctasia rested her head on Erystalben's shoulder and said
wearily, "People will not believe that there's no such thing as
a love-philtre, no matter what one says."

Erystalben kissed her temple. "I am astounded by the depths
of my jealousy," he said. "I don't remember this first love of
yours, but I despise him nevertheless. If he weren't dead, I'd
take pleasure in killing him myself."

"I never could make you understand my feelings for
Thierran, any more than I could make him understand about
you."

"That's because I understood his feelings for you, and he
mine. I've known you only since yesterday, 'Tasia, but I want
you to think of no one but me. And I know just how to
accomplish that, without the aid of spells."

Nyctasia sat up and regarded him with a challenging air, one
eyebrow lifted. "And how is that, pray?"

He grinned. "Simply by confessing that I'm thoroughly
exhausted."

Nyctasia was on her feet at once. "For someone who only
met me yesterday, you know me remarkably well," she
admitted. "Come along—back to bed with you straightway."

"I don't need more sleep, I've had sleep enough for a legion.
I just want a bit of rest."

"No matter. It's time I had another look at your arm, so
you'll have to lie down, like it or not as you choose."

"My arm feels fine, so long as I don't disturb it."

"That's well, but I'm going to change the dressing anyway,
so you may as well save your breath."

"And to think I've been wondering how such a mild, sweet
maid could be ruler of a city!" Erystalben complained, well
pleased with his success at making her forget her lost love.
Seeing that it pained her to speak of him, he had determined to
distract her. Not only was he grieved at her distress, but it
grieved him all the more to see how much she still cared for
Lord Thierran. A dead rival could sometimes be the most
difficult to defeat.

He hissed with pain as Nyctasia carefully removed the
bandages and examined his torn flesh. Satisfied that it was
healing cleanly, she spread a greyish ointment on a clean piece
of soft cloth and laid it over the wound, then bound fresh
bandages around his arm. "Sorry, love. I tried to be quick."

"You do it well," he said reassuringly. And it was true, she had a deft, expert touch with the materials. "You could be a physician."

"I don't believe I could, not truly, though I'd like to learn. From the first, I studied texts of healing above all else, but I was seeking a way to cure myself, not others—and perhaps I still am. A true healer ought to be selfless."

"And have you known many who were so?"

"Well, no, not many," laughed Nyctasia. "There's something in that." She leaned down to kiss him and said, "You stay right there for now. This is the last of my unguent of mendersleaf. I'll fetch more from an apothecary in Chiastelm while you're resting. I'll be back by dark, I should think."

"Why not send someone for it?"

"The herbalist's an old friend of mine. I want to have a good gossip with her. She'd like to know that you've come home." And Maegor wouldn't give Elixir of Painshade to a messenger, but Nyctasia said nothing of that yet.

"Do I know her?"

"You've met her, but you don't know her well," Nyctasia said evasively. The two had not taken to one another, in fact. "I'll give her your regards, shall I? And don't stir from that bed until I'm back, you mark me!"

From long habit, Maegor did not greet Nyctasia by name before her other customers. She merely chided, "Must you bring that monstrous hound of yours in here? There's scarce room enough as it is. Take him out back at once, and don't let him dig up my herb beds!" No listener would have supposed that the Rhaicime of Rhostshyl was being addressed in such a way.

"Yes, Maeg," Nyctasia said tamely. "Come, Grey." She led him out through the storeroom, pausing to steal a handful of currants from the bin.

Only when she'd rid the shop of everyone else did Maegor join Nyctasia in the kitchen garden. Greymantle, recognizing her scent as that of someone who'd often given him nice meaty soupbones, fawned on her shamelessly until she shooed them both into the kitchen. "I might as well give you a meal too, 'Tasia. You look as if you haven't eaten in a fortnight, as always, and I see you've been into the currants already."

"No one ever lets me have sweets enough," Nyctasia

lamented. "I don't need a meal, Maeg. I've come for some Painshade."

Maegor frowned. "Again? If you're still troubled by sleeplessness—"

"It's not for me, it's for 'Ben," Nyctasia said with a smile. "He's come back."

"Oh, 'Tasia, I'm glad for you! But—why does he need Painshade? Is he ill?"

Nyctasia related what little she knew of Lord Erystalben's plight, including his mishap with Greymantle. "I'm not sure what to make of these dreams of his," she concluded. "He's not said much, but I don't like the look of it."

"A spell of Perilous Threshold . . ." Maegor mused. "He was fortunate to lose no more than his memory. Still, he's to be pitied. It's a hard welcome, to find you at last, only to be attacked by your dog, and then to learn that you're about to be married to someone else."

"In the *vahn's* name, how do such rumors get about? I haven't even *met* Aithrenn of Ochram, much less agreed to a marriage-treaty. But the matter seems to have been settled without me. Even here in Chiastelm it's common knowledge! I suppose there's nothing for me to do but consent, since it's plain that everyone on the coast approves."

"Erystalben won't approve."

"He wouldn't have liked it before, but now, I'm not sure. He's changed, Maeg. It's as if . . . well, do you remember the divination I nearly always used to receive when I cast the lots?"

Maegor nodded. "The number fourteen.

> 'To thee hath fallen the fourteenth lot:
> To have thy desire, yet have it not.'

The most ambiguous of the answers."

"Yes, and the two texts closely agree on the augury for fourteen, though they differ for most numbers. The Celys Oracle says:

> 'Thou hast cast the lot Fourteen.
> Now good and ill thou liest between.
> Thy wish the fates will not fulfill,
> Yet in a manner, so they will.'

I always favored the interpretation that one may win one's heart's desire, and then discover that one no longer desires it. But since I lost 'Ben, my desire has been for his return, and now I have him back—and yet I don't. He doesn't know me, and I hardly feel that I know him."

"But you care for him still?"

"*Vahn*, yes! As much as ever. Isn't that strange?"

"No, not so very strange. Perhaps you never really knew him."

"Maeg, I know you thought 'Ben proud and cold, but—"

"Never mind, 'Tasia. Certainly you knew him better than I. But sometimes the ones we love best are those we know least. That is no secret." She stood and lightly caressed Nyctasia's cheek. "I'll give you the Painshade, if you insist, but are you sure that he must have it?"

"No, not altogether, but there's none at the Smugglers' House, and I want to have some at hand, in case he should need it while we're there."

"Very well, but don't give it to him unless it's necessary. It's not to be trifled with."

"I know. I'll be careful, though it's never done me any harm."

"You haven't lost quantities of blood—or your memory—recently. And even so, because it's never harmed you before, don't suppose that it never will. You oughtn't to take it any oftener than you can help."

"I don't, Maeg, honestly. And I mix it very weak."

"That's of no consequence. You're so small and slight that a weak draught affects you as a powerful one affects others. Once in a great while, it won't hurt you, but taken any oftener it could be dangerous."

"Well, don't worry, Maeg," said Nyctasia, with a sudden wicked grin. "Perhaps 'Ben won't need it, and once he's healed and has his strength back, I expect I'll have much less trouble sleeping at night!"

But the following night, he woke again, shivering and groaning in terror, as Nyctasia bent over him, softly calling his name. He clutched at her desperately with his good hand, so hard that he hurt her arm, but she only stroked his face and said, "You're all right now, 'Ben. You're here with me."

Again, he had been walking aimlessly through the Forest,

listening to the whispers and the distant singing, when a grey
bird lit on his shoulder and stole one of his golden earrings.
He'd followed it frantically, knowing the danger of letting the
Yth keep anything of his, but the bird had led him on, flitting
always out of his reach. It would alight for a moment, then take
wing just as his hands were about to close upon it, drawing him
ever farther into the depths of the Forest. Finally it swooped
low over a pool to drink, and let the earring fall, then flew off
into the trees with a liquid trill of song.

When he leaned over the pool to retrieve the earring, he saw
his reflection appear, with its one earring on the opposite side
from the one he still wore, but the face seemed to smile at him,
though he was not smiling himself. It was but a trick of the
moving lights and shadows on the water, he thought, yet it
frightened him nevertheless, for no reason that he could call to
mind. The image shattered and melted away as he reached into
the pool, groping for the gleam of gold at the bottom. But what
his fingers felt, half buried in the soft silt, was the features of
a human face.

Snatching back his arm in horror, he stared down into the
pool, but saw only his reflection re-forming as the water grew
still again. But now it wore two earrings, and it grinned at him
in triumph.

Somehow this nightmare had left him more terror-stricken
than all the others, and this time he told Nyctasia everything
that he had dreamt from the first. "Could a—a creature of the
Yth take on the form and flesh of a human being?" he asked her
afterward.

"Yes . . ." Nyctasia said uneasily, "but it couldn't leave
the Forest, 'Ben. Nothing of Yth-kind will set foot outside the
Forest. They believe it would be their death."

"But suppose it no longer knew itself for an Ythling? What
then?"

"No, no, put such mad fancies out of your head, love. Such
a thing cannot happen, in very truth. It's only the old ballad
you're dreaming of, the song of the demon bridegroom—"

He shook his head. "I know no song like that."

"You do, 'Ben, I've sung it for you many times. You may
not remember it while you wake, but you know it still, for
you've dreamt it from first to last. The true groom is lured
away by the spell-song and taken by the Forest, and a
demon-creature returns in his place. But it's only a song.

Nothing of the sort has happened to you, I promise you! It's as I told you, 'Ben—no Ythling ever shed such human blood as you did!"

She couldn't see his face in the darkness, but she felt him relax a little, and heard his breathing grow calmer. She believed all that she had told him, but she wished she were as absolutely certain as she'd pretended to be. What disturbed her was not the unlikely idea that he might be some inhuman creature spawned by magic, but the realization that she didn't care what he was, as long as he was hers again. "It's the spell of Perilous Threshold that's made you a stranger to yourself," she said confidently. "But you're not a stranger to me, believe me."

"I believe you," he answered flatly, "but I want to leave for Rhostshyl today, do you understand?"

"You're right, I think. We'll go," Nyctasia promised. "I've made arrangements, we can set out whenever we choose." It might be wiser to wait until his arm was further healed, but his peace of mind was worth the risk of an uncomfortable journey. And even if Rhostshyl failed to fulfill his hopes, still Nyctasia had begun to suspect that he might be better off anywhere than at the haunted Smugglers' House.

15

Nyctasia was rather alarmed to be met on the road to Salten not only by Corson but by Lord Therisain and an escort of guard as well. Since she and Erystalben were traveling slowly, she had sent a messenger ahead to inform a few of her trusted allies of her coming, but this had been a mere courtesy on her part. She had not expected a retinue to accompany her on her return to the city. She had guards enough from the Smugglers' House in attendance.

They had evidently been watching for her approach, for they galloped to meet her, causing her escort to surround her with swords drawn, until she recognized Corson in the lead. "What is it?" she called, as they drew near. "Is something wrong?"

Lord Therisain greeted her coldly. "Was this necessary, Nyctasia?" he demanded.

Thinking that he referred to her sudden disappearance from Rhostshyl, Nyctasia replied, "It seemed so to me. If the city cannot survive a few days without me, it is in a poor way indeed. Has something happened in my absence? Is Tiambria all right?"

"There, now do you see?" Corson broke in impatiently. "I

told you she knew nothing about it. Nyc, Tiambria's fine, it's the Lady Lhejadis—she's been poisoned, and everyone thinks you were responsible."

"What else are we to think, when you vanished on the very morning Lhejadis was stricken?" Therisain asked in an angry whisper, drawing Nyctasia apart from the rest. "Are you completely mad, 'Tasia? This was the worst possible thing to do at this time!"

"Jade?" said Nyctasia, still bewildered. "Oh, *vahn*, no! Don't talk nonsense, Therisain. I'd no reason to poison her."

He had not actually expected her to deny it—not to him. "Who else had a reason? She maligned you openly, everyone knows that."

"All the more reason for me to spare her! I'd only confirm her slanders if I silenced her. My best defense was to let her be."

"Eh—but that's what I hoped to make you see," Therisain said uncertainly. "That's why I came to fetch you. If you make haste you might be in time to save her."

"What! Do you mean that she's still alive?"

"She was this morning, but the physicians haven't much hope for her. If you—"

"Why didn't you say so at once, man, in the *vahn's* name? There's not a moment to lose!" Wheeling her horse around, she trotted back to Erystalben and leaned from the saddle to kiss him quickly. "I'm sorry, love, I can't wait for you. I must get to the city without delay. Stay in Salten tonight as we planned and rest that arm—promise me!"

"All right, but what—"

"I've no time—don't worry—I'll see you soon. Therisain, you remember Erystalben ar'n Shiastred. He doesn't remember you, but he'll explain that. See that he reaches his people. Corson, you'll come with me—?" Without waiting for anyone to reply, she spurred her horse to a gallop and was soon riding as fast as she dared through the village, with Corson close behind her and Greymantle racing at her side.

Nyctasia had sent word only that she was coming, not where she had been, but Corson was not much surprised to see that Lord Erystalben was with her. Little could surprise Corson anymore, where Nyctasia and her affairs were concerned. When they stopped to water their horses at a farmhouse, she only asked, "It is him, isn't it?"

She thought Nyctasia hesitated for a moment before answering, "Yes. Oh, yes, it's 'Ben."

"I was afraid of that."

Nyctasia sent her a sidelong glance. "He suspects that you want to kill any man who takes an interest in me."

"Rutting insolent jackass!" Corson blustered, her face flushing. "He's welcome to you—and you to him! The pair of you deserve each other." Determined to change the subject, she asked, "How did you know Lord Collarbone was at the Smugglers' House in the first place?"

"I didn't know. I went there to look for myself, and found him."

Corson didn't ask her to explain this cryptic remark. In her experience, Nyctasia's explanations generally created as much mystery as they dispelled. "Well, why's his arm in a sling? He was all right when I left him."

"Greymantle misunderstood his intentions toward me. I was so shocked to see him there that I all but swooned, and when 'Ben tried to catch me, Grey attacked him."

Hearing his name, the dog trotted over to them, wagging his tail and still panting from his long run. Corson patted him. "Good lad, Grey! I couldn't have done better myself."

"You needn't gloat, Corson. He nearly bled to death."

"I came to warn you he was there—it's your fault if you go haring off like that without letting me know."

And if Jade dies that will be my fault too, Nyctasia thought grimly. If I'd let Therisain know where to find me, he could have fetched me back sooner to save her. And now he thinks I don't trust him. That probably vexes him more than the belief that I'd poison Jade. I must show him some sign of my faith and favor soon. It won't do to occupy myself so with reconciling my enemies that I forget my friends.

It was just to get away from such concerns that she'd gone to the house by the sea, and she still believed that she'd been right to do so. But perhaps she'd had no right to be so secretive, after all. Did the Principles not say, "The only one who is free is the one who has no heart"?

"You're right, of course," she said to Corson. "I won't do it again, I promise you." In spite of everything, she could still surprise Corson from time to time.

Though Nyctasia had been suspected of poisoning the Lady Mhairestri, the accusation had never been widely believed. The matriarch had been so advanced in years, and her health so uncertain, that folk were ready enough to accept her death as the course of nature. But Lhejadis, who was young and strong, would be another matter. Her death would not only look like Nyctasia's work, but would seem to confirm the rumors about Mhairestri's murder as well. Lhejadis was the perfect target for those who wished to discredit Nyctasia.

"Why didn't I foresee this and warn her?" Nyctasia reproached herself. "I sent the children away, to protect them—thank the *vahn*!—but Jade was always in greater danger than they." As Erikasten had argued, Mhairestri's followers wanted to see Leirven and Deirdras take their places among Rhostshyl's rulers. But Lhejadis was of no great value to them. To check Nyctasia's power would be well worth the sacrifice of a pawn like Jade.

"But she'd never have believed a warning from me," Nyctasia thought. "And if I'd tried to send her away, she'd have refused to go." Lhejadis was not a child, nor a commoner like Rehal, nor was she Nyctasia's ward, like Erikasten. She was of age and might do as she pleased, and if Nyctasia had forced her into exile, it would have been said that she'd been murdered. But now that would be said anyway, and with better reason! It seemed that any action or failure to act would have endangered either Lhejadis or Nyctasia herself.

"I should have protected Jade somehow, in spite of herself," Nyctasia brooded. "I never gave a moment's thought to her safety. Yet how could I have protected her save by dying myself? If I'd died as a child, Jade wouldn't be dying now, and Mescrisdan and Thierran would still be alive. Jade would be Rhaicime, and Mescrisdan's wife instead of his widow. The family would have found a wife for Thorn by now—some girl he scarcely knew, who'd not have come between him and Mescrisdan as I did." Yes, she'd have had to die to save them. Jade had felt cheated of her title, but that alone would not have destroyed her. It was Mescrisdan's jealousy that had doomed them both.

While Nyctasia had been a bedridden invalid, Mescrisdan had not resented his brother's partiality for her, or the time he spent with her. It was Thorn's duty, Nyctasia was his betrothed. He himself was expected to pass time in the company of his cousin Jade, whom he would one day marry, and he, like Thorn, had been taught his duty to his House. And 'Tasia was

weak and sickly and lonely—Thorn felt sorry for her, anyone
could understand that. She would probably not live many years
longer anyway, though he had learned not to say so before his
brother.

Sometimes he even went with Thorn to visit her, and she
always welcomed him warmly. It was pleasant, on a rainy day,
to listen to 'Tasia's songs and stories, to look at the books on
falconry or history, with their colorful, detailed pictures.
Combing the woods for wormbane or stormcloud mushrooms
was a game the brothers could share. And 'Tasia could always
tell them apart at a glance, which gratified them both.

But when she'd emerged from her seclusion, everything had
changed, leaving Mescrisdan alone and embittered. At first the
physicians had allowed her to be carried out to the gardens
where she might sit on the terrace, swathed in shawls, to take
the sun. But in time she'd begun to walk along the garden
paths, with Thorn beside her feeling very important and
responsible, because he'd been told not to let her tire herself.
Then before long she was running, slowly gaining strength in
limbs long unused to any exertion. And each day it seemed she
ran a little farther, and Thorn with her, farther away from his
twin.

The stronger Nyctasia grew, the less Thorn cared for
anything or anyone else. 'Tasia must be taught to ride, to shoot
a bow, to fence. She only knew how to play the harp and write
like a scribe—she had years of lessons to make up for! She
must learn to dance, to hunt. When Thorn wasn't taking her to
ride to hounds, or practicing fencing moves with her, or
sneaking off with her to go somewhere forbidden, he was
boasting about her or making plans for her. Mescrisdan was
soon heartily sick of the sight of her, and of the very sound of
her name. If he accompanied them on one of their outings,
Thorn hardly seemed to know he was there. If he suggested to
Thorn that they go hawking or riding, that they visit the market
square, he always wanted to bring 'Tasia along. It was hurtful,
it was unfair—these were the things he and Thorn had always
done together.

Mescrisdan was too young to be sent on a diplomatic
mission, as Nyctasia was later to do with Erikasten, and he
received little sympathy from his elders for his resentment and
discontent. It was quite proper for Thierran to be taken up with
Nyctasia, he was told—but two could play at that game. He too

had an affianced. From loneliness and spite he turned to Lhejadis, and in her he found an unexpected ally, for she had her own grievances against Nyctasia. She was too well bred to admit, even to herself, that she was disappointed by Nyctasia's recovery, which would deprive her of the rank of Rhaicime, but she soon found other grounds for her dislike. Nyctasia was conceited, Jade complained to Mescrisdan. She gave herself airs. She prided herself on her singing and boasted of her learning. She thought herself cleverer than her cousins, and disdained to join in their games. She was only a scrawny, whey-faced little brat, after all. To all of which Mescrisdan readily assented. Already, unwittingly, Nyctasia had made enemies.

Mescrisdan sought out Lhejadis's company more often, and her evident pleasure at his attentions soothed his wounded feelings. Indeed, consoled by one another, the two might well have outgrown their childish jealousies in time, but within a few years Nyctasia had made more powerful enemies among her kin, and their disapproval of her fanned the embers of Mescrisdan's and Lhejadis's rancor. By siding against Nyctasia over the question of the sovereignty of the Edonaris, they won the favor of the Lady Mhairestri and her faction. They willingly joined in the conspiracy against her, which cost Mescrisdan his life, and with his death Lhejadis's resentment of Nyctasia had grown to a seasoned, unrelenting hatred, the hatred that had proved her undoing.

"The *vahn* knows I never meant her harm," Nyctasia said to herself, "but she lost title and husband because of me. She mustn't lose her life as well!" Curse them, they had chosen their time to strike well, when she was not there to work a spell of healing! But she would spare no effort to save Jade, she determined, if it was not already too late.

When she arrived at the palace of the Edonaris, she ran straight to Lhejadis's chamber, ignoring everyone, courtiers and kin alike, who tried to report various matters of urgent concern to her. A petition of redress required her attention. Certain distinguished scholars had arrived from the east. Lord Aithrenn was in the city. Emissaries from Heithskor awaited an audience with her. "I've no time for that!" she snapped. "Corson, see that I'm not disturbed!" She admitted no one but the court physicians, and then, having consulted with them, dismissed them as well.

"Don't let anyone but them near me," she instructed Corson. "Only you and they are to watch over me—and Greymantle, of course."

"You mean to do one of those healing-trances of yours, eh?" Corson said with a frown. They always left Nyctasia weak and exhausted, sometimes dangerously so.

"There's nothing else to be done, I'm afraid. The physicians are right, it's bloodbane poisoning, there can be no doubt." She lifted Lhejadis's limp hand and showed Corson the greyish tinge at the base of her fingernails. "It's a silver-poison—the same that killed Mhairestri. They've not neglected any detail that might bear witness to my guilt, the swine! Still, it's to my advantage that bloodbane's a slow-working poison."

"Slow? It killed the matriarch quickly enough."

"Yes, but she was old and ill. Jade's in her prime. That's why she's living yet. I commend the physicians—what can be done they've done, but that doesn't amount to a great deal. Only spell-healing can turn the tide now. You didn't object to it when I did it for you, as I recall."

"I was in no condition to object to anything! Besides, that was different. I wouldn't have been dying if not for you and your rutting poisoned earrings."

"And Jade wouldn't be dying if not for me," Nyctasia said sadly, "though I no more poisoned her than I did you. That's why I must do the same for her."

"That's no reason. It's one thing to risk your life for a friend, and another thing to do it for an enemy."

"So it is," agreed Nyctasia, "for the first risk is undertaken for one's own sake, and the second for the sake of another. Is not the latter the nobler deed, then?" As she spoke, she never turned her gaze from the still, waxen form of Lhejadis, and Corson could sense that already she was withdrawing from the world of the living, to seek the world of the dying.

At no time in her life had Nyctasia more wanted to live than she did now. Her plans for the city seemed daily nearer to being fulfilled, and new possibilities had presented themselves, beyond what she had imagined when she'd first returned to her homeland. And now Erystalben had returned as well. . . .

But Lhejadis's death would jeopardize her position, and with it all her hopes for Rhostshyl's future. And she owed Jade this chance, surely, whatever the danger. She would take what precautions she could, but her duty in this matter was manifest.

"If I've not come to myself by morning, separate us, and summon the physicians to me," she said to Corson.

"And suppose they can't rouse you, what then?"

"That will depend," Nyctasia said distantly, "on what happens to Jade." She sat on the bed beside Lhejadis and began to pull off one of her own boots. But then, unexpectedly, she chuckled and instead held out her foot imperiously to Corson.

In reply, Corson made an unladylike gesture with which Nyctasia was not familiar, though it was not difficult to interpret its significance. She grinned and shook her head reprovingly as she tugged at the boot again. "I can't think why I tolerate your disrespect, woman."

"I'll tell you why," said Corson. "It's because you're so fond of me, remember?" To Nyctasia's surprise, she came over and pulled off the other boot for her, then suddenly caught her up in her arms and kissed her roughly. "Be *careful*, Nyc, you mooncalf, will you?"

"Don't worry, sweeting, I will." Nyctasia returned the kiss, but as Corson laid her gently back on the bed, she could see the faraway look in her eyes once more. Nyctasia turned to Lhejadis and drew the motionless figure to her, pressing her lips to Lhejadis's temple, where the heart's beat makes itself felt. As Corson watched uneasily, Nyctasia settled back with her arms about her cousin, and gradually grew as still and lifeless as she. Corson suddenly saw the family likeness between them, which had never been apparent to her before. With a shudder, she cursed and drew the curtains about the bed.

◆　◆　◆

Lhejadis discovered that the nearer she approached to the waterside, the closer and more heavy the air around her was becoming, until she seemed to be moving against an almost substantial pressure. It was not easy even to draw a breath of this dense, different air, but she found that if she breathed and moved very slowly, she could continue her progress, little by little, through the thickening atmosphere, toward the sea. The air was gradually turning to water, she realized, and at the shoreline there would no longer be any difference between the two.

She understood, now, that her slow approach to the sea was necessary to allow her to enter it, that by the time she reached the shore she would be prepared, able to dwell beneath the waves as she had dwelt hitherto above the earth. Such a transformation could not be accomplished suddenly; one must grow accustomed to the new element slowly, by degrees. She would stop here for a time and rest before going on. There was not far to go.

She had been aware from the first of the boat, guided by two oarsmen, that had been slowly moving towards land from across the water, even as she had been moving across the land towards the oceanside. But now she saw that this vessel did not so much skim atop the sea as pass through it, as a bird passes through the air, and now it sat offshore not floating on but in the water, as a fish rests, hanging suspended in the depths. This boat would not bear her over the waves but down into them, slowly descending through the shafts of green light that pierced the water, ever lower, carrying her to her new home. She longed for that serene, silent journey, but she knew that she could not hasten to it; she must wait until the sea-air had done its work. She was content to sit and rest for now, breathing deeply, languidly, drawing the sea into herself along with the air, and feeling it enter her as she would soon enter it. Soon they would be one. There was no hurry. The boat would wait for her, and already each breath was a little easier than the last.

When she heard someone call from far behind her, she turned slowly, with a drifting motion, to look back at the distant figure struggling through the sand towards her. But what lay behind was no longer of interest to her, and she soon turned away, a little more quickly than before, to gaze once more towards the still, calm waters.

Nyctasia called again, but it was useless—she would never reach Jade in time. She was too far ahead, and it was too difficult to move. Not only did the deep, soft sand impede her, but the very air sought to hold her back. Whence this Resistance, what did it mean? Her own limbs seemed to weigh her down, and it was all she could do to raise her head or put one foot before the other. She, who was said to be light as thistledown!

"Float, if you're tired, *float*," suggested a calm voice that seemed to come from near at hand. But no one was there. And how could she float when she was so heavy? "I shall never get on," she thought confusedly, "unless I leave myself behind."

But had she not already done so? "*Neither shore nor sky*," she whispered, "*Neither earth nor air*." Yes, she need not go to Jade, she had only to remember that *she was already with her*. And then she was. "Sister," said Nyctasia, embracing her, "come home with me."

But the other stood and pulled away from her. "Let me be. You have no hold on me."

"I have. I love you," Nyctasia answered, and the truth of her own words took her by surprise. "I'll not leave you."

"No? Then I shall leave you." Lhejadis laughed and made for the water's edge, moving almost swiftly now, with an easy, effortless grace.

And only then did Nyctasia understand what task she had undertaken. Lhejadis had not been poisoned—she had taken poison. She did not want to live, and it would therefore be far more difficult and dangerous to save her. . . . But there was not time for Nyctasia to consider the consequences of her decision, for Lhejadis was even now stepping from the shore and raising her hand to summon the waiting boat. *Don't hesitate, act!* Nyctasia thought wildly. She would not have entered those dark waters by choice, but she willed herself once more to join Lhejadis, and seized her arm to pull her back to shore.

"Let me go! You cannot hold me!"

"I must," cried Nyctasia, gripping her tighter. "It's my duty! Come with me—please—wait!"

But suddenly it was no longer Lhejadis who fought to escape her, but a hissing serpent whose coils slid freely through her hands. *Neither form nor feature,* Nyctasia gasped, as, almost without thought, she made of her hands powerful talons to clutch the creature fast. A great sea-eagle rose from the shore, with the serpent caught in its claws.

And then the serpent too had vanished, and a tiny white moth fluttered from the raptor's grasp. But even as the eagle became a bat and swooped after it, the moth was gone, and Nyctasia saw Lhejadis herself beneath her, not falling but slowly sinking down through the liquid air.

At once Nyctasia was beside her, but now it was she who was seized and held, and Lhejadis laughed at her, exclaiming, "Why, if you won't let me go, you'll come with me, cousin!"

And as the black waters closed over them both, Nyctasia, despairing, saw the boat gliding swiftly toward them. In the bow, a dim, misty figure leaned forward, his arms outstretched, reaching for her. In the moment before the darkness claimed her, she knew him for Thierran.

16

When she'd heard Nyctasia cry out desperately, Corson had
torn open the bedcurtains to find the two women locked in a
deathgrip so fierce that their nails had drawn blood from each
other's arms. Which of them was trying to escape she couldn't
tell, and didn't care—she meant to take Nyc away *now*. It still
lacked some hours till dawn, but her instructions could rot, as
far as Corson was concerned. She'd seen Nyctasia's healing-
trances before, and they'd never resulted in a struggle of any
sort, much less a savage conflict like this. This *couldn't* be
what Nyc had intended. And even though Corson was far
stronger than both of them, she was hard put to force open their
rigid hands and separate them.

Once released from Lhejadis's cruel embrace, however,
Nyctasia yielded and fell limp and motionless. She scarcely
seemed to be breathing as Corson carried her through the
torchlit corridors, sending the first guard she passed to waken
the palace physicians.

Now she lay in her own bed, sometimes as still as stone,
sometimes lost in dreams and delirium, whispering words too
soft for Corson to hear, reaching out for something or someone

only she could see. Once she sobbed heartbrokenly for a few minutes, but then fell silent and seemed to sleep peacefully for a time, with a half-smile playing about her lips. Greymantle lay at her feet by day and night, despite the physicians' orders that he be removed from the Rhaicime's bed. When anyone but Corson tried to take hold of him, he growled very convincingly, displaying his long teeth, and when Corson tried it, he whimpered so pathetically that she hadn't the heart to put him out.

"He'll let you be, now he knows your scent," she assured the physicians. "He doesn't interfere with anyone who attends to Her Ladyship. Besides, if I don't let him stay, he'll sit outside and howl, and that will disturb the Rhaicime. No, it won't help to take him to the kennels, or anywhere else. If that dog gets to howling, he'll disturb all of Rhostshyl, believe me."

Corson felt like howling herself, less from sorrow than frustration and helplessness. She watched over Nyctasia almost as steadfastly as Greymantle, but she knew that there was nothing she could do to help her. She was afraid for Nyctasia but couldn't protect her—it was maddening! She thought of going back to Chiastelm, since she was doing no good in Rhostshyl, and Steifann had expected her to return in a few days, but she knew she wouldn't leave until Nyctasia's fate had been decided one way or the other. "She's been in this state three days," she wrote to Steifann, "and the rutting physicians won't say yes or no about her, or tell me how long she's like to stay this way. I don't believe they know any more about it than I do. They just poke her and listen to her heart and look in her mouth and feel how cold her little feet are. Then they mutter together and say she's no worse and no better. I could do that myself. So I don't know yet when I'll be back—" Corson paused to shake her cramped hand, then read over what she'd written. It didn't satisfy her, but she found writing too much of a chore to start over again. Finally she scratched out the last word and carefully wrote "home" in its place, adding, "but don't worry about me."

When she'd rested her hand, she went on with the rest of the news. A letter was an unusual event for her friends at the Hare, and she might as well make the most of it. "I tried to send Trask back with a party of travelers, but he wouldn't have it. He's got my 'Malkin teaching him to read—and the Hlann knows what else—and he says he might not have such a chance

again. That's so, after all, and he really is working at his
letters, so I let him stay. It's not as if he's much use to you there
anyway."

It would be too much trouble, Corson decided, to explain all
about Nyctasia's ill-fated meeting with Lord Erystalben and
its consequences. She could make a good story of it when
she returned, if all went well. She refused to think about the
possibility that all would not be well. Nyc would recover, she
always did. . . .

Corson turned resolutely back to her task. "That fellow with
no memory," she wrote. "He's giving trouble already, I knew
it would be so. It's no secret now. Nyc said he's the one I took
him for, a Jhaice of the House of Shiastred, and some of his kin
agree, but the rest deny it and claim he's an impostor. Nyc's the
only one who can settle it, and both sides want to lay an appeal
before her. Half of Rhostshyl is demanding an audience with
her about one thing or another. There were rumors about that
she'd vanished again, like before the war, so now no one
believes that she's just too sick to show herself.

"I know that much because Trask brings me all the news and
gossip. That one hears everything, you know. But I haven't left
Nyc all this time, I even sleep here. Anyone could do away
with her easily while she's so defenseless. Her enemies have
been quiet of late, but they might think this a good time to
strike. I mean to stay by her till she's come to herself, and
then—" *And then I'll kill her myself for putting me to all this
worry,* she thought, but she was tired of writing, so she
concluded, "I'll fly straight to Chiastelm and not stop for wind
or welter. I wish I was there with you right now, even though
you make me do the work of three. And you'd better be lonely
for me too, else when I get there I'll slaughter you and that ugly
bitch Destiver both!" There. That would do well enough.

Corson folded and sealed the letter, then, hearing Nyctasia
call out again, she dropped it and hurried to her bedside. "I'm
so tired," Nyctasia said clearly, but she was still asleep, her
lips moving soundlessly now, her brow creased with fear or
anguish. Greymantle looked up at Corson with a whine, and
she stroked his head.

"I know, Grey, I miss her too." There was no one else like
Nyc, Corson thought glumly, no one else who could take her
place. She was crazy, and she drove Corson crazy, but without
her life would be so rutting *dull.* Corson smoothed Nyctasia's

forehead, then bent down and kissed her. "Don't die, Nyc, you silly chit," she said fiercely.

The black waters had engulfed Nyctasia and swept from her all memory of her struggle with Lhejadis, of the fall that had left her drowning in fathomless depths of darkness. She knew only that she had been drifting in the darkness for a long time, and that the darkness was not only all about her but within her as well, for she felt neither fright nor impatience nor curiosity. She was neither contented nor discontented. She was merely a part of the darkness, of nothingness.

But now it seemed that the tide of darkness was receding, leaving her stranded on some unknown shore. She was beginning to grow aware, first of herself, then of her surroundings. She was, after all, someone—a being separable from the shrouding darkness—and she must therefore be somewhere. But where? And how had she come to be there?

She could feel, now, that something hard and unyielding lay beneath her, and as she stared into the darkness her eyes began to grow used to the gloom at last, and she made out the dim shapes of things—arches and columns with great long blocks strewn among them. She recognized the place, then, and with the recognition came remembrance of herself, of her life—but not of her death. She was lying on a bier in the family crypts beneath the palace of the Edonaris.

The only light was the faint glow from a wall-torch in the stairway behind her, but it sufficed, for Nyctasia knew the crypts well. It was the first of the forbidden places she had made Thierran bring her, as soon as she was strong enough, to see if it looked as she had so often imagined it during her illness, when she'd expected that she would soon lie there forever. To visit it living, to visit it and *leave*, had been a triumph for her, and it had become one of their favorite hiding-places, since no one thought to look for them there. She remembered the first time they'd descended the long, winding stairway together, lamps in hand, half-afraid that they'd be caught and sent back, half-afraid that they wouldn't.

Thierran had come there once before, with Mescrisdan, each daring the other to go on, neither wanting to stay. They'd done no more than make their way to the far wall of the innermost chamber, looking around them as little as possible, and then hasten away again, honor satisfied. The venture had done little to dispel his apprehensions about the dismal place, but he had not let Nyctasia see that he feared it. "There's nothing to be afraid of," he assured her boldly, as if every corner of the crypts had long been familiar to him. "It's just a lot of great stone boxes with statues lying on them, that's all."

And Nyctasia had answered confidently, "I won't be afraid if you're there, Thorn." How could he disappoint her after that?

They'd explored everything with growing courage, blowing the dust from the carved faces of their ancestors' effigies— "This one looks like you, 'Tasia"—and trying to make out the ancient inscriptions. It had been daunting at first to think that a like sepulchre waited for them, a tomb they would share since they were to be husband and wife, but the place had soon lost its terrors for them as they found nothing to frighten them but shadows and spiders.

"We might not be buried here," Thorn had said defiantly. "We might be lost at sea. We might be eaten up by wolves."

Nyctasia had taken up the game at once. "We might be captured by pirates and sold into slavery in a foreign land."

"We'd be ransomed," he pointed out.

"So we would," she said, disappointed. Then, drawing on the many stories she'd read, she suggested, "Well, we might wound an enchanted stag, in the hunt, and be changed into trees, or fall asleep for a thousand years, and when we come back there won't *be* an Edonaris palace, or even a Rhostshyl. . . ." But that they could not imagine, any more than they could truly imagine their own deaths. They knew that the crypts would one day claim them, but even to Nyctasia that day had seemed unimaginably distant.

But she remembered as well the last time they had visited the crypts together, in secret, on the day of her mother's death. They had stolen away to discuss some childish scheme of their own, but they had not been there long before they'd heard the bells tolling the death-knell, and they'd known that it could mean nothing else. The court physicians had not held out much hope for the Lady Teselescq's recovery, and Nyctasia had been duly warned to expect the worst, but she had not believed them. If she, the weakling, the sickly one, had survived their dire prognostications, how could her strong, iron-willed mother do less? The women of the Edonaris usually lived to a great age.

The message of the bells therefore found Nyctasia unpre-
pared, and came upon her as much as a shock as a sorrow. She
could not greatly grieve for her mother, whom she had rarely
seen, but the tidings of her death were most unwelcome
nevertheless, for Nyctasia had now inherited the rank of
Rhaicime. She would not assume the full responsibilities of the
title until she came of age, of course, but she would be
expected to take a much more serious interest in the family's
affairs from this time on. Lady Mhairestri would insist that she
be trained to fulfill her future obligations as one of the heads of
the House and rulers of the city. There would be endless
instruction in civil and municipal government, diplomacy,
judicature and magistracy. It was not a pleasant prospect, but
Nyctasia was an Edonaris and knew where her duty lay. At the
sound of the bells, she and Thierran had only exchanged a
stricken look, then resignedly returned to their own apartments
to change into suitable mourning clothes. Nyctasia's childhood
was over. She was twelve years old.

After that, they had shunned the crypts, without needing to
discuss the matter. Now that someone they had known was
entombed there, the place had become too real for comfort, no
longer a secret retreat from the world for them alone. Nyctasia
had not seen it again until her return to Rhostshyl, when she
had first paid her respects to the memory of those fallen in
battle with the Teiryn, and then returned not long afterwards to
witness the formal interment of the matriarch Mhairestri. But
she had visited the crypts more than once since then to lay
wildflowers at the tomb of Thierran, and see that it was well
tended.

She rose and went to it now, finding her way easily despite
the murk. As she leaned over the effigy of Thierran, she let her
long hair fall about his face, as she had used to do when they
were alive, and she saw the white marble of his eyelids darken
as her tears touched them. It seemed altogether natural that
those stone eyes should open and look up at her, and that his
cold lips, when she kissed them, should part and speak to her.

"For shame, 'Tasia, you know it's forbidden to play down
here. Will you never learn to behave?"

Was she 'Tasia, she wondered, or Nyc? Was she dead or
alive? But these questions did not seem of great importance. "I
always led you to do what was forbidden," she said.

"But you're too old for such games now, my dear. You have

work to do, and no time to waste. Hurry now, before the curfew rings."

"Oh, Thorn, I'm so tired. Let me stay here with you. You've always taken care of me."

"Rest then, little one, but not here. Come, I'll take you back."

Arms of stone lifted her, and she settled her head on his shoulder gratefully and closed her eyes, feeling safe and sheltered. Soon they were ascending the stairs. "Do you remember, when I fell out of a peach tree in the orchard and hurt my leg?" she asked sleepily. "You had to carry me all the way back."

"I remember."

"And then they punished *you* for letting me climb the trees! It's so unfair. Everyone who loves me suffers for it. . . ."

"I didn't mind, my heart. I liked to be punished for your sake. It made me feel a hero."

"Ah, there's no pleasing them," sighed Nyctasia. "They bade me learn the harp, and then scolded me for practicing too much. 'A lady ought not to have calloused fingers like a laborer,' Lehannie told me. I said, 'I see. A lady should play the harp, but she shouldn't play it *well*.' And Mhairestri slapped me for disrespect. Quite right, too, that was no way to speak to my aunt. All the same, Derry and Raven shall climb the trees in the orchard if they like, no matter what the gardeners say. Thorn . . . ?" She yawned. "Thorn, do you think it was Mescrisdan who told Mhairestri that we went to The Lame Fox? How else could she have found out? But maybe she had us followed, I never thought of that."

He laid her down carefully on her own bed and drew a coverlet over her. "There, now you'll be all right, 'Tasia."

"Mmm, that's nice, I feel much better now. Thorn, I think Mescrisdan told her. He was angry because we didn't take him along. But how could we? I *told* him, it was just that the two of you would have drawn too much notice to us, being so alike. I didn't mean to . . . Thorn, don't go—stay with me!" she cried, and opened her eyes, only to find Corson bending over her.

"Nyc? Are you—"

"Corson? Where—"

Both were interrupted at once by Greymantle, who jumped to his feet, barking excitedly, thrashed Corson with his heavy tail, and licked Nyctasia's face repeatedly. By the time they had succeeded in getting him out of the way, both had forgotten their questions. Nyctasia remembered that she had dreamed of Thierran, but nothing that had come before, save that she had attempted to enter into a healing-trance with Lhejadis. But this was her own bedchamber—why was she here, not with Jade? If they'd been separated without her knowledge, it could only mean that she had failed. "I lost her," she said, grief-stricken. "Poor Jade!"

"No you didn't," said Corson. "She came 'round days ago. She's still weak, but the court leeches say she's out of danger."

"What! How can that be? I don't understand."

Corson shrugged. "If you don't, no one does. She wants to see you, and she's given it out to all and sundry that you didn't poison her, or the matriarch either. She says she took blood-bane herself. She's not been told that she half-killed you too."

"Herself . . . !" breathed Nyctasia. "Fool that I am! I should have seen that from the first! But then how—? I must go to her at once." She rose hastily, then, catching sight of herself in the mirror, she threw open a chest and began to pull out fresh clothing. "I suppose a bath can wait," she said regretfully.

"But, Nyc, shouldn't you rest? You can't just—" But Nyctasia wasn't listening, and Corson gave it up. She could see for herself that Nyctasia was perfectly well. "Rutting magic!" she muttered. More dead than alive one moment, hale as a hare the next. It was unsettling, it was contrary to nature. Well, she'd just deliver the letter to Steifann by herself, then. He was rutting well going to see it, after she'd gone to the trouble of writing the thing.

"No, Grey, you stay here," Nyctasia was saying. "Jade doesn't need you galloping about her sickroom. Corson, I shan't be long. Would you wait for me here—and order a bath for me too, please, if you will. I'll just see Jade, and then I want to speak to you. There's so much to be done. Could you raise a force of mercenaries for me, do you think, to augment the city guard? Mostly for show. We'll discuss it presently—"

Corson grabbed her on her way to the door. "If you think to go running about the palace unarmed, without even Grey for escort, you can think again," she said grimly. "I swear you've begun to believe the moonshine you let others believe about you. Take the word of a soldier, Nyc, once you start to think you can't be killed, you're as good as lost."

Nyctasia seemed about to argue, but wisely changed her mind. "Yes, very well—you know best. But I can't bring you into Jade's presence. You see, she's never spoken of it, but she must know that it was you who killed Mescrisdan. She blames me, of course, not you, but for me to call upon her with you in attendance would look like a deliberate insult."

"By all means, far better for you to be in danger than for the Lady Lhejadis to be insulted! I'll see you to the door and send another sentry to stand guard, but Grey's to stay with you, and you'll wear a dagger at the least!"

Hlann's blood, what am I to do with her? Corson thought. She'd have to have a strict talk with Nyc before she left, and with some of the palace guard as well. Someone had to keep an eye on Her Witlessness when Corson was away. But, having seen to Nyctasia's security for the present, she set out to find Trask and tell him to make ready to leave for Chiastelm in the morning.

Lhejadis looked happier than Nyctasia had seen her since they were children. Despite her pallor and her drawn, ailing appearance, she seemed to glow with a new peace and contentment, and she greeted Nyctasia joyously. " 'Tasia, I've been longing to tell you—I've had a vision, a Manifestation, and it's healed me in body and spirit!"

"You remember it?" Nyctasia asked, astonished. "But that's remarkable, Jade—I've never heard of anyone who remembered a healing-trance." She sat on the bed and took Lhejadis's hand, saying eagerly, "Tell me everything! What was it like? Did you see me? Did I speak to you?"

"You, 'Tasia? How could you be there? You're neither dead nor dying. No, don't you see, it was Mescrisdan! I was with him. But he sent me away, because the Law of the *Vahn* forbids us to choose death over life."

"So it does," said Nyctasia, and fell silent, lost in wonder. Jade remembered the healing-trance no more than she. *Mescrisdan* . . . That was the answer to Jade's recovery, then—the last answer she would have imagined. "What else did he say to you, cousin?"

"If only I could remember it all! I can recall the sense of it, now, but not the words. I only know . . . that I was wrong to believe Mhairestri. She was to blame for Mescrisdan's death, not you. She sent him to kill you that night, and she'd no right—"

"Mhairestri sent him? But he and Thorn were together."

"Thorn thought they were to capture you, but she told Mescrisdan not to bring you back alive. He agreed for my sake. She promised him that she'd see you stricken from the family records as a murderess."

"I see. And you knew of this?"

"But, 'Tasia, we thought it was true! She told us that you killed her brother, her twin, and I'd swear she believed it herself. Mescrisdan was to avenge him."

"Great Uncle Brethald," Nyctasia mused. "Did Mhairestri also tell you that he tried to poison me, twice, or did she neglect to mention that detail? Both times he failed because he hardly knew me at all. He offered me poisoned wine at dinner, not knowing that I didn't drink spirits. I only sipped at it, as a courtesy, but that made me ill enough to guess at his game. Then he poisoned a pair of earrings that had been his mother's, for his share of her jewels was to come to me. But the fool didn't take the trouble to find out that I never wore gold. Really, the carelessness of the man was disgraceful," she said bitterly. "If you intend to murder people, you must first make a study of their habits, the greenest assassin knows that much."

"We shouldn't have listened to her, but how were we to know what Brethald had done?"

"You weren't to know, but you may be certain that Mhairestri did. Brethald probably acted at her behest." Nyctasia rose and began to pace about the room. "Mhairestri should never have convinced me it was my duty to concern myself with the interests of our House and the governing of the city. That's what set me to studying the family chronicles and the City History in earnest. But they taught me that there were no grounds for our claim to rule of Rhostshyl, no just cause for our continued feud with the Teiryn.

"Like a little fool, I thought that those facts would change matters, if only my elders knew them. It never occurred to me that they had known them from the start. Before these inconvenient discoveries of mine, Mhairestri and I could tolerate one another, but once I became a threat to her ambitions for the Edonaris, she was determined to be rid of me, and she didn't do things by half-measures. She sent assassins after me more than once. But to try to use Mescrisdan! He was no murderer—I daresay he only agreed from fear of refusing Mhairestri to her face. We were all afraid of her. But he probably never meant to see it through, Jade. Mhairestri should have known that he'd not succeed where skilled killers had failed."

Lhejadis shook her head sadly. "She tried again when we first heard rumors of your return. And even when you were in the city. It was when that failed too that she told me you couldn't be killed, that the spells protecting your life were too strong."

"Mhairestri believed that?" Nyctasia's tone seemed to dismiss the idea with contempt, but she did not deny it outright.

"Yes, but she said that no spell could protect your reputation, and that your disgrace would serve our purposes as well as your death. There seemed no other way to prevent Tiambria's marriage to Jehamias ar'n Teiryn. Mhairestri didn't believe you'd be able to obtain Tiambria's consent to the match, but when you did—"

"Jade! Do you mean to say that you knew Mhairestri meant to take poison? And you did nothing?"

"Did you ever succeed in turning Mhairestri from her purpose, when she'd made up her mind?"

"Well, no, but didn't you tell the others, at least?"

"She was dying already, 'Tasia, or so she said. She told me she hadn't long to live—mere days perhaps—but now I wonder if even that was true."

"Very likely it was," Nyctasia said thoughtfully. "The signs were there. Who but Mhairestri would think to make use of her own death to strike a blow at her enemies?"

"We agreed that if her death didn't put an end to your plans, mine should follow, to confirm your guilt."

Nyctasia caught her breath. She had thought that nothing could shock her, but this confession chilled her to the bone. "Oh, no, Jade. Mhairestri told you to—? She gave you bloodbane?"

"I asked her for it. I didn't want to live, I only wanted vengeance."

"My poor Jade, you may have thought it was your own idea, but I'd wager my fortune that Mhairestri trapped you into asking for the poison."

Lhejadis only shrugged. "I hadn't the courage to take it,

after all, even when Leirven and Deirdras disappeared. It was my duty to stop you, in the only way possible, and I thought that if I'd done it sooner I might have saved Emeryc's children. I despised myself for my cowardice—I, an Edonaris!—but still I couldn't bring myself to it. Then when Erikasten, too, was sent away—"

"But, in the *vahn's* name, 'Kasten's gone to the Midlands, to Vale—there was no secret about that!"

"So he said, but I thought you'd deceived him, that he would never return, like Rehal and the children."

"I was afraid of that," sighed Nyctasia. "Jade, Rehal is soon to be married, and I'll prove to you that she and the children are alive, if you'll swear to me not to tell the others where they are—at least, not yet." It was a bold step to take, perhaps a dangerous one, but Nyctasia felt strongly that now, if ever, was the time to confide in Lhejadis despite the risk, and she did not attempt to resist the prompting of her spirit.

It was Lhejadis who hesitated. "No, don't tell me . . ." she said slowly. "I don't want to know more than the others, but neither do I want to betray your trust. If you assure me that they live, that suffices."

Nyctasia nodded, relieved. "That is wise." She kissed Lhejadis and said, "I'll go, you need your rest. If I send you a cordial to give you strength, will you dare to drink it, do you think?"

"I believe I shall," she said, smiling. "But, 'Tasia, you must . . ." She paused, gathering her resolve, and went on with an effort, "You must understand—Mescrisdan—he meant to carry out Mhairestri's orders if he could, and I encouraged him to it. We believed what we wanted to believe. You must forgive us, 'Tasia, you must forgive us both!"

Nyctasia embraced her. "What does it matter what we've done, Jade? We all did things we regret, and failed to do what was right, but we must forgive one another, and forgive ourselves as well. Only the future matters now. When I think of the past, I find I have forgiven all and everything."

And even as she spoke, she realized that it was true. She had forgiven everyone, even Brethald, even Mhairestri, yet when or how she had done so was a mystery to her. She too had been healed, though it was not her healing-trance which had brought this to pass. Her magic had failed completely, but she was not disappointed.

17

Trask protested at being dragged back to Chiastelm, but he didn't give as much trouble as Corson had expected. "I don't see why I have to go just because you're leaving," he argued. "Why can't I stay here on my own?"

"Because someone at court has to be answerable for you—and don't think that 'Malkin will take responsibility for you, because if I know that one, he won't."

Trask suspected the same thing. 'Malkin had only so much time for his new pupil, and expected him to keep his distance when he wasn't wanted. Trask was not to make demands on 'Malkin's attention. He was not to put himself forward or presume to be familiar with 'Malkin before others. But, all the same, 'Malkin did take an interest in Trask's education, praising his determination to better himself, and his quickness to master what he was taught. And this was more encouragement than Trask had ever received from anyone else.

"How can I learn to read if I leave now?" he complained.

Corson considered. It was hard on Trask to lose such an opportunity, but she couldn't leave him to shift for himself at court—Nyc wouldn't hear of it. "Well, listen, Nyc wants me to muster a troop of mercenaries for her, so I'll be back and forth between here and Chiastelm a good bit, and you can come with me, if Steifann gives you leave."

Trask brightened. "I can deal with Steifann," he said confidently.

"Huh," Corson snorted, "I daresay you'll fare better with 'Malkin like this anyway. He'll grow tired of you if you're underfoot too much. If you come and go, you'll not wear out your welcome so soon." She hesitated, and said uncomfortably, "Trask, don't expect too much from 'Malkin. That one's not to be counted on. He really cares for no one but himself."

"I know," said Trask. "I think a courtier has to be like that. Lucky for me that I am." He grinned. "Truth to tell, he's no more tired of me than I am of him."

Trask felt that he really could do with a rest from 'Malkin's overbearing ways and his insistence on keeping Trask in his place. He was even beginning to understand why both Nyctasia and Corson claimed that court custom and ceremony were a nuisance. Such things fascinated him as much as ever, yet it would be rather a relief to let down his guard for a while, and not have to think every moment about acting and speaking correctly. Always provided that he could come back soon, of course. . . .

" 'Malkin's a high-handed bastard," he agreed, "but he's been nice to me, you know, Corson, in his way. So long as he's willing to teach me, I don't mind playing toady to him. And absence lends charm, they say. Maybe he'll miss me if I'm gone for a while."

"You really *are* a disloyal little cur, aren't you?" Corson said, laughing. How could she have thought it necessary to warn Trask against growing too attached to 'Malkin? He could take care of himself.

"Well, Asye's teeth, Corson! If I don't look to my own interest, who will?"

"Steifann would," Corson pointed out.

"All right, Steifann, I grant you—but there aren't many like Steifann. I'm loyal enough to him, you know, but he can't give me a chance to make anything of myself."

"No," Corson said thoughtfully, "there aren't many like Steifann. Come along and take your leave of Nyc—and don't pester her to let you stay, either, because I happen to know that she'd rather have a mad dog loose at court than you."

"I haven't the least intention of pestering Her Ladyship,"
Trask said loftily. "Not about that."

Nyctasia was sequestered with her court officials and advisors, all intent on informing her of a great many matters that
demanded her immediate attention. Lord Aithrenn had arrived
in the city during her unexplained absence, she was told, and
to make matters worse, he had presented himself at the palace
after her return, only to be told that the Rhaicime was unable
to see him. Now it seemed that nobody knew whether he was
still in Rhostshyl or had returned to Ochram.

"But why wasn't he offered accommodation here?" Nyctasia
demanded, dismayed at this breach of courtesy and hospitality.

"He was, my lady, but he declined. It is to be feared that he
interpreted Your Ladyship's failure to confer with him person-
ally as a deliberate affront."

Nyctasia sighed. "If he chooses to be offended, it can't be
helped. I cannot be expected to receive people when I'm
insensible and half-dead. There's nothing to be done about it at
present, at all events. What else have you there?"

While a clerk gravely consulted a list, Lord Therisain broke
in impatiently, "Half the House of Shiastred is demanding an
audience with you."

With a start of guilt, Nyctasia realized that she had hardly
given a thought to Erystalben's return. "Indeed?" she said.
"What do they want of me?"

"Well, some want you to recognize Erystalben formally and
restore him to his place, and the others want you to withdraw
the impostor you've inflicted upon them."

"Impostor, is it? How dare they! Of course he's 'Ben—I
ought to know."

"So ought his father to know, one would think, but he denies
that this stranger is his son."

"I see! So Lord Descador finds his nephew a more satisfactory heir than his son. I suppose I ought not to be surprised at
that. He never did think 'Ben suited to his position, and now
that he's lost his memory . . ." She shook her head. "I can
compel the Shiastred to acknowledge him, of course, but I'd
best see 'Ben before I take any steps at all, and learn what his
wishes are in the matter."

"He's been trying to see you for days," Therisain observed,

"but your bodyguard would give entrance to no one." His tone was resentful, and Nyctasia hastened to explain.

"I expected to recover long before you returned from Salten with 'Ben, else I'd have left orders that you were to be admitted." She had made a point of receiving Lord Therisain before anyone else. "Though there's nothing we could have done for one another, after all." Turning to the clerk, she said, "Send word to Lord Erystalben to attend me this evening, if he will. He's to be admitted to my chamber whenever he arrives. What more is there?"

"The Lord Anseldon desires a word with you, my lady."

Nyctasia nodded. "I want to see him as well, and the Lady Elissa both. Inform them that I shall be pleased to receive them at their convenience. What remains?"

"Messengers from the governors of Heithskor await Your Ladyship's notice."

It might be as well, Nyctasia decided, to let them wait. "Presently, presently," she said with a negligent wave of her hand. "Ask their business and report it to me. Is that all?"

"No, my lady. The Lohannes have requested a hearing concerning the redress owed them by the Anderleys for the burning of their storehouse."

"Then the Anderleys have not yet made restitution? The judgment against them was decisive, was it not?"

"Entirely so, my lady, but they have sought to circumvent the obligation by disowning Jacon ash Anderley, and disclaiming responsibility for his deeds and debts."

"Clever," said Nyctasia, "but it won't do. Had they disowned him before the fire, they might have had grounds for appeal, but it's plain that they were behind the business. They're only angry with Jacon for being caught at it. Send them a warning letter from me, and another to the Lohannes with my respects, and due apologies for the delay, saying that I'm attending to the matter. Just bring them to me to be approved, signed and sealed."

"As you will, my lady. And a pair of physicians from Celys, with letters from Your Ladyship, seek to present themselves."

"Very good. They must be the Master Scholars Anthorne and Tsephis—arrange an audience for them directly. Now—"

But she was interrupted by Corson and Trask, who arrived at that moment, unexpected and unannounced, without having requested an audience or stated their business to anyone.

Nyctasia was officially not to be disturbed while conferring with her advisors, and Corson took considerable pleasure in flaunting her unique position at court by ignoring this prohibition. There was not a guard in the palace garrison who dared deny her admittance to the Rhaicime at any time, and, in Corson's experience, Nyctasia was only too glad to be disturbed on such occasions.

"Ah, Corson, there you are," she said, quite as if she had sent for her. "You are in good time—we have just concluded our affairs." She stood, to dismiss the others politely, remarking in a businesslike tone, "We must discuss the reinforcements to the city guard." But as soon as the rest had taken their leave, she hugged Corson and exclaimed, "Thank the stars you chased them off, pet! I was on the point of perishing. Do you think you could sneak me out of the city again, as you did before? It won't be as easy this time, I warn you. I only had to elude my enemies then, but now I want to escape my allies."

"Poor little Nyc. Are your people bullying you, then? I'll kill the lot of them, shall I?"

"Ah, would you? I'd appreciate it very much."

"But if you want to run off again, you'll tell me first, next time! Is that understood?"

"Yes, Corson. I suppose I must put up with *your* bullying, since I've no one who can kill you for me. Except perhaps Greymantle?"

The dog looked up, waved his tail once, said, "Hruf?" and went back to sleep. There were no threatening scents in the room. He was familiar with Corson and Trask, and considered the first a friend, and the other harmless.

Corson pointed a warning finger at Nyctasia. "Not even Grey can save you if I decide to teach you a lesson, so you'd better do as I say, or you'll regret it."

Nyctasia laughed and threw herself down on a couch, feeling much refreshed. After the morning's formalities, Corson's threats were as welcome as a cool breeze to a laborer. "I never should have made you a Desthene. You were bad enough before, but now—!"

Trask, who'd been awaiting an opportunity, now came forward and made Nyctasia his best bow. It was quite an accomplished and graceful performance.

Nyctasia applauded. "Bravo, brat. Well done!"

"Then can I come to the wedding?" he asked eagerly. "*Please*, Nyc?"

Nyctasia threw up her hands. "If I hear another word about this everlasting marriage—! I am *not* betrothed to the High Lord Aithrenn, I've never seen the man, I don't even know where he is!"

"You don't?" said Trask, surprised. "He's staying at The Golden Horn, isn't he? That's where he was a few days ago."

Nyctasia stared. "If you want to know what's taking place in the city, don't ask someone in the palace," she said finally. "It doesn't do to forget that."

"And if you want to know what's taking place in the palace, don't ask someone in the palace either," said Corson wryly. "The only folk who know anything are gossipmongering minions like our Trask."

"No, they're not the only ones who know tidings of the palace," Nyctasia corrected her. "They're the only ones who'll *tell*. What else have you heard about His Lordship?" she asked Trask.

"Only what everyone knows," Trask said with a shrug. "They say he's older than you, but a fine-looking man still, and that he has half-grown children who are his acknowledged heirs, though he's never had a wife."

" 'What everyone knows,' indeed! Everyone but me, it seems—I've had no time to make inquiries. I've sent spies into Ochram, of course, but I haven't received their reports yet. I might better question one of my own scullions, apparently, or any idler in the marketplace."

Corson was skeptical. "It's probably just rumor, Nyc. Why would the High Lord stay at the Horn when he could have lodgings here in the palace?" She turned on Trask. "Tell me that if you know so much."

"His Lordship didn't tell me his reasons! I just—"

"Oh, I can guess his reasons readily enough," Nyctasia put in. "He means to take this chance to have a good look at the city, without interference, and see how badly she was wounded by the war, before he commits Ochram to any irrevocable union with her. And very prudent of him, too. He naturally assumes that I'd show him only what I wanted him to see."

"Would you?" asked Corson, curious.

"No, I'd insist that he see everything—not because I'm honest, but because his spies have no doubt reported the truth to him already. It shows a commendable diligence on his part to take the trouble to confirm the condition of the city for himself."

These considerations did not interest Trask. "But aren't you going to marry him, Nyc?" he persisted. Having seen the splendor and pageantry of the Lady Tiambria's wedding, he'd been looking forward to Nyctasia's with great anticipation. And what better occasion for displaying his newly-acquired skills and courtly graces?

"Greymantle, kill," Nyctasia moaned, pointing to Trask. "Attack. Maim. Mangle."

Greymantle good-naturedly got up and ambled over to Trask, sniffed him, licked his hand, and then sat down beside him, looking to Nyctasia for further instructions.

"Bad dog, Grey," she said fondly, at which he clambered onto the couch, crowding her into a corner, and laid his great head on her knee adoringly.

Since Greymantle had failed to rid his mistress of Trask, Corson offered to do so, for a very modest fee, but before they could seal the bargain, their transaction was cut short by the arrival of a page with a letter for Corson.

She recognized the seal—a prancing hare—as the one she sometimes used to send messages from the Hare, but she'd never seen it on a letter directed to herself. The only missives Corson had ever received were instructions from her employers or orders from her commanders. "It's from Steifann," she said in wonder, looking at the letter as if she had no idea what to do with it. "He's never written to me before."

"How could he?" Trask asked reasonably. "He's never known where you were before, when you weren't at the Hare, stupid."

"That's so," said Corson, so entranced that she didn't even bother to swat Trask for his insolence. Steifann was thinking of her! He'd sent her a letter!

"Aren't you going to read it?" Nyctasia asked, turning away to hide her amusement.

"Oh. Of course I am," said Corson, flustered. Suppose it was bad news, she thought suddenly. What if the Hare had burned down, what if Steifann had been robbed, or had broken his leg, or worse? What if he needed her—and her not there? She tore off the seal, and nearly ripped the letter in half in her haste to unfold it.

Trask tried to look over her shoulder, eager to see if he could recognize any of the combinations of letters he'd learned, but Corson pushed him away, mindful of those lessons in reading. He couldn't have learned much yet, she thought, but one couldn't be too careful where a sly thing like Trask was concerned.

"Well, what's he say, then?" Trask demanded. "Don't be such a bore, Corson! Steifann always reads us *your* letters."

"Only part of them," Corson said smugly, savoring the coarse but gratifying endearments with which Steifann addressed her. "And you can hear part of this one. He wants to know what in the name of several dozen perverted demons is keeping me so long in Rhostshyl—and he says that it had rutting well better be something important. He says he hopes you're behaving yourself, Trask, and—" she turned to Nyctasia with a mocking grin— "he congratulates you on your coming marriage, Nyc."

◆　　◆　　◆

Nyctasia hadn't time to grant a personal interview to every student or scholar who sought to address her, and she was rather sharp with the clerk who informed her that a group of students was demanding to see her.

"What of it?" she said impatiently. "Students are always demanding to see me."

But these particular students, she was told, claimed to have been specially invited by Her Ladyship to visit her at court. "Impossible," said Nyctasia. "I summoned only certain select scholars, and if this lot were among them they'd have letters from me to prove it. You know that."

"Yes, my lady. But they assert that they met Your Ladyship last week in Rhostshyl Wood, and that you promised to receive them on your return. And they insist that Your Ladyship will confirm their story. Shall I send them away?"

Nyctasia began to laugh. "I beg your pardon, sir, they're quite right. I'd forgotten them. Show them in." So they'd found her out already. She must have been pointed out to them at a distance, as the Rhaicime. It would be amusing to see them again; they'd been a merry crew, and good company. And she was particularly interested in the man Wren, who'd interpreted her dream with such insight.

But to her disappointment he was not with the others, and they seemed to know very little about him. He and his companion had joined them on the road, and left them before they'd made their way to the palace. "But it was he who betrayed you to us, lady," one of them told her with a grin. "He said, 'It's no use your looking for the Rhaicime in Rhostshyl, she's on her way to the coast. That was she who crossed our path in the wood last night.' We thought he was daft, of course, but when we arrived here, we learned that Your Ladyship really wasn't at court, and no one knew where you'd gone."

"And then folk told us what the Rhaicime looked like—"

"We heard that she'd always a great guard-dog with her, too, just like our boastful palace scribe."

"So it seemed that Wren was right after all, but how in the *vahn's* name did he know, Rhaicime?"

Nyctasia's look was absorbed and pensive. "In the same way that he knew the meaning of my dream," she said quietly. "I hope our paths may cross again one day."

She soon sent the students to 'Malkin, who could be trusted to assess their abilities for her and find them work. He was really making himself quite useful, Nyctasia thought.

But the Master Scholars Anthorne and Tsephis had come to Rhostshyl at Nyctasia's express invitation, and were not to be so summarily dealt with. The pair were among the most celebrated of the scholar-physicians of the Imperial University, and only the opportunity to consult certain long-lost works of the legendary healer Iostyn Vahr could have drawn them from the capital to an insignificant coastal city-state like Rhostshyl.

After an exchange of formal courtesies, Nyctasia bade her distinguished guests be seated, and patiently answered their questions about the manuscripts from the Cymvelan library, before raising a concern of her own.

"I had, I confess, another reason for inviting you here," she said frankly. "A personal matter. My sister Tiambria is with child—her first. The women of my family have no unusual difficulties in giving birth, but as Tiambria is rather young, it would ease my mind a good deal if you would consider acting as her physicians."

"Youth is entirely in a mother's favor," Master Anthorne said curtly. "Are we to understand that you make it a condition that we be midwives to the Princess Tiambria, if we wish to make a study of these texts?" His command of Common Eswraine was stilted but flawless, and Nyctasia had no difficulty understanding him.

But she was accustomed to testing others, not to being tested herself. Matching his tone, she replied coldly, "Rhostshyl is not a monarchy, sir. Tiambria is a *Hlaven*, not a princess, and I have set no conditions whatsoever. It would be criminal, in my estimation, to deny such knowledge to any reputable scholar. I meant to ask as a favor that you undertake my sister's care, but much as I should like her to have the benefit of your skill, I would not allow anyone to attend her who did not wish to do so. That would hardly be to her good." She stood and bowed to her visitors in a manner that conveyed due respect, but little cordiality. "Arrangements will be made at once for you to see any of the Cymvelan books that interest you." *That should satisfy them*, she thought. *And put them in their place as well.*

The two scholars exchanged a look, then stood and returned Nyctasia's bow. "That being so, we shall be honored to serve as the Lady Tiambria's physicians," Dame Tsephis said with a smile.

Nyctasia had barely time to congratulate herself on the successful conclusion of this interview before a page announced the Lord Anseldon and the Lady Elissa. She sighed and took a moment to commune with the *vahn*, gathering her strength for another difficult encounter. But, contrary to the expectations of all concerned, the meeting did not prove unduly disagreeable or acrimonious.

Having spoken with Lhejadis, Anseldon and Elissa could no longer suspect Nyctasia of poisoning either her or the matriarch Mhairestri, and they had thus been forced to face the likelihood that she was guiltless where Emeryc's children and Erikasten were concerned as well. They found themselves in the uncomfortable position of owing her an apology for their previous accusations, and, being Edonaris, they would not shirk their duty.

But Nyctasia forestalled them by greeting them at once with humble and quite sincere apologies for having suspected them of poisoning Lhejadis in order to incriminate her. She too was reconsidering her views about the safety of the children.

After receiving her confession, it was far easier for Nyctasia's elders to make their own amends with grace. Mutually reassured, the three parted company on better terms and with more goodwill than at any time in the past.

All in all, Nyctasia felt that she'd earned a rest. She sent her page to order a hot bath.

18

For the first time, Nyctasia regretted having cut off her long hair, years ago, to defy her family and to allow her to disguise herself more easily as a common student or harper. At last lying once more beside Erystalben in her great bed, she would have liked to sweep her hair across his bare chest, as he'd always loved, but she contented herself with trailing her fingertips down his throat and along his collarbone. Her maid had considered it most improper to admit him while her mistress was bathing, but Nyctasia had thought it an excellent idea. Surely by now his arm must be nearly healed, she'd reasoned. . . .

He caught her hand and kissed it. "Now you'll have to take another bath," he teased.

"Mmm, so will you. You can share mine. You'll stay the night, 'Ben?"

"I may stay permanently, if you'll have me. I'm more welcome here than among the Shiastred."

"You've not remembered them, then?" Nyctasia asked, rather guiltily. Really, she thought, she might have given him a chance to tell her that before, instead of greeting him like a starving woman offered a leg of mutton.

He didn't answer at once, but drew her close again and toyed with the soft, crisp hair at the back of her neck. She smelled faintly of mint. "No," he said finally, "but it's not only that I don't remember them . . . what troubles me is that I don't particularly *like* them."

"But you never did. I told you that neither of us could get on with our families."

"You did, but I didn't realize . . . I've *heard* them at it, in the *vahn's* name! They either want to be rid of me altogether or use me to influence you. They deliberate over how secure your position is, because they're afraid to offend the ruler of the city by turning away her favorite. But if they acknowledge me as heir instead of Jhasteine, they may forfeit the alliance with the House of Lesevern—and then suppose you fall from power?" His voice was disdainful, but Nyctasia could feel the anger in his hands. "None of them cares a straw whether I'm Lord Descador's son or not, only whether I'd be an advantage or disadvantage to the House of Shiastred. It's not quite the homecoming I'd anticipated."

"I'm sorry, 'Ben. I tried to warn you. They'd accept you readily enough, I daresay, if you abandoned your claim to the Jhaicery."

"I've done so already, it would seem. They say that Lord Erystalben renounced his position formally before he left the city. But did he—did I? How am I to know?"

"If you did, you said nothing to me about it. Still, you might well have done so. It would have been the responsible step to take, since you didn't intend to return. And you always felt that you'd have no time for your studies, as head of the House of Shiastred. But if you doubt their word, I can see to it that they recognize you as heir to the Jhaicery, never fear. It's for you to say."

"A pox on the Jhaicery, and the Shiastred with it! I don't know that I want any part of them, even if they are my kin."

Nyctasia kissed the corner of his mouth. "Then stay with me, 'Ben," she murmured.

"As your consort, perhaps? You didn't tell me, in Chiastelm, that you were soon to be married to the ruler of Ochram."

"Am I never to hear the end of Aithrenn brenn Ochram! I didn't tell you of the matter because I never gave it a thought. Nothing whatsoever has been settled, or even discussed yet, but even if I marry the High Lord, that's of no consequence to us. You know a marriage-treaty's purely traditional—it means nothing."

He was silent for so long that Nyctasia grew anxious. She knew that he was not asleep. "'Ben? Answer me, love. I'd refuse the alliance for your sake if I were free, but I must do whatever's best for the city—I've no choice. Rhostshyl is your rival, not Lord Aithrenn."

"But will your bodyguard allow the union?" he asked with bitter humor.

"That's what she asked me about you."

He sighed. "I've no right to make demands on you, I know that," he said resignedly, but broke out in frustration, "If I could but feel that anything here belonged to me! Rhostshyl promised me all, but it's given me only a family I can't care for, a title I can't lay claim to, a woman I can't make my wife—*Vahn* help me, if only I could feel that I belonged here—!"

I'm going to lose him again, Nyctasia thought with a sudden hopeless conviction. She held tightly to him and said, "Perhaps you will remember in time, 'Ben. You've not been here long. The city may yet awaken your memories."

"You don't believe that, do you?" It was not really a question.

The time had come to tell him the truth, Nyctasia saw. "No," she said gently. "I'm not at all certain what to expect, but I don't believe that you'll recover your past without some further sacrifice. A spell of Perilous Threshold does not return what it has taken."

He had grown so still that she could barely feel him breathe. "What sort of sacrifice?" he demanded in a low hiss.

"I don't know. I've made little study of spellcasting, and still less of spellbreaking, but . . ." She too let her voice sink to a whisper. "I have books here that belonged to the Cymvelans, and you might find the answer to such a question among them."

"Books? What books are they?"

"Such books as Khressen's *On the Securing and Sundering of Spells*, and the forbidden *Mastery of the Invited Powers*."

"No one has those books, they were destroyed—" Yet until she had named them, he had not realized that he'd ever heard of them.

"The Cymvelan Circle had them still, and I keep them now—under lock and key, you may be sure. I've shown them to no one. I haven't read them myself, nor do I mean to read them, but you may do so if you choose—if there's no other way." It might be a mistake, but it was the only hope she had left to offer him. "You know what they are, 'Ben. Do you want to read them?"

"I have to read them!" he said passionately. "I have to know who I am, now. I could just bear to be a stranger to myself when I was among strangers, but here where I'm known to others, yet know them not, it's maddening. Whatever the price, I must believe I'm Erystalben if I'm to live his life. No one else—not even you—can believe that for me. If the books can give me that, I must have them, don't you understand?"

Nyctasia could only embrace him and promise, "I'll try, love. I'll try." Then they were locked together again. Yet lying in his arms at last, in her great bed, as close to him as she could be, she sensed once more the growing distance between them.

19

"Wren . . . !" said Nyctasia. "*Aithrenn*, of course. How blind I've been! I can't even accuse you of duplicity, my lord, since I was equally guilty. But you had the advantage of me, it seems. How did you know me?"

Lord Aithrenn chuckled, enjoying her astonishment. "You'd been described to me, my lady—dog and all. And the way you talked of the Rhaicime made me suspect you as well. But I wasn't sure of you until the next morning, when you described your dream, that all of Rhostshyl followed you to the sea, rejoicing."

"But I never told you that! I said only that Rhostshyl marched to the sea, not that I led the way or that it was a festal procession." She had chosen her words deliberately at the time, and remembered them.

Leaning toward her, serious now, he said, "There was no need for you to tell me, Rhaicime, for I knew. I had the same dream that night—that the people of Ochram journeyed with me to the gates of Rhostshyl, coming after me with song and celebration." He sat back again, silent, allowing Nyctasia time to realize the significance of his words. He knew exactly what they would mean to her.

Nyctasia too was silent for a time, lost in thought. But now her thoughts were fixed on the future, after dwelling so long on the past. At last she said, "It would seem that this decision has already been made for us. Are you satisfied with your scrutiny of Rhostshyl? You've seen the destruction and poverty in the city?"

He nodded. "It was no more than I expected to see. The one thing that surprised me was the talk of invasion from Heithskor."

"Why, my rumor-mongers have done well, if you heard that! But it's all moonshine and mirrors, I assure you, devised to unite the troublesome factions in the city. If the governors of Heithskor thought to take advantage of Rhostshyl's weakened state, the power of the Alliance would soon change their minds, as you know. Only the consequences of our civil warfare need concern you."

"As to that, this proposal of mine *is* one such consequence. Before Rhostshyl's ruin, the Rhaicimate would never have entertained the idea of union with another municipality. It is I who seek to take advantage of Rhostshyl's losses."

He was right, Nyctasia realized. The very people who now urged her to accept his offer would have scorned it when Rhostshyl's power was at its height. No other city—not even the thriving port of Ochram—would have been thought worthy to share that power. Not without reason had Rhostshyl been called the proud city.

But now the advantage seemed all the other way. "I see the benefit of such a union for Rhostshyl," she admitted, "but what does Ochram stand to gain by it now?"

"Oh, a great deal, Rhaicime, I trust. Prestige, for one thing. Rhostshyl has not lost her name and reputation. But that is the least of it. Ochram is built on the rock of the coast—we need grain and dairy-goods that we can't produce ourselves. We need arable land." He held up a hand to forestall Nyctasia's objection. "I'm aware that Rhostshyl hasn't food enough for her own people at present, but that will not always be so. When her estates are again fully cultivated, they can easily supply Ochram with farmstuffs—at favorable terms of trade, of course. By the same token, we will gain a ready market for our imported goods and fish, offered on the same terms."

Nyctasia only nodded encouragingly and said, "Yes?" as a polite indication that she was still waiting for him to come to the point. Mutual trading privileges were all very well, but they did not require two cities to merge their interests to the extent of a bond of union.

Lord Aithrenn sipped his wine and continued in the same unhurried manner, "More than prestige or provisions, however, Ochram needs space to grow. We are hemmed in on three sides by the sea and the cliffs, and by Rhostshyl Wood on the fourth. Our success as a mercantile port has swelled our populace beyond what our borders can reasonably hold, but we're unable to expand those borders. The city's growing too crowded already, and that leads, of course, to crime and sickness. Now, Rhostshyl has recently suffered a great loss of her citizenry. If the two cities were one, under the law, our people could make good that loss, without forfeiting their guild-rights or violating yours."

"So you mean to swallow up Rhostshyl on your way east, do you?" said Nyctasia, sounding amused. "Yet my advisors believe—and I agree—that if the two do indeed become one, that one will be Rhostshyl. This city too is growing, sir. Since you traveled here with a band of students, you must know something of the scholarly work being carried out at court?"

"My claims to scholarship are as modest as Your Ladyship's are renowned, but I have heard reports that you were in possession of the fabled Cymvelan library. It seems to be more than idle talk."

"It is indeed. Many of the greatest scholars living are gathering here to consult the Cymvelan books, and I intend to make it worth their while to stay. And where scholars go, naturally students follow. My intention is no less than to make Rhostshyl the center of learning in the west, to rival Celys in the east."

"Why, this becomes more and more interesting," Lord Aithrenn said thoughtfully. "In a word, you are speaking of the Maritime University."

"Exactly! If my plans bear fruit, Rhostshyl will become a far more important and illustrious city than she ever was before. Ochram may be no more than the portal to Rhostshyl, in days to come."

He waved this aside with a smile. "Ochram would be a great trading harbor, with or without Rhostshyl in our backyard. This design of yours, should it come to pass, will be altogether in our interests. The students you anticipate will naturally dock at Ochram on their way to the university. And just as students follow scholars, merchants and artisans follow students. Rhostshyl will need bookbinders, copyists, victualers, clothiers, shoemakers. . . ."

"Very likely we shall. And of course guild-rights would be extended to the tradesfolk of Ochram, were we bound by such ties as you propose. But do not deceive yourself that you will be allied to a dying city, or that you will build on her ashes."

Lord Aithrenn grinned. "Certainly not, Rhaicime. Such an idea never entered my mind. In witness to which, you will find me as determined as ever to pursue the treaty, despite your plan to restore Rhostshyl's fortunes by bringing down a horde of students upon us. We'll have to double the night watch, I suppose."

"Or lock up our young people," Nyctasia agreed. "But students are free with their money, whatever else may be said against them." She raised her goblet to click against his. "Then as long as we understand one another, sir, let us leave to posterity to see which city will devour the other. We can relieve you of some of your overflowing populace, and grant tracts of land for your use as well—particularly if you employ Rhost-shylid laborers to clear it and harvest your crops."

"Willingly," he said, "but as to clearing the land, now, that brings me to the most important of Ochram's needs that Rhostshyl may fulfill."

At last, thought Nyctasia, and said, "I am all attention, sir."

"Wood," said Lord Aithrenn, striking his hand against the arm of his chair. "Wood for the shipyards of Ochram. At present, we have to bring timber from the south, at great expense—with Rhostshyl Wood at our very doorstep! Hitherto, the Rhaicimate has been adamant in its refusal to allow the trees to be felled, but now, surely Your Ladyship will agree, Rhostshyl needs the revenues more than the forestland."

"The woods are valuable hunting-grounds," Nyctasia explained, and this time it was she who gestured for him to hear her out. "But there could be no possible objection to the clearing of a road through Rhostshyl Wood—on the contrary, a road is precisely what my plans require. It's absurd for travelers to have to skirt the wood or brave the bandits. Rhostshyl should be directly linked to the seaways, all the more so if we're to join our two cities. What's wanted is a broad, safe thoroughfare, one that can't easily be ambushed by robbers. It should be patrolled by road wards day and night, so that even a lone student, who doesn't know a sword from a spindle, may travel it without peril. Of course, to accomplish this, a wide swath through the wood would have to be cleared of timber. I've long contemplated the need for a direct route to the coast, but I lack the resources to carry out such an undertaking, since the war has depleted the City Treasury."

"Yet from what I've seen in the streets of Rhostshyl, you have people enough who'd be glad of the work."

"The difficulty is not in finding laborers, but in feeding them. Now Ochram, as Your Lordship has been at some pains to point out, is a wealthy and flourishing city. A roadway to Rhostshyl would benefit your people as well."

Lord Aithrenn surrendered with a laugh. "So you'll have a road and food for the hungry of Rhostshyl."

"And you will have a road and wood for the shipwrights of Ochram. I feel confident that we can reach mutually acceptable terms in this matter." She consulted a list she had drawn up earlier, and asked, "Have you made a study of Rhostshyl's laws? I am not, I must admit, familiar with those of Ochram. There may be differences which will have to be reconciled if our people are to enjoy citizenship of both municipalities."

"The disparities are mainly minor, but in certain cases the laws of Rhostshyl are considerably more lenient than our own. I've been trying to bring about these very changes for some time, and I have been opposed by influential merchant interests on the City Council, but now I mean to take this opportunity to get my way. The Council wants the alliance with Rhostshyl, you see. I shall report to them, with your leave, that you make it a condition of your consent to the treaty that our laws be brought into conformity with those of Rhostshyl in these particulars. You would oblige me by confirming this fiction."

"Done," Nyctasia said with relief. "Consider it an unalterable demand on my part, sir."

"Many thanks, Rhaicime. Shall we say spring for the ceremony, in keeping with tradition?"

"An auspicious time. My sister's child is due in the spring. You have been told, I trust, that I myself am barren? You must not look for an heir from this union of ours."

He shook his head. "I've heirs enough to satisfy the city."

Nyctasia knew a moment's confusion before she realized that when he said "the city," he meant of course Ochram, not

Rhostshyl. "My late brother's daughter is my heir," she informed him, "unless my sister should bear more than one girl-child before my niece comes of age. I've never thought that likely, as we are not a prolific family, but then neither did I think to see her with child so soon, so I suppose that anything may yet happen. Our lines of descent must be made clear and indisputable by treaty, lest either side should try to lay claim to rule of both cities, in the future, and set off wars of sovereignty."

"True," he said soberly. "We don't want to repeat the wars of Kehs-Edre. Far safer not to mix our lines, now or in later generations. Perhaps we can establish a prohibition to that effect. But our envoys can attend to these details, if you and I are agreed as to the essentials."

"I believe we are," said Nyctasia. "In the spring, then?"

"In the spring. I shall, of course, send you a formal invitation to make a state visit to Ochram in the meantime."

"I shall look forward to it, sir."

Lord Aithrenn kissed her hand, and she suddenly began to laugh. At his quizzical look, she shook her head helplessly and said, "Forgive me—everything seems to be happening so quickly. I was thinking of a time when I was first learning to ride, and a horse ran away with me. No one could catch the beast, and I didn't know how to control its flight, so I just held fast and kept my seat as best I could. In my ignorance, I had great faith that my mount knew what it was about.

"In time it stopped to graze in a field, while I waited to see what it would do next, and my people caught up to me. I don't recall what my feelings were, but I'm told that I said, 'How exciting, but it makes one quite giddy, doesn't it?' I had no idea at all what danger I'd been in. And now I feel my plans have run away with me. . . . We can only hold tight and hope that all turns out well. It's exhilarating, without doubt, but it *does* make one giddy!"

20

Matters continued to progress at a dizzying pace during the months that followed, and Nyctasia was kept so busy that she was hardly aware of the passage of time, as autumn gave way to winter, and winter wore on toward spring. Preparations for the marriage-alliance alone could have occupied most of her hours, had there not been so many other claims on her attention as well. Not only must arrangements be made for the ceremony itself, but the terms of the treaty necessitated endless discussions of diplomatic precedents and jurisdictions. Dignitaries from Ochram arrived almost daily to confer with Nyctasia and her advisors. It was settled at last that the formalities would begin in Rhostshyl with Nyctasia's vows, carried out in a simple court ritual, and would then proceed to Ochram for the conclusion of the solemnities, and the festivities to follow. This arrangement satisfied the counselors of both parties by giving precedence to Rhostshyl, but prominence to Ochram. For the court and Council of Ochram meant to host an impressive celebration that would demonstrate to the entire Alliance the importance of their city. A tournament of sporting contests would be held, musicians, acrobats and troupes of actors would perform, and all the city would be feasted amid revelry and splendor. Nyctasia was only grateful that the City Treasury of Rhostshyl would be spared the expense of such extravagant displays. She was officially invited to the court of the High Lord, she duly accepted, and the visit took place and was over all in a few days' time. Corson accompanied her as bodyguard, but Nyctasia refused absolutely to bring Trask along. She promised, however, to let him come to Ochram for the wedding.

Scholars from near and far continued to gather in Rhostshyl, even during the winter, when the traveling was most difficult. As their numbers grew, so grew Nyctasia's confidence that her dream of the Maritime University would indeed be realized. She began to speak of it openly, consulting with those who came from Celys, and from most she met with an enthusiasm for the idea as keen as her own. To be part of the creation of a new university was an unheard of opportunity for a scholar to achieve a position of influence and authority. Nyctasia, who had never been to the Imperial University herself, needed a good deal of advice about how such an institution should be governed, and her learned visitors were more than willing to supply it. She sent for architects, and commissioned plans for the great halls she hoped to have built, just outside the city walls. At times the Fourteenth Divination haunted her with its mocking uncertainty. When she had cast the lots, years ago, to learn whether she would ever attend the University, she had received only that same unsatisfactory answer, but now she was struck by its unexpected fitness. True, she had not been granted her desire to study at Celys, but it began to seem ever more likely that she would, after a fashion, attend the University. . . .

Corson came and went during the winter months, usually bringing Trask, who was always eager to show Nyctasia his latest accomplishment. "Steifann's vexed with you, Nyc, for letting him learn to read," Corson told her. "Now he has to lock up his letters, or that one will read them out to the whole taproom."

"That wasn't my doing, far from it," Nyctasia objected. "Tell Steifann he'd do better to leave the letters lying about, and lock up Trask instead."

Though the time sped for Nyctasia, to Corson the winter seemed to drag on endlessly. It was a relief to be able to escape to the court now and then, when life at The Jugged Hare began to feel too confining. It was no time for long journeys, but an occasional visit to Rhostshyl helped to satisfy her restlessness, and she was always willing to escort Nyctasia's couriers to and from Ochram. Her appearances were frequently a relief to Nyctasia as well, for Corson often took it upon herself to rescue her from the others, the better to have Nyctasia's attention to herself.

As spring approached, Tiambria complacently grew enormous, but remained as willful and lively as ever, scorning all suggestions that she rest quietly and let others tend to her. She declared that she felt wonderfully well, and worried her young husband Jehamias to distraction. Nyctasia too was rather alarmed for her, though she concealed her fears from Jehamias, but Master Anthorne and Dame Tsephis informed her that nothing was amiss, and that the signs were all favorable.

"The physicians say we're to let her do as she likes," Nyctasia assured Jehamias. "And we may as well accept their advice, since she'll do as she likes anyway."

Corson too had her say on the matter. "Physicians are all very well when you're sick or wounded," she stated, "but your sister's not ailing, she's just carrying a child. What good are a lot of leeches to her? What she wants is a good midwife."

Nyctasia felt as surprised as if Greymantle had offered his opinion. "Corson, you amaze me. How do *you* know about such things?"

"I don't. But Walden does. He said to tell you to send for his wife Omia. She doesn't usually go so far as Rhostshyl, but Walden says she'll come as a favor, since you're a friend of the house."

"I'm honored," said Nyctasia, "but tell them they needn't worry. I have the best midwives in Rhostshyl at hand. The physicians will only assist in case of need."

"The best in Rhostshyl, maybe, but I'll wager that among the lot of them they've not borne as many brats as Omia—nor birthed as many. And she's never lost a babe, nor a mother either. Oh, Walden wants her to have the glory of delivering a baby Rhaicime, I know, but all the same he's right. There's no better midwife on the coast. Anyone in Chiastelm will tell you the same."

Nyctasia asked only one person in Chiastelm, and when Maegor sent back a message warmly confirming Corson's claims, she quickly made arrangements to accept Mistress Omia's services. In days to come, she would employ such magical healing arts as she possessed on Tiambria's behalf, but at present she had done all in her power for her sister.

With all these matters to attend to, Nyctasia saw little of Erystalben, who found that the Rhaicime of Rhostshyl was a different woman from the mistress of the Smugglers' House. It was one thing to be on intimate terms with a stranger who cared for one, and quite another thing to make claims on the time of the ruler of a city. He immersed himself in study of the books of spells and counterspells that now seemed to hold his only hope. He had not yet remembered anything of his past, and his dreams of the Yth had not ceased. Nyctasia saw him growing more distant and withdrawn, but with the passing of the winter she had less time than ever to devote to him.

When she received word from Corson that another shipment of books had arrived at the Hare, Nyctasia was astonished to realize that the trade route through the Valleylands to the east must have been clear for some time. The spring thaw had come sooner than seemed possible. She could not spare the time to go collect the books herself, but she sent 'Malkin to take charge of them, and gave him a letter to deliver to Corson as well.

'Malkin was still curious about The Jugged Hare. Nothing in Trask's descriptions of the tavern had made it clear to him why the Rhaicime of Rhostshyl should make a habit of visiting the place, nor had the sight of the Hare itself explained the mystery. It was perhaps a little larger, and cleaner, than most—clearly a prosperous concern—but still it was only a common ale-house like hundreds of others he'd frequented in his student days. Hardly the haunt of Rhaicimes, he thought. 'Malkin had been in far shabbier establishments, and more recently than he'd have cared to admit, but after his months at court, the Hare looked barely respectable to him. He felt an unwonted sympathy for Trask.

He'd arrived in Chiastelm too late in the day to think of starting back till the morrow, so he'd taken a room at one of the better inns, then had a meal, bathed and changed his travel-worn clothes before going about his business. He didn't expect anyone at the Hare to notice or care how he looked, but as the Lady Nyctasia's courier and emissary it behooved him to make a decent appearance nevertheless. It was therefore nearly closing time before he arrived at the Hare, and the taproom was almost empty. Corson was nowhere to be seen, but 'Malkin recognized Steifann from Trask's description and asked him where Corson might be found.

Steifann regarded him with marked disfavor. Not the usual sort of good-for-nothing reaver Corson kept company with, but a scoundrel of some sort, no doubt. "You're not a Rhaicime in disguise, are you?" he asked with a scowl.

"Er . . . no, unfortunately," said 'Malkin.

"Good. The last time I threw one of Corson's lovers out of here, it turned out I was dealing with a Rhaicime, and it was an awkward business all 'round. But you—"

"The Lady Nyctasia, do you mean?" 'Malkin interrupted, diplomatically ignoring the threat against himself. "Did you actually lay hands on her? I took her for a servant-wench myself when I first saw her, and gave her a friendly pat on the posterior. Now *that* was awkward if you like—"

"Oh, you're that one," said Steifann. "Well, I wouldn't think you'd want anything to do with Corson, then."

"I don't," said 'Malkin, with unmistakable sincerity. "But I have to fetch Lady Nyctasia's books from her, and deliver a letter to her. If I had my way, she'd be food for crows. Of all the insufferable savages it has ever been my misfortune to meet, that one is the most treacherous and vicious!"

Far from resenting this vilification of Corson's character, Steifann altogether approved of 'Malkin's attitude. There were far too few people, in his opinion, who wanted nothing to do with Corson. "Isn't she, though?" he said genially. "I don't know why I put up with her. Once the City Governors made me close my doors for a week after a fight she started in here. Fined me a pretty penny, too. I sent her packing then and there, I can tell you, but no matter how often I put her out, she always turned up again."

"That's nothing to the trouble she can cause! We were both jailed for nearly a fortnight in Larkmere, once, because she attacked an officer of the night watch. And that wasn't the worst of it—"

Steifann clapped him on the shoulder. "Come have a drink! Corson's in the back. Trask!" he called, "Fetch some of Nyc's fancy wine for our guest!"

"Why, it's 'Malkin. What are you doing here?" Corson

asked. "Have you lost your place at court already? We could do with another scullion, if you're out of work."

"I've come for Nyc's books, of course," 'Malkin said curtly, sounding as if he had never referred to Nyctasia in any other way.

Taking his cue from this, Trask said—omitting the "sir"— "'Malkin, welcome to the Hare! It's not the palace, perhaps, but we serve as fine a wine as you'll find outside the Valleylands." He poured 'Malkin a generous measure of a tawny gold wine, and presented it to him with a playful bow.

"This *is* good," he said appreciatively. "It has a nice bite to it."

"That's why they named it after me," Corson said with a snap of her teeth.

"We were just talking of you," said Steifann. "Our friend here was telling me a most interesting tale. Let's have the rest of it."

He and 'Malkin were soon exchanging stories like old acquaintances, vying to tell the worst tale of Corson's misdeeds and evil temper. Corson denied most of it, but no one heeded her, and the others soon began to contribute details to Steifann's accounts, or relate episodes of their own.

"Don't forget the first time she came in here, either," Walden put in. "We knew then that Steifann had met his match at last."

"Now that was all your fault, 'Malkin," said Corson. "It was not long after I parted from you, and I was doing everything you disapproved of, just to spite you—gambling and drinking and looking for trouble—"

"I remember that night!" Trask said gleefully. "She looked like a drowned cat. Stinking drunk, too, and she ate a lot of food without paying for it—"

"Then she had the gall to flirt with me," Annin recalled. "Without a penny in her pockets, either!"

"Steifann tried to throw her out, but she got the better of him."

"She fights dirty," Steifann explained. "Very dirty. Filthy." It was one of his favorite stories.

"She all but tore the place apart," said Walden. "Chairs and tables went flying—"

"Only one table," Corson protested.

"Then she *chased* Steifann into his room," Trask continued, "and they didn't come out for a week."

"Now *that's* not so," said Steifann. "It can't have been more than two or three days."

Walden took up the tale again. "And then they staggered into my kitchen one morning with their arms 'round each other, grinning like a pair of idiots, and all he said was, 'This is Corson. She's going to stay for a while.' Then they ate everything in sight and disappeared for another few days."

"Well, what could *I* do?" Steifann asked innocently. "She took advantage of me. I can hold my own against a dozen common brawlers in a fistfight, but that one's a trained killer. I was just a helpless victim of—"

The others hooted him down.

"I was a little wild in those days," Corson admitted, when the tumult subsided.

"Huh—you're not what I'd call a ewe-lamb nowadays either," said Steifann.

"Well, I can't help that. Nyc says I'm encourageable."

"*Incorrigible*," 'Malkin sighed. "Here, I'd almost forgotten, Nyc sent you this letter."

Corson read it through quickly and started to laugh. "It's an invitation to the celebration of the marriage-alliance," she reported. "Nyc wants me on hand, in case there's trouble, and I'm to bring Omia to Rhostshyl because she may be wanted at any time. Then she says that anyone else who wants to see the festivities should come along, and—listen to this—'but under no circumstances should you neglect to bring Trask'! What do you make of that?"

"Corson! Does it really say that?" Trask demanded.

"See for yourself—you're such a keen reader." Trask grabbed the letter and began to spell it out, muttering to himself. Corson turned to 'Malkin. "I suppose Nyc's betrothal has kept you out of her bed, eh?"

He shook his head regretfully. "No, it's Lord Erystalben who's done that. The betrothal's merely a formality, but Shiastred's another matter. When she has time to think of anyone, she thinks of him and no one else. It's certainly a pity. We were getting on so well before he appeared." He spoke as one disappointed, not of a romance but of an opportunity.

"Cir-cum-stan-ces," Trask read triumphantly, then suggested to 'Malkin, "You could poison him."

"That's not much in my line, I'm afraid. But perhaps someone else will do it for me. I'm not the only one inconvenienced by his return. They say there'll be trouble if he tries to press his claim to the Jhaicery. As for me, I have the University to console me. I'll be one of the Master Scholars of Rhostshyl—a provost at least, if not a chancellor. I could never have attained such a position in Celys, where I'm not known to anyone of importance. Yes, I know it was your doing that I'm known to the Rhaicime, Corson, you needn't remind me."

Corson grinned. "I was just going to ask, Master Scholar, do you want to see Nyc's books now? They're locked up safely. I haven't let Trask get at them."

"I wouldn't have hurt them," Trask complained. "I've finished with the things you gave me, 'Malkin. There's no library here, you know. How am I supposed to practice?"

"Not with these books," 'Malkin said firmly. "I'll send you some new texts to work on, but you stay out of the Rhaicime's books if you want to stay out of trouble, my lad." He finished his wine and followed Corson to Steifann's quarters to inspect the shipment, checking each volume against a list. When he was done, he replaced them carefully in the chest and relocked it. "It's probably safest to leave them here till tomorrow," he said as they returned to the kitchen. "The *vahn* knows where my escort is spending the night."

"I'll bring them 'round to you in the morning," Corson offered, "so you can make an early start. Tell Nyc I'll—no, I'll give you a letter for her! I need to practice my penmanship."

"Very well. I'm staying at The Golden Arrow," 'Malkin said, with a glance at Trask. He thanked Steifann cordially for his hospitality and wished the company a good night.

Trask looked after him wistfully. If he was really to attend Nyc's wedding ceremony, he had a dozen questions to ask 'Malkin, but there was all the evening's cleaning yet to be done, to ready the tavern for tomorrow. He sighed and picked up a broom, wondering if he could get away without mopping the taproom.

But Annin, who didn't miss much, took the broom from him and shooed him out with it. "Run along then, and catch him—we can do well enough without you," she said briskly. "You'd not do a good job of it anyway."

21

Nyctasia was wakened by the unexpected warmth of the early spring night. She pushed away the covers, taking care not to wake 'Ben, and drew back the bedcurtains to let in the mild breeze from the open windows. The heavy weight across her feet proved to be Greymantle who, as usual, had managed to climb onto the bed during the night. He jumped down, at Nyctasia's kick, and curled up with a sigh on the sheepskin rug at the bedside.

By hearth-light and moonlight she looked at 'Ben to see if he was sleeping peacefully. She herself was always so exhausted of late that she slept easily and well, but 'Ben often slept fitfully, still plagued by cruel doubts and dreams. She had more than once awakened in the night to find that he was no longer beside her but had gone to pace the garden walks alone, or had returned to the library to pursue his studies by candlelight.

Watching him sleep, Nyctasia was as much struck by his dark beauty as when they had first met. He bore scars now that she had not seen before, but he rarely spoke of what had befallen him during the last two years, and she did not press him to do so. He seemed as anxious to forget his recent past as

to remember the rest, and he could no more do the one than the
other. His search of the Cymvelan books had thus far suggested
only one way to break the spell that bound him—to return to
the Yth where that spell was evoked.

"It is, in essence, a question of elemental Balance," he'd
told Nyctasia. "To regain what I've lost, I must give up what
I've gained. I never won my freedom from the Yth; I took it,
and paid too dearly for it. But if I surrender it, I may gain it
again—on my own terms, this time." He had determined to
wait only until the roads were clear in the spring and start for
Hlasven then, if he still had remembered nothing and had
discovered no other solution.

He'd informed Nyctasia of this decision only a fortnight
before. "I'm not wanted here, you know it as well as I," he
said. "For the *vahn's* sake, Lord Descador has offered to pay
me to go!"

"*I* want you here," Nyctasia had answered fiercely, but he
shook his head and looked away.

"No, you want *him*—Erystalben. When you look at me, you
see him, and your face lights. But then you remember who I
am, and your look turns to pity. You once told me that
Rhostshyl was my rival for your love, but Shiastred is my true
rival. Can you understand how jealous I am of the man I was?"

"I know what you suffer, 'Ben, and I suffer with you. It is
pain you read in my eyes, not pity. Yes, I want you to recover
the past we shared, but I want it for your sake, not for my own.
To me you are Erystalben whether you remember or not, and
I'm afraid, 'Ben—afraid that if you return to the Yth, alone,
you may find yourself again, but I may lose you again. If
there's no other way, then wait until I can go with you—"

"What do you take me for, 'Tasia? I'd not let you risk the
Yth on my account!"

"Two together are far safer against the Yth, believe me. I
know the ways of the Yth now, and I don't fear its tricks. With
my help, you may find what you seek, but you know that I
cannot leave the city now, with so many things unsettled. Wait
a year—less, perhaps. Once Tiambria's child has been born,
and Jehamias has come of age . . . when the alliance with
Ochram is on firm ground, and the University well enough
established that I can appoint chancellors to look after its
interests in my absence. Wait until then, and I swear this time
I'll not fail you."

He had neither consented to this appeal nor refused it, but Nyctasia was confident that she had persuaded him to stay, at least for the present. If only she felt as confident that she had been right to do so. . . . She was troubled by his continued preoccupation with the dangerous Cymvelan books, and she knew that he was still tormented by nightmares of the Yth. It seemed all too likely that he would not be free of them until he returned there, and Balance was restored . . . Even as she lay looking at him now, she saw him shudder in the grip of a dream, and he whispered, "Old, so old! No, it can't be!"

He'd thought he had been wandering through the Forest for an hour at most, but when he saw himself in the pool, his reflection was that of an aged man, and he knew that he had been lost in the Yth for years, for scores of years. He woke suddenly with a frightened gasp, and said wildly to Nyctasia, "I'm old, old! It's too late!"

She drew him to the side of the bed and pointed to her tall, shining mirror. "Look at yourself, love. You've not changed."

He stared into the mirror for a long while, then said with a deadly calm, "I'm sorry I wakened you, 'Tasia, you need your rest. Go back to sleep—I'll get on with my work. I'll not sleep again tonight." He rose to return to the library, nearly falling over Greymantle, but Nyctasia held him back. She suddenly knew just how to make him forget his evil dream.

"You didn't wake me," she said. "The warm spring air did that. Don't you feel it? It's so beautiful, there's a breeze that smells of blossoms. . . . It gave me the most splendid idea about how we might pass the rest of the night—a far better idea than yours. I didn't like to wake you, but now that you're awake anyway . . ." She leaned close and whispered her suggestion, circling his waist with her arms and nuzzling his ear.

He laughed softly. "Mad Lass, I almost believe you're in earnest."

"But I am. Why shouldn't we? It's a fine, fair night. What better way to spend it?"

"I can't think of one," Erystalben admitted. "Very well, but on one condition—that hound of yours stays here!"

Despite the late hour, there were others stealing through the gardens to enjoy the inviting night, Nyctasia noticed with amusement. "How everyone always carries me about," she murmured dreamily, cradled in Erystalben's arms like a child.

"Everyone? Who else has been carrying you about, pray?"

"Why . . . no one else," said Nyctasia, puzzled by her own remark. "I don't know why I said that. I must have been talking in my sleep." But why had she felt that someone had carried her somewhere, not so very long ago? "My brother Emeryc once carried me out here at night, but that was when we were children. He wanted to show me the game of floating candle-ends downstream in the dark, but of course the night air was thought to be bad for me, so we had to sneak out of the palace in the dead of night. Then he carried me, lest my nurse should see my slippers wet with dew."

"A brother's right I'll allow," Erystalben conceded. "But henceforth no one is to carry you anywhere without my leave." His arms tightened around her as he spoke, and Nyctasia smiled to herself in the darkness.

"I'll issue an edict to that effect," she promised. "I'll appoint you First Bearer to the Rhaicime, with all the dues, duties, obligations, rights, perquisites and prerogatives pertaining to the office."

"And what are the duties and prerogatives of the position?"

"I shall explain them all to you presently—in private," said Nyctasia.

She had shown him the walled garden once, during the winter, and he went directly to it now, only pausing to let Nyctasia take the key from its hiding-place. Not until they were within its walls did he set her down, kneeling to lay her on the young spring grass, and kissing her eyes and lips before he released her. Nyctasia clung to him, but he laughed and said, "I think I should close the door, don't you?"

"Be quick about it, then," Nyctasia ordered. But before he could obey, two darkly cloaked and hooded figures slipped swiftly through the door and blocked the way, daggers drawn at the ready. Nyctasia had time for only a moment's regret that she hadn't heeded Corson's warnings more faithfully. Neither she nor Erystalben was armed. "Teiryn or Edonaris?" she demanded, scrambling to her feet.

"Shiastred, I think," said Erystalben. As the two started forward, he took a step toward them, as if to meet their attack, but the intruders never reached their quarry. They crumpled suddenly to the ground, without a cry, before they even came within striking distance of Erystalben. "You should not have persuaded me to stay, 'Tasia," he said. "The delay has made Jhasteine impatient."

Nyctasia let fall the handful of earth she had seized to throw, and slowly came to stand at his side. One look at the attackers was sufficient. She did not trouble to listen for their heartbeats. "'Ben," she said heavily, "what bargain have you made?"

He put his arm around her shoulders. "Do not ask that if you prefer not to hear the answer, love." When she made no reply, he asked, "Should I have let them kill us both?"

Nyctasia turned away. "Do what you must, 'Ben, but not here. Not in my city. Take the books and go."

Outside the garden, he took her in his arms again. "Am I to come back, when I can claim what is mine in my own name?"

Holding tight to him, Nyctasia thought, *'Ben, where are you? Yes, come back to me. You have never come back to me.* But aloud she said, "I command you to do so. Who is to be my Bearer, if not you? And always let me know where you are—always. It may yet be that I shall come to you."

She had the unknown attackers buried secretly in the garden, then locked the door and threw the key over the wall. She knew that it would be many years before anything grew there again.

22

Nyctasia made good her promise to bring Trask to Ochram for the celebration of the marriage-alliance. He was not allowed to attend the court ceremony in Rhostshyl, but Corson, who was present as Guard of Honor, assured him that the proceedings had been nothing but dull talk and bowing.

But the festivities in Ochram more than made up for this disappointment. The spectacle and pageantry were all that he'd hoped, even surpassing the magnificence of the wedding of Lady Tiambria and Lord Jehamias. As a member of Nyctasia's retinue, Trask was a guest of the court, and was admitted everywhere. He found himself mingling with folk of every degree, and—thanks to 'Malkin—he knew better than to make any extravagant claims about his own position. When asked about his place in the Rhaicime's party, he merely replied with charming humility that he was no one at all, a lowly commoner of no family, in whom the Lady Nyctasia had been kind enough to take an interest. This ingenuous response had just the touch of truth needed to make it acceptable, without actually revealing anything about Trask's social standing. 'Malkin was of course too occupied with courting patrons of his own to have time for Trask, but when he happened to encounter his pupil he felt that Trask was doing him credit, and gave him a wink of encouragement.

Nyctasia had never taken an interest in him before, but it would seem that she did so now. It must be the manners he'd learned from 'Malkin that had changed her mind, Trask thought. She had sent for him specially, after all, and even seen that he was provided with a suit of beautiful new clothes for the occasion. Trask loved these elegant garments, though left to his own devices he would probably have chosen something a good deal more showy. 'Malkin had told him that ostentation in dress was in poor taste, and Trask accepted the idea, but he couldn't help thinking it a shame that folk who could afford brightly-dyed stuffs should content themselves with dull colors. Still, he had no fault to find with the butter-yellow silk shirt he'd been given, which made his hair glow like molten gold. Even Corson had been impressed when he'd shown off his new outfit for her. "Look at our princeling!" she'd said with a whistle. "If I didn't know better, I'd think you were someone decent, not a piece of filthy Chiastelm wharf scum."

Trask let his fellow guests draw their own conclusions about his origins, and he was taken for a student, or the son of prosperous tradesfolk, or even a bastard of good blood—but not, apparently, for an underling from an ale-house. Caught up in his role, Trask himself all but forgot what he was and where he came from. He was hardly surprised when Nyctasia summoned him to join her for the actors' performance, though he knew that this was an honor any courtier would envy him. He made Nyctasia a low bow and thanked her very properly for this unlooked-for token of her favor, but she only said, "Sit down and watch the play, Trask—the play, not the audience."

She didn't present him to her other guests, but perhaps that was not to be expected. They might be nobles of exalted rank who'd be insulted if Nyctasia introduced a commoner to them. But never mind, he thought—merely being seen in the Rhai-cime's company would confer distinction upon him in the eyes of all who saw him. He smoothed his hair and sat up straighter. 'Malkin was always telling him not to slouch.

Then a burst of trumpets announced that the play was about to begin, and before long Trask had forgotten everything else, even his own ambitions and appearance. The actors had partitioned off the far end of the hall with curtains about the dais, and when two of the troupe pulled back the draperies

Trask saw that they'd transformed the platform into a forest glade with trees and grass and flowers—and could that be a pond? He had sometimes seen traveling bands of mummers put on a crude play in the marketplace, but a polished performance like this, indoors, with elaborate properties and scenery, was a completely new and fascinating experience to him. The trees were of painted wood and gauze, the flowers of cloth and wire, the grass a green carpet, and the pond must of course be a mirror, he realized. Yet all was somehow arranged so cleverly, so charmingly, that the scene was somehow thoroughly convincing, without looking at all realistic. Trask was already captivated, but when the actors entered, in their ornate costumes, and delivered their elegant, dramatic speeches, he was awe-stricken, exalted as if by some long-awaited inspiration. Those who portrayed nobles were more lordly than the real aristocrats who were watching them. The swordfighters were more dashing than real soldiers of fortune, who, in Trask's experience, were more likely to be vulgar louts like Corson than debonair, witty bravos. The bandits were more cunning and clever than real robbers—and Trask had known plenty of thieves in his day. And the princess, when she stood revealed (it seemed that the leader of the bandits had been the princess all along, it was rather complicated) was undoubtedly more majestic than any true daughter of royalty. True, Trask had never seen anyone of regal blood, but he had instinctively grasped the secret of the theater: *everything* on stage was better than in reality. Everything was as it ought to be, not as it was.

Trask watched the play from beginning to end in a state of feverish intensity that left him exhausted. While the audience applauded, some throwing flowers, coins, or sweets wrapped in gilded lace, he only sat stunned and speechless, consumed with desire.

It was Nyctasia's duty, as guest of honor, to summon the leader of the troupe and commend the performance on the court's behalf. When all had taken their bows, and the curtains had been drawn again, she turned to Trask as if he were her page, and said, "Go present my compliments to the actors, Trask, and fetch me the man who played the king."

As if in a dream, Trask rose unsteadily, murmured, "Yes, Nyc," and hurried away, his eyes still fixed on the curtain.

The master-actor bowed to Nyctasia with a grace that Trask envied, accepted her congratulations with eloquent thanks, then startled Trask not a little by pointing to him and asking, "Is this the one you mentioned, my lady?"

"Yes. A likely lad, don't you think? He's nothing but a nuisance to me, but you might find a use for him, no?"

Trask held his breath.

The director of the troupe looked him over with a professional eye. The boy was at a usefully indeterminate age— young enough to pass for a lass, if they were short a girl, but old enough to fill any number of minor men's roles with a little padding and a false mustache. They could always do with a spare man-at-arms, a herald, thief, beggar or page. He'd do for an urchin, too, for another year or so. Then with a few years' training behind him he'd be just the right age for a young hero of romance—and he'd have the looks for the part as well. And besides, a boy who enjoyed the patronage of a Rhaicime might well be valuable in other ways. . . .

"Can he read?" he asked at last. It wasn't necessary, of course, but it was useful for learning long speeches.

"Yes!" cried Trask, but both ignored him.

"So I'm told," said Nyctasia. "And he has a good deal of native ability. He's an excellent mimic, as I know to my cost. He learns quickly, and remembers what he's taught. You'll not regret taking him on."

"Mind you, he can't expect a wage till he's trained, my lady, and not much then. He'll be working for his keep and training for two years at the least."

"I would gladly pay you a 'prentice-fee to take him," said Nyctasia. "Just keep him out of my way!"

"Done!" said the actor, laughing. He bowed again and gestured to Trask. "Come along and make yourself useful, youngster. There's everything still to be packed away."

"Yes, sir," Trask said breathlessly. He too bowed to Nyctasia, imitating the older man's flourish. "Nyc—I mean, Your Ladyship—" he began, but Nyctasia cut short his words.

"Don't thank me," she ordered, "thank Annin. I expect you'll pass through Chiastelm on your way north. Now please go away."

Trask didn't see what Annin could have to do with his good fortune, but he felt so dazed that anything seemed possible. "Yes, my lady," he said, and followed his new master without another word. Perhaps if he was careful and didn't question his luck, he thought, he could keep himself from waking up.

23

Nyctasia was dreaming of bells again.

Even deep in the crypts, she had heard the bells heralding her mother's death, and now, as Tiambria's time drew nigh, the echo of their knell haunted her dreams and made her start anxiously at any bell that sounded. Her concern for her sister, and for the child who was to unify the city, drove all other matters from her mind, and she allowed more of the responsibility for Rhostshyl to fall to others, and left much of the business of the budding university in the capable and willing hands of 'Malkin. So occupied was she with thoughts of Tiambria that she rarely even found herself brooding over the loss of Erystalben. She devoted herself to study of the great scholarly works on the healing arts, poring over all that was written about childbearing and its dangers, but she learned nothing that Dame Tsephis and Master Anthorne had not told her.

The same fears tormented Lord Jehamias. "Your own mother died in childbed, did she not?" he asked Nyctasia wretchedly. "And Briar is—"

"*No*, Jehame. I've told you, Teselescq would have recovered fully if she'd given herself time to heal, as her physicians advised. She made light of their warnings and went riding far too soon after the twins were born. She was seized with such pains that she lost her seat and suffered a terrible fall. It was her own willfulness that killed her."

He groaned. "But that's just the sort of thing Briar would do."

"Yes, but Briar has you and me to keep her from killing herself, brother. Teselescq's husband was an old man who took little interest in her—theirs was purely a marriage of duty. But if you ask Briar to do as her physicians order, just to spare you worry, I daresay she'll oblige you."

"Perhaps she may, but suppose she refuses?"

"Jehame, Briar knows what happened to our mother. But even if she refuses to listen to reason, nothing of the sort will happen to her, because I'll have her locked up if necessary! Teselescq was of age, you see, but Briar is still my ward, by law. So you needn't worry—between us, we'll take care of her in spite of herself." It was all perfectly true, but it comforted neither of them much.

"Still, I wish there was something I could do now," said Jehamias. "You're a healer, 'Tasia, you'll have your spells to do, but I can only wait. They won't even let me stay with her. Mistress Omia says I'd only be in the way."

"She said much the same to me, and she's right, I'm afraid. I may be a healer, but I'm no midwife, nor even a physician. I can't very well put Briar into a healing-trance while she's giving birth, so I can be of little help till the child's born—and she'll probably not need me, then. All I can do when the time comes is undertake a trance-spell myself, to try to create an Influence to lend her strength. It may well come to nothing."

"Even that's more than I can do," sighed Jehamias.

"But you can help me, Jehame, if you will. I need someone to attend me, to see that nothing disturbs me, and to recall me from the trance at the proper time. Someone who cares for Tiambria would best serve the Influence, you see."

Jehamias had of course been eager to help, to feel that he could be of some use to his wife at such a time. Tiambria's confinement therefore found him secluded with Nyctasia, watching over her anxiously as she sat stiffly upright in a narrow chair, silent and motionless, unaware of him or of anything save her inner visions. Greymantle lay at her feet, not sleeping but perhaps creating an Influence of his own to guard her.

She had given Jehamias various tasks—most of them quite meaningless—to keep him occupied. He tended the fire carefully, felt Nyctasia's pulse from time to time, and dutifully tried to concentrate his thoughts on the Discipline that Nyctasia had said would somehow assist her in her efforts. But as the hours passed without word of Tiambria, he paced the chamber more and more, waiting and worrying, while Nyctasia's trance gave way to mere dreams, dreams of great iron bells.

The tolling of the bells reached her even far beneath the earth, and she turned to her cousin in dismay, only to find that he was not Thierran, but Jenisorn brenn Vale. "There's nothing to fear, Nyc," said Jenisorn, laughing. "It's the harvest-bells. The Royal Crimson are ripe, the Crush has begun! We must hurry, or the fruit will lose its flavor."

Of course, this dark underground passage was in the wine-cellars of the Edonaris vintnery, not in the crypts of the palace. Her mother had died long ago, she was safe in the Midlands, far from Rhostshyl and its mournful memories. She followed Jenisorn up the stairs at a run, the sound of the bells growing ever louder as she neared the light at the head of the stairs.

She raced through the doorway, despite the deafening clamor, into the abandoned tower on the crown of Honeycomb Hill. The bell-rope thrashed wildly from side to side, but Nyctasia caught it and pulled as hard as she could, lest the bell should fall silent too soon. She was dragged and shaken to and fro by the weight of the bell, and the ground trembled beneath her as the shattering noise fractured the supports beneath the tower. At any moment it might collapse and crush her, but Nyctasia could not abandon her duty. Mortal danger threatened the valley, and only she could sound the warning in time. Someone called to her from nearby, and she wondered, in the midst of her frantic efforts, why he should use her old nickname, when she was known in Vale only as Nyc. . . .

" 'Tasia!" cried Jehamias, shaking her awake at last. "Come, the bells have sounded—the birth-peal! Twice, 'Tasia, they've rung it twice. It must be *twins*!"

◆   ◆   ◆

"As soon as one begins to cry, the other joins in," Tiambria said despairingly. "Did 'Kasten and I do that?"

"You certainly did," said Nyctasia. "And you didn't stop it till you were ten years old."

Tiambria laughed. Sitting up in bed, supported by pillows and cushions, she looked wan and weak, but pleased with herself. "But what ails the creatures now? They *can't* be hungry again so soon. Jehame, do send for a nursemaid. Tell her to take them away and drown them."

"They don't want a nurse, they want their aunt," said Nyctasia. "Don't you, my pets?" She picked up one of the swaddled infants and asked it, "Now are you my niece or my nephew?" The child stopped crying and gazed at her in solemn, wondering silence. "Never mind, you're sure to be one or the other," she said, tucking it into the crook of her arm and deftly scooping up its twin with her free arm. It too stopped its whimpering as Nyctasia bounced them both gently up and down.

Jehamias, who was still terrified to hold even one of the babies, watched her in awe and alarm, and even Tiambria murmured, "Do take care, 'Tasia."

"Ho, you forget that I was carrying both you and 'Kasten about when I was twelve. I daresay I could juggle these little mites if I tried." She knelt down and offered the babies for Greymantle's approval. "What do you think, Grey? Will they do?" He sniffed them with interest, wagging his tail, then began to lick their faces, pleased with their milky scent. One of the twins gurgled with delight, and the other immediately echoed the sound.

"'Tasia, don't let him do that!" Tiambria protested. "Anyone would think you were raised in a kennel! Give them to me." She held out her arms for the twins.

Nyctasia grinned at her disapproval. "Nothing's cleaner than a hound's mouth," she teased. "Oh, very well, Briar, you may have this one." She let her sister take one of the twins from her arms, and pretended to toss the other to Jehamias. "Do you want one too, Jehame? No?"

"I'll thank you to stop using my daughter for a shuttlecock," laughed Tiambria. "And stop tormenting poor Jehame, too. What demon's gotten into you? Give me that child!"

"I shan't. I think I'll keep this one," said Nyctasia. "Anyone can see that she takes after me, just look how pretty and clever she is." She sat on the bed near Tiambria and held her tiny niece close to her heart, crooning a song to her as she rocked her. The baby made contented, sleepy, suckling sounds, and yawned.

"Can't you even sing them a proper lullaby?" Tiambria scolded in a whisper.

"They like it," Nyctasia retorted, and sang softly:

> "Oh, I could complain
> That my life is a curse,
> That love's a murrain
> That no healer can nurse.
> But let me explain—
> Things could always be worse!"

About the Author(s)

J. F. Rivkin is the shared pseudonym of two writers who live on opposite sides of the country. They coauthored the first two books of the Silverglass series, *Silverglass* and *Web of Wind*. The next two volumes, *Witch of Rhostshyl* and *Mistress of Ambiguities*, were written by the East Coast J. F. Rivkin, while the West Coast J.F. is the author of the third volume of the RuneSword series, *The Dreamstone*, and is currently writing two books on time-travel and dinosaurs.